WOMAN STRANGLED — NEWS AT TEN

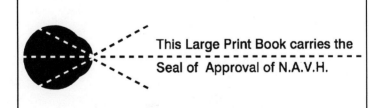

This Large Print Book carries the
Seal of Approval of N.A.V.H.

WOMAN STRANGLED — NEWS AT TEN

LAURIE MOORE

THORNDIKE PRESS

A part of Gale, Cengage Learning

GALE
CENGAGE Learning™

Detroit • New York • San Francisco • New Haven, Conn • Waterville, Maine • London

LIBRARY OF CONGRESS CATALOGING-IN-PUBLICATION DATA

Moore, Laurie.
  Woman strangled— new at ten / by Laurie Moore.
    p. cm. — (Thorndike press large print core)
    ISBN-13: 978-1-4104-1894-4 (alk. paper)
    ISBN-10: 1-4104-1894-4 (alk. paper)
    1. Women television journalists—Fiction. 2. Texas—Fiction.
  3. Large type books. I. Title.
  PS3613.O564W66 2009b
  813'.6—dc22   2009017504

Published in 2009 by arrangement with Tekno Books.

Printed in the United States of America
1 2 3 4 5 6 7 13 12 11 10 09

For my daughter Laura,
who shares my love of
words and writing,
you're the reason I do all that I do.

ACKNOWLEDGEMENTS

Many thanks to those who graciously assisted me in my technical research: former engineering supervisor Tom Unterberger, KTVT-TV Channel 11 Dallas/Fort Worth; investigative reporter Brett Shipp, WFAA-TV Channel 8 Dallas/Fort Worth; and investigative reporter Marty Griffin, KDKA-TV Channel 2 Pittsburgh.

And a special thanks to Jim Palmer, Tarrant County Constable (Ret.) for trading war stories with me.

CHAPTER ONE

Aspen Wicklow sat on a tobacco-colored leather loveseat in the foyer of WBFD-TV, just outside station manager J. Gordon Pfeiffer's office. She hoped anyone seeing her at close range wouldn't notice she'd pressed her knees together to keep them from shaking, or that her confidence waned in inverse proportion to each minute Pfeiffer kept her waiting for their interview. Sneaking a peek at the compact makeup mirror attached to the fabric facing of her handbag, she studied her carefully lined eyes for smudges. The extra swipe of dark mascara had thickened her copper lashes, giving them a luxurious look. And her lids, shadowed with the palest hint of purple, made her green irises sparkle like six-carat gemstones next to fiery red curls that framed her face and bounced past her shoulders. After deciding she looked chic in the hand-me-down designer suit, she discreetly snapped the purse closed. Her gaze dipped to her freshly polished pumps. Shoehorned into a pair of borrowed Ferragamos that were a half-size too small, she let out a slow breath and settled into the sofa back. From her appearance, employees wouldn't guess that she was down to her last seventy-five dollars and the rent was due.

She'd spent no more than a few moments rehearsing the *Please hire me* speech in her head when a disturbance erupted inside Pfeiffer's office. Whipcrack voices that took on the demonic strains of a Beatles record played backward filtered out through glass walls. Without warning, a burly man with thinning brown hair, wire-rim glasses and a baked-potato nose that glowed bright red yanked the door open. He made a thumb gesture, *Get lost,* and a strikingly handsome male with laser-like blue eyes, a tropical tan and perfect bone structure stormed out in the vapors of fury.

With his sandy blond hair made into a halo by the morning glare slanting through the windows, Aspen recognized Stinger Baldwin immediately. Each Thursday, she'd glue herself to the six o'clock newscast to watch the tall, sturdy-jawed investigative reporter or his colleague, Tig Welder — the real celebrity at WBFD — deliver the *Public Defender* spot. Later, as she stood in front of her bathroom mirror while getting ready for bed, she'd mimic their delivery using her toothbrush for a microphone. Whether recreating reports of price gouging at the gas pumps or exposing corruption at City Hall, she'd furrow her brow enough to telegraph concern in all the right places.

The sad stories were the ones Aspen couldn't duplicate. When a customer-cheating airplane mechanic's use of inferior or damaged parts for small aircraft overhauls ended in tragedy for the owners of a Cessna-152, her composure disintegrated into sobs before she could finish imitating Stinger Baldwin's news report.

During those practice sessions, recreating evening broadcasts in the serenity of her bedroom, she realized empathy would do her in. She'd never cut it as a news anchor or an investigative reporter because she couldn't remain stone-faced while reporting the news. That's why she'd applied for a research assistant position.

"Clean out your office and don't come back," Pfeiffer yelled with a terrible intensity. To his secretary, an older, porcelain-faced woman with dark hair upswept in a chignon, he said, "Call security. Have him escorted out."

Baldwin's slitted gaze cut to Aspen. She tried to avoid his drill-bit stare but her eyes strayed toward him of their own volition.

He spoke three words. "Run like hell."

The wait for her nine o'clock appointment turned into a hostage situation. If thugs charged in with Uzis and stitched bullets across the wall, it wouldn't surprise her.

Her first instinct was to melt into her surroundings until she was no longer visible. Unable to pull it off, she sat perfectly still and tried to take her pulse by looking at the wall clock. Her eyes slewed to the secretary's desk, where a plaque with the name *Rochelle LeDuc* carved in block letters sat prominently on the blotter. Aspen assumed the stylish lady with the telephone receiver in her grip was Rochelle.

The woman punched out numbers on the keypad. "We need Security in Mr. Pfeiffer's office," she announced calmly, as if summoning the guards. But Aspen noticed a manicured finger depressing the switch and knew in an instant she'd called no one. Rochelle's berry-stained lips curled up in a polite smirk.

Aspen thought her heart might beat right through her chest. She wanted to bolt from the room. To escape the public beheading playing out in WBFD's lobby and reschedule her appointment by cell phone from the sanctuary of her car.

Startled into embarrassment, Pfeiffer had an abrupt mood change. He moved in close, extended his hand and spoke in the brandy-smooth baritone of a schmoozer.

"You must be Ms. Wicklow. Come in, Aspen. I've been looking forward to our meeting." He gripped her elbow and guided her into his office, as if the tantrum she'd just witnessed could be undone by this small act of reversal.

Rochelle's eyelids fluttered in astonishment. She lip synced, *Hold my calls* as her boss simultaneously issued the same over-the-shoulder directive at her. Nearby, the assignments desk hummed with the air traffic of at least thirty competing police frequencies scanning the airwaves for the next breaking story. Employees jockeyed for position as keyboards clacked, phones clamored and faxes went off.

Inside Pfeiffer's office, Aspen waited intently as his eyes drifted over her application. Her skin tingled with enough electricity to power the west end of Dallas.

"Impressive credentials." Pfeiffer tented his hands on the desk.

She knew he didn't mean a word of it.

She'd graduated from the University of North Texas with a Bachelor of Arts in Radio-Television-Film and a minor in psychology. It wasn't as if she'd earned an RTF degree from the Columbia School of Broadcasting. If her credentials had been that impressive she would've started looking for work at the other fifteen TV stations in the Metroplex, not the one with the lowest ratings.

Pfeiffer set the application aside. "Tell me about yourself. What you like to do on your days off. Interesting places you've been. Whether you have pets. Things like that."

I only go places that don't charge admission.

I've started hanging out at places that demo free food.

My boyfriend dumped me for an exotic dancer a few months ago.

There's more gas in my stomach than my ten-year-old Honda.

I couldn't get a date in a men's prison with a handful of pardons.

She took a deep breath and flashed her sweetest smile. "No pets. There's a stray that hangs around my house but I try not to encourage him. I spend a lot of time roaming the Kimbell Museum. And the most interesting place I've ever been was my

14

grandmother's kitchen." The rest of the sentence, the *Please give me a job* begging part, slid back down her throat.

"What's so interesting about Granny's?"

She called up a memory from childhood, when she'd sit on a stool and watch her grandmother bake specialty cakes shaped and iced like shoes, handbags, jewelry boxes, cartoon characters, and classic cars. When a couple of Hollywood celebrities discovered the old lady, they enticed her to move to LA and bankrolled her shop.

Pfeiffer listened with rapt attention. "Fascinating."

His eyes had the glazed look of a man wanting chocolate. He cleared his throat and got down to business. "Your application indicates you're here for the research position."

I'll take anything. Please give me a job before I get evicted.

"That'd be nice."

Pfeiffer grimaced on his exhale. "Tell me about your family."

The question surprised her. The sanitized adaptation, the one reserved for strangers, went like this: *They're older people, living in a nursing home.* In an unguarded moment, the version she unloaded on Pfeiffer was the truth, the whole truth and nothing but the truth.

"Divorced parents. My father's much older than my mother. I recently placed him in a nursing home that specializes in Alzheimer's patients."

"And your mother?"

"Three weeks ago, my mom was in a bad car accident. You might remember this since WBFD covered it. Lady hit head-on by a drunk driver going the wrong way on Interstate Twenty? She has a closed-head injury with serious short-term memory loss, so I ended up putting her in the same care center."

A flicker of recognition registered in the station manager's eyes. He remained cordial but detached.

Aspen shifted her gaze to the window, a huge wall of plate glass overlooking downtown Fort Worth. The next part would be hard. She didn't want to see the weight of Pfeiffer's judgment in his stare.

"It wasn't something I wanted to do since it's common knowledge among friends and family that my folks hate each other. But I'm on a shoestring budget at the moment so it made sense to place them in the same facility instead of driving all over town to visit them."

Don't be nice. Don't be understanding. Give

me a job.

Pfeiffer eyed her hair with cold scrutiny. "Is that your natural color?"

"Yes." Aspen tugged nervously at the hem of her skirt, a tropical wool number with tailored gussets that accentuated her shape, in a Kelly green so bright it gave her hair the look of copper coils.

"Good. Don't change it." He leaned back in his oversized chair. "Think you'd be interested in a position other than behind-the-scenes research?"

"I'll scrub toilets if it'll get my foot in the door."

The station manager laughed. Not one of those patronizing chuckles, but a huge belly laugh that caused his shoulders to heave.

Then the contours of his face hardened. "Do you scare easily?"

She felt the muscles tense along her back. Little hairs on her arm stood straight out. Words of truth forming in her head didn't make it out of her throat — she still slept with a nightlight and steered clear of biker gangs, alligators and things with scales or fangs.

"I can hold my own."

"Good. I'm giving you Stinger Baldwin's job. Against my better judgment, of course. You'll be my new investigative reporter. Just don't screw up."

Aspen's mouth gaped. Pfeiffer's offer struck like a harpoon to the brain.

He rose from his place behind the desk, snagged a jacket that had been hooked on a brass peg and shrugged into it. "There's one thing I have zero tolerance for. The cardinal rule of journalism is to cover the news; you don't become part of it. Never become part of the story. It's the quickest way out the door."

She'd watched Stinger Baldwin getting the heave-ho. Had the veteran reporter become part of the story?

Pfeiffer wagged his finger in a "no" motion. "Don't break the law. Don't do anything that'll end in a body cavity search. And get everything pre-approved. I'm not paying off any lawsuits."

Aspen sat inert as a gas. Just to make sure she'd heard right, she parroted the offer back to him. "*You* want *me* to replace Stinger Baldwin?"

"Right." His face creased into a broad smile. "And since Tig Welder's been slacking lately, you might just light a fire under him, too. If you want the job, see Rochelle. Get her to show you around and pick up your first assignment. Be ready to go on the air a week from Thursday night. We're heading into sweeps month."

She leaned forward, awestruck, and extended her hand. "I won't let you down." The clench in her stomach told her otherwise.

Pfeiffer pumped vigorously. "One more thing . . ." He pointed at her throat. "What's that hanging around your neck?"

Aspen caressed the gold ring — her own personal good luck charm — held by a rope chain. "It's a claddagh. An heirloom passed down from my grandmother. It signifies love, friendship, loyalty and fidelity."

"Get rid of it. If we want you to wear jewelry, we'll supply it."

CHAPTER TWO

Despite the station's thermostat being set on the chilly side, Pfeiffer's assistant, Rochelle, stood beside the open drawer next to her desk with a small, battery-operated fan clutched tightly in her grip. Tendrils of hair blew back from her alabaster skin as she held the personal fan inches from her face. She gave her cheeks the once-over, moving her hand clockwise, stopping at the neck for a few seconds, then hooking a finger into the front of her knit shell and aiming the current of air at her cleavage.

She flicked off the switch and tossed the little fan back in the drawer. After slamming it shut, she snatched an incoming fax off the machine. Her eyes drifted over the page. She gave an aristocratic sniff and promptly pleated it into a fan, which she used to resume cooling herself.

"Follow me." Without a preamble, Rochelle pivoted on one alligator shoe and took off down the hall.

Aspen hurried to catch up.

They entered a large room across from the studio, sectioned into cubicles.

"Welcome to Production — the neurological center of WBFD's brain. Here's where the work gets done." A paper airplane sailed into their airspace. "See all these people? They're fact-checkers, cameramen, computer wizards, gophers, interns, electricians — you name it, we have it." A triangular-folded paper shot past them. One of the employees had "kicked" a field goal through the finger-shaped goalpost of a colleague. The secretary shook her head in disgust. "Too many freaks, not enough circuses."

Aspen lagged a few steps behind as Rochelle skirted the corner and pointed down the hall toward a wall of offices. "Here's where the big wheels work. Bill Wallace usually leaves as soon as the morning show's over. You can meet him later. Steve Lennox left to run an errand. You ask me, it's a good thing he's pretty. The guy's so stupid he couldn't figure out how to keep from tripping over a cordless phone."

The first door stood slightly ajar. Rochelle poked her head through the opening.

"New employee," she announced to the

21

willowy blonde seated behind the desk, her head bent in concentration, hunting and pecking on the computer keyboard. Aspen recognized Misty Knight immediately.

The phone bleated, shearing Misty's concentration. She gave them a finger wave, mouthed *Hello* and picked up the line.

"Don't refer to her as the weather girl unless you're good at ducking coffee cups," Rochelle said under her breath. "Misty's our meteorologist." She pulled the door closed, shook her head and mumbled, "Sharp as the leading edge of a BB."

WBFD's ambassador of orientation headed down the corridor and paused at the next office. "Want to meet Tig Welder?"

Did she ever.

She'd flirted with the idea of making him her mentor ever since one of her professors invited him to speak to her class. Besides being the most drop-dead gorgeous, middle-aged man she'd ever met, she admired him for his goal-oriented quest to win the Peabody Award. Golden-throated Tig wanted to report the news for CNN. Or get his own talk show. Anything to break into the national market.

The man sitting behind the big mahogany desk had his back to her. Had it not been for the telephone pressed against one ear,

Aspen would've guessed he'd been staring out the window, surveying his kingdom of viewers. Rochelle tapped on the doorframe and he swiveled his chair around.

"Gotta go," he said into the receiver. "Be ready at eight. If you're late, I'll take one of my other girlfriends." He flashed a mouthful of porcelain-veneered teeth like a Great White eyeing his next meal. Down went the phone. "Well, well, well. What do we have here?"

"Tig Welder, meet Aspen Wicklow. Stinger's replacement."

Tig's grin faded. He stood and extended his hand, but his penetrating anthracite eyes were anything but friendly. He exchanged pleasantries, made a *Let's do lunch* invitation that rang hollow and ran out of things to say.

"I'm new at this, so I hope you don't mind me asking questions from time to time," Aspen said.

Tig meshed his fingers together. "We're colleagues but we're also competitors. It's sink or swim here, toots. And don't even think about filling the anchor slot. When Bill retires, it goes to me." To Rochelle, he said, "Did you explain to Investigative Reporter Barbie how things work around here?"

Rochelle flashed a fake smile. "Tig's kind of a superstar —"

"I wouldn't go so far as to use the word superstar," he said, clearly enjoying his celebrity.

"— so Gordon lets him pick and choose his assignments. You have to get up pretty early in the morning to scoop Tig."

Tig's grin went suddenly stern. "Say, Rochelle, I expect you to call Red Hot Tunes before the end of the day. Tell them to quit sending crap to my house. Thirteen CDs for a penny — who're they kidding? By the time you pay all those inflated postage and handling fees, the album's double what it costs retail."

"I feel for you." Rochelle gave him a mournful headshake, but the lack of sympathy in her gaze suggested otherwise. "I could've warned you not to enroll in their little program. Once you order, they dog you like a Nazi war criminal."

"Tell them I didn't sign up for those damned rap CDs and I'm not going to pay for them. Get on that right away, okay?"

"When it comes to helping you out, I'll stop at nothing," she deadpanned.

While he scrawled down the number for her, the telephone rang. With a brusque hand wave and a "See you around, Barbie,"

Tig swiveled his chair away and took the call.

Ten feet further down the hall, Rochelle mumbled, "I often visualize him tied to a chair, with duct tape over his mouth, just to make myself feel better. He's an insufferable prick but he's good at his job. He gets up early in order to get down here and sift through the consumer tips before anyone else has a chance at the primo investigations."

"What time does he get here?"

"Four-thirty every morning."

"Then I'll be here by four."

"I like your spirit, kid. You remind me of when I was young and stupid." Rochelle lopped an arm around Aspen's shoulders in the way of a favorite aunt. "I think we can help each other."

They arrived at Stinger Baldwin's empty office. His nameplate still remained affixed to the outside of his door, so Rochelle slid it along the metal track that held it in place and pocketed it.

"Welcome to the Taj Mahal," she said cheerfully. "Don't fret. If you do your job right, you won't have to spend much time here. Tig, Misty and the news anchors get the big offices."

Aspen could've cared less. Sure, it was the

size of a roach motel. But it had a door, a telephone and a small desk pushed up against the wall. Best of all, it came with a paycheck.

She turned to Rochelle, confused. "What did Mr. Welder mean about the anchor position?"

"Bill Wallace is taking an early retirement. Last week, he told Gordon he'd been diagnosed with a mysterious ailment and now Tig's lobbying for the job. It'd serve him right not to get it. That back-stabber may think he's a big shot, but Stinger was the fair-haired boy Gordon had in mind to replace Bill."

"Did Mr. Welder have anything to do with Mr. Baldwin getting fired?" Aspen said, fishing.

"You're a smart cookie, so let me give you a word of advice. The way to survive in this cutthroat operation is do your job and don't ask questions that don't directly concern you." She faced Aspen head-on. "What machines can you operate?"

"I can work a coffee maker."

"Don't let on to anyone or you'll get stuck making coffee everyday. Can you work a computer, copier, fax . . . can you type?"

"Yes."

"Good. Then you'll be able to write letters, make your own copies, and fax whatever you need." Rochelle's falcon-eye stare demanded that Aspen agree with the terms.

"What if there's an emergency and I need your help?"

"Plan your itinerary so that there's not one. The only people around here who expect me to drop everything and coddle them are Gordon, because he's the boss; Misty, because every time she has another cosmetic surgery her brain cells die under anesthesia; and Tig, because he's a horse's ass. Anyone lacking power, influence, clout or mental defects is expected to carry his own weight."

The tour ended back at the assignments desk, the clearinghouse for breaking news.

"By the way," Rochelle said with a smile, "I love your Escada."

Aspen blinked. She hadn't expected anyone to recognize the couture brand and hoped the station manager's assistant wouldn't get the idea she didn't need the job. After all, the designer suit had been hastily plucked from her mother's closet. "How'd you know?"

"It still has the tags on it."

Aspen's confidence tanked. While she contorted her head to look beneath each arm, Rochelle reached out and plucked the tags from the back of her collar.

Then she handed over the rumpled fax. "Here's your first job. Tig already pirated the good ones, but do what you can with it. If you don't care for the subject matter —" she pointed to a box "— here's where you'll find the consumer tips. Rummage around and find a story you like."

Irritated as a sopping wet badger, Rochelle flopped into her chair, slid open the desk drawer and reached for the personal fan. She flicked on the switch and leaned her head back. The whir of spinning blades put a smile back on her face.

Aspen un-pleated the fax. Her eyes scoured the page. The prep school cafeteria exposé had all the earmarks of a disgruntled employee behind it. Surely there had to be at least one interesting lead left in the tip box. She rifled through the emails and sorted through the faxes.

One complaint caught her eye.

A car mechanic had sold a BMW out from under a customer when she failed to pick it up after repairs were made. In the printed email, the complainant identified herself as Margo Drummond Sommervel. The car belonged to her sister and Margo Sommervel wanted the sleazy mechanic investigated for ripping people off.

Aspen's heart fluttered. She clutched the email to her chest and tried not to panic.

She knew Margo and her sister from their college sorority days. Neither had acted particularly congenial to Aspen. Her clothes never quite came up to par and she didn't have money to squander on trendy accessories when the dormitory bill had to be paid. The Drummond sisters ran with rich girls and lived at the sorority house. After graduation, Margo married a City Councilman. Her sister, Caramel Janine, took a position as a purse buyer for Harkman Beamis, a high-end department store new to the area.

"I'll work on a couple of these," Aspen said. She gave Rochelle a furtive glance.

"Mechanic stories are a dime a dozen, hon. They're where you turn when you can't find anything more interesting to report."

Aspen rattled the fax. "I want to hedge my bets in case this cafeteria lead doesn't pan out."

"Suit yourself."

But there was another reason for safeguarding Margo Sommervel's complaint. Caramel "Candy" Drummond was the same young woman whose story WBFD and competing stations had been covering for the past ten days. Caramel Janine Drummond, the mayor's niece, had gone missing.

CHAPTER THREE

The cafeteria lead that began at the city's premier prep school turned out to be a total bust. Aspen could hardly expect to corroborate the tipster's claim that the headmaster was receiving a kickback from the food provider when she hit a wall of silence. According to the headmaster, they'd had disgruntled employees who whistle-blew problems that didn't exist. If WBFD had proof, then bring it on.

Before returning to the studio, she dialed the phone number for Margo Sommervel. She didn't identify herself other than to say she was an investigative reporter with WBFD assigned to follow up on the mechanic complaint. When she asked to drop by for a chat, Margo agreed. Motoring through the west side of Fort Worth in a company car, Aspen located the sprawling ranch home in the fashionable Ridglea neighborhood. High-end autos were parked up and down the street, as well as in the driveway.

A block away, Aspen locked the vehicle and walked.

Margo Sommervel appeared at the front door wearing turquoise Capri pants, a gauzy, over-sized shirt and a pair of aqua leather espadrilles. Glossy platinum hair fell past her shoulders to the middle of her back. Recognition flickered in her pale blue eyes as the past came rushing back. A questioning smile died on her face.

"You're Aspen Wicklow. What're you doing here?"

"I called about the mechanic complaint you sent in. I'm with WBFD-TV."

"You're the investigative reporter?" Margo said with the kind of dumbfounded expression one might expect from someone who'd just been asked to sample a new cookie dough, only to learn after swallowing that it contained powdered earthworms and other vile ingredients. She sucked air. "They must be paying you a bundle. Is that a Judith Leiber handbag? Those cost eighteen hundred dollars."

Aspen held it aloft. "Do you like it?"

She wasn't about to tell Margo her purse was a knock-off purchased at a wholesale place in the Asian district of Dallas. That she didn't have eighteen hundred dollars. And if she ever did get such a windfall, she wouldn't be so shallow as to fritter it away on a purse. Assuming she went off the deep end and spent that much for a Judith Leiber minaudière, she'd at least be smart enough to make damned sure the artisan who created it came with it.

Practically salivating, Margo kept her eyes riveted on the handbag. "I asked my husband, Biff, to buy me one for Christmas using my sister's discount at Harkman Beamis. He said I must be nuts to think he'd be stupid enough to throw away his hard-earned cash — and here you have one. Imagine that."

Aspen nodded. Well, what kind of greeting did she expect from someone in the midst of a missing persons investigation, whose brain had been strip-mined by fashion magazines, clothes catalogs and trunk shows?

"May I come in?"

"Of course." With an exaggerated eye roll, Margo thunked her forehead with the heel of her hand. "Where are my manners?" Her face relaxed into resignation. In her favor, the Drummond sisters were big on etiquette. Aspen should know. Margo herself had chastised her for using the wrong fork at a sorority house dinner. "I apologize for the parking problem. We're running a sweat-shop out of my living room, putting together flyers with my sister's picture on it and running a phone bank . . ." Her voice trailed off. A frown creased her forehead. "You're aware Candy's missing, right?"

"I've been following the story." A lame response considering there was a dragnet out for her.

Margo gave Aspen a somber nod. She motioned her through the house by way of the living room, a well-appointed area with leather furniture tastefully arranged below the glassy-eyed stares of safari trophies mounted on the walls.

"Biff spends most of his time here," she explained, continuing down a long hall with Aspen in tow.

They ended up in the master bedroom, a posh expanse of Italian Provincial furniture: a California King dressed in Waterford linens and four crystal chandeliers mounted on the ceiling, dressed with vintage chains and drops. Margo removed a file folder from an antique secretary and walked to a cur-tained area along one wall. She drew the drapes open, exposing a set of French doors that led to an outside patio with a wrought iron bistro table and chairs.

Aspen assumed her sorority sister took her morning coffee here. And why not? They stepped outdoors into the equivalent of an English garden and Margo offered her a chair. With the file lying squarely in the middle of the table, she folded it open and retrieved what appeared to be a time-line.

"Would you like a Vodka Collins?"

"I'll take lemonade."

"I find large quantities of Stolichnaya help." The pampered princess's haughty expression fell. She slid into one of the chairs, folded her hands and hung her head. "You must hate me."

I do, Aspen thought. But she said, "For what?"

"Oh, come now." Pale blue eyes turned watery. "We were the mean girls."

"Water under the bridge."

"I'm sorry. Sorry if I hurt your feelings. Sorry I wasn't nicer to you. And now you're here to help and I feel really bad because Candy and I went out of our way to snub you."

"We can talk about this another time. Why don't we take a look at your notes and see what's here?"

Twenty minutes later, Aspen was looking through documentation while Margo ran down events that led to the sale of the BMW.

It went like this: Candy took the Beemer to Pop's Auto Salvage and Repair on the fifteenth of the month. She signed a work order accepting the estimate and authorizing them to fix it. A few days later, the mechanic left a message on her answering machine telling her the car was ready. And he said he preferred the payment in cash.

Aspen took notes. "How do you know what was on the message?"

"I went to check on Candy when she didn't show up for our regular Saturday lunch at Pierre's and heard it for myself."

"You have a key to her place?"

"I do now. I didn't then. I broke a window and crawled in." Her expression changed. "She didn't show up and that was unusual for Candy. We were reared to be on time. It's rude to be late." A shadow fell across the table. "Oh, look. Our drinks are here."

The housekeeper placed a tray between them, selected a glass and handed it to Margo. She vanished as quietly as she'd materialized.

Aspen steered the conversation back to the message as her hostess sipped from the crystal tumbler. "If I understand your complaint correctly, the mechanic sold the car?"

Margo gave her a vigorous head bob. "A few days after I filed the missing person's report, I drove out to Pop's Salvage with a friend to pick up Candy's car. He said he sold it for scrap. A thirty-six thousand dollar automobile. I reported it to the police, but they said they couldn't do anything since it's a civil matter and they don't investigate civil matters."

Aspen did an eye squint.

Margo consulted her timeline. "This is criminal. He shouldn't be able to get away with it."

"I admit it seems a bit unethical," Aspen said reflectively, "but it does state the terms of forfeiture in the contract. I think this is what they call a mechanic's lien, but you should talk to a lawyer and verify that through him."

"Already did."

It appeared Pop's had the right to dispose of the car. The only ambiguity was whether Candy had received notice through the telephone message machine. Still, the contract provided for that. It clearly stated in bold type that a telephone call, whether the agent spoke to the customer directly or left a message, served as notice. The consumer's signature served as an agreement to these terms.

"May I have copies of your file?"

Margo nodded. "I'll drop them by the station whenever you say."

"If it's all the same to you, I don't mind picking them up." She was thinking of Tig Welder and how he might pull rank to get his hands on a story about a missing car belonging to a missing person. She retrieved her handbag from the seat of a bistro chair and stuffed her notes inside.

As she stood to leave, Margo said, "There's more."

Aspen settled back down.

"When I left the mechanic's, I was so angry I wasn't watching where I was going. I ran, head-on, into a guy who was lurking around outside the fence. After we exchanged a couple of embarrassed *Sorrys,* he started in asking questions about why I was there."

Aspen listened intently. Margo's speech had started to slur in inverse proportion to her disappearing drink, leading her to believe that the glass contained more than plain lemonade. She dug out her pen and paper and proceeded to add these boozy recollections to her notes.

According to Margo, this young man told her that a female friend sent him a text message telling him she had to go visit a sick aunt in Rhode Island. She wanted him to feed her cat while she was gone for the week. When he let himself in with a spare key hidden in a fake plastic rock, he saw the light blinking on the answering machine and screened her messages. One was from a mechanic telling her if she didn't come pick up her car it would be sold for scrap.

"He told me he'd been trying to get this girl, Gabrielle, to seriously consider him as a boyfriend. He said they've known each other since high school and he'd always had a crush on her but Gabrielle was one of the popular girls —" Margo averted her eyes.

The rest of her story tumbled out in a hyperventilating rush. "He said he decided to settle her bill and retrieve the car himself to impress upon her what a good guy he is, and since the bill was under eight hundred dollars, he could manage until she came back. Only when he arrived at the mechanic's, the car had already been sold. He said he left a message on Gabrielle's cell phone but she never phoned back. Then he called himself a fool for trying to help her, which he claimed is the story of his life."

Margo heaved a deep sigh and the vapors of alcohol traveled into their shared space.

Aspen poised her pen to write. "What's his name?"

"I knew you'd ask that. I didn't get it." She heaved a resigned sigh. "You're thinking I'm still a bitch, aren't you? Because of what I said about Gabrielle being one of the popular girls? I saw the look on your face. Please don't be mad at me. If you'll help me, I'll find a way to make it up to you. I promise. Candy, too. She'll make it up, too."

"That won't be necessary. This is my job. How well I do it, or don't do it, doesn't hinge on whether I get anything out of it other than a job well done."

"No, but I was thinking . . ." Margo stared at Aspen's naked ring finger ". . . if you're not dating anyone, Biff and I have a friend we could introduce you to. He's not the handsomest guy in the world but he's good-natured and funny; and even though he's between jobs right now, he'll make a good catch one of these days."

Let me see if I get this right . . . nitwit wants to fix me up with an ugly guy who's unemployed but has a great sense of humor.

"I'm not interested." Aspen smiled sweetly. Inwardly, she wanted to smack Margo so hard her clothes went out of style. "But thank you for the thought."

"Are you gay? Because Candy knows a lesbian who works in the fine china department at her store. She's supposed to be pretty."

Aspen stiffened. Words came out even and metered. "I'm not gay. And I don't need help getting dates."

Actually, what she really wanted to say was that she couldn't imagine anyone in the world being so bad off they'd need either of the Drummond sisters' help.

"I didn't mean to offend you. I just thought . . . since I never saw you with a boyfriend . . ."

"No offense taken."

But watching Margo's house shrink in the rearview mirror, Aspen felt the heat of shame rise to her cheeks. Margo Sommervel and her sister were the shallowest people she'd ever met. It'd serve them right if she didn't lift a finger to help either of them.

Did she need up-and-coming Margo to find her a date?

She most certainly did not.

Aspen checked her watch. She had just enough time to return the car to the station, check the tip box at the assignments desk, drop by Tranquility Villas to check on her parents and meet her online date at a popular Mexican restaurant by seven o'clock.

Tears cut a track down her carefully made

41

up face.

Stupid Roger. How dare he. Leaving her for a bleached-blonde stripper. Of all the low-class, ill-bred things to do to a person.

Her vision blurred. The memory of his parting insult rang in her ears.

"For God's sake, Roger, the least you can do is have the common decency to tell me why you're dumping me."

"Just remember — I didn't want to hurt you."

"Out with it."

"Fine. You want to know the real reason? You're just not that interesting."

Chapter Four

Aspen returned to the news station to find Rochelle standing near the door to J. Gordon Pfeiffer's office with her hand cupped to her ear. When they locked eyes, the secretary put a finger to her lips in the universal gesture of quiet. A furious, muted argument broke out behind the walls. She mouthed, "Tig," and hand-swatted the air to shoo Aspen away.

Inside her office, WBFD's novice reporter searched for her notes on the cafeteria story. She discovered them shredded in her trashcan. Stunned speechless, she headed back to Rochelle's desk with a palm full of confetti.

Ten paces from the desk, she overheard the secretary talking on the phone to Red Hot Tunes in a low, conspiratorial tone.

"He wants to change the CD selection from rap to black metal. How should I know? Just pick something satanic and send it to him." Glancing Aspen's way, her demeanor abruptly changed. She sat up rigid, reached across the blotter, grabbed a paddle fan from a local funeral home that had gone out of business years ago and swiped it through the air in front of her face. "And don't let it happen again, do you hear me? He does not want rap music coming to his house. Understood?"

She hung up and swiveled her chair around to face Aspen head-on. "Does it seem hot in here to you?" Without waiting for an answer, she reached for the drawer, pulled out the battery-operated fan and aimed it at the beads of perspiration glistening above her upper lip. "I'm working in a blast furnace. It's as if I leave home every day just so I can drive straight to Hell where Satan bitches all day about shit that I don't have any control over, and in the grand scheme of things, doesn't matter. And all the lesser demons scurry around making work for me. And people wonder why the highlight of my day is reading obituaries." With sweat still dotting Rochelle's hairline, she placed the little fan back in the drawer and unexpectedly cheered up. A disturbing smile angled up one side of her face. "May I help you?"

Aspen showed her the confetti. "These

papers had the names and phone numbers for my contacts on the prep school investigation. Who'd do such a thing?"

"I wonder." Rochelle shifted her eyes in the direction of Gordon and Tig, animated behind the glass, in the throes of a nasty pow-wow. She expelled a wistful sigh. "I often have to remind myself that not everyone hates Tig. After all, a lot of people don't know him."

She pulled a small plastic wastebasket out from under her desk and thrust it close enough for Aspen to dust paper chips off her hands.

"How come Mr. Welder's got it in for me?"

Rochelle lifted one thin black eyebrow until it formed an inverted "V". The fax at the assignments desk went off, shearing her attention. She pointed toward the incoming text and made an observation. "If I were you, while Tig's temporarily out of commission, I'd rein in my paranoia and see if that's something of interest to you."

Infuriated, Aspen strutted over to the assignments desk. She pulled out the latest tip as it rolled off the machine and unfurled the curl of paper.

"Prison overcrowding," she said in a voice stripped of enthusiasm. "Sounds boring."

Rochelle sighed. "Might as well check it

out. You never know who you'll meet on these little escapades." She reached into the drawer, pulled out the hand-held fan and started airing out her cleavage again. "Stinger once put together a story that started out as an entertainment piece on the Fort Worth Zoo. By the time he finished, it turned into an exposé on black market reptiles."

Aspen blinked.

"Speaking of snakes —" limpid gray eyes cut to the boss's office "— Tig's in there lobbying for Bill's anchor position again. Gordon doesn't want him to fill the slot because he doesn't trust him. Word of advice: No matter how bad things get, don't ever lie to Gordon. He has eyes like an ocular lie detector. He can just look at you and know when you're trying to buffalo him. Remember, hon, the secret of success is sincerity. Once you can fake that, you've got it made."

Aspen took a deep breath.

Rochelle appraised her in a glance. "The camera will love you and that's why Tig doesn't. Too bad you don't have more experience . . . and confidence. Why, if you were ever to get Gordon's attention with a good story, you could steal that job right out from under that conniving bastard."

Aspen folded the fax and stuffed it into her purse. Might as well check out the prison-overcrowding situation now that the cafeteria story was shot to hell. "I'll be here at four in the morning."

Rochelle pulled open the drawer again, pushing aside the battery-operated fan and pulling out a bottle of calcium pills. She twisted open the cap, shook out a few tablets into her palm and slammed them back in her mouth. Washing them down with a Styrofoam cup of water, she grabbed the fan by its shaft, hit the switch, flopped against the chair back, saucer-eyed, and resumed airing herself out.

Aspen turned to leave, but the secretary called her back.

"Want to grab a bite for supper?" Rochelle inclined her head in Aspen's direction. "I'm thinking of swinging by Wild Dick's on the way home. Maybe pick up a Dickburger and O-rings." She switched off the fan and rested it in her lap. "Who am I kidding?" Rochelle sat up straight. She leaned in conspiratorially. "I'm going over there because one of my friends' daughters talked to a good-looking man at the bar. When he invited her home with him, she said no. Later, he ambushed her in the parking lot as she was getting into her car. He cracked her head open with a tire tool, abducted her, raped her and left her for dead out in the middle of no-damned-where. That was a month ago. Since then, I've been stopping by every evening hoping he'll return. I have a little something for him." She hoisted her handbag from the floor. Fingertips whitened against the heft as she rested it in her lap. Rochelle patted the purse knowingly.

"You're asking me to come along as bait?" Aspen stared, incredulous.

"I'm merely inviting you to share a Dickburger."

"I can't tell you how much I'd like to do that," she said, sarcasm brimming, "only I have a date."

"Boyfriend?"

She didn't want to get into the whole, embarrassing *dumped-for-a-stripper, got desperate, resorted to an online dating service* explanation, so she said, "First date," and left it at that.

"Then you should wipe that mascara out from under your eyes and powder your nose. It's as red as a Kojak light. And one more piece of advice —"

Mortified, Aspen halted in her tracks.

"— Gordon hates crybabies. Every time Southern Methodist University sends us a new crop of interns, one of these numbskulls ends up making them cry. Don't ever show your face in here again with tear-tracks on your cheeks or you'll never hear the end of it."

The owners of Tranquility Villas Care Center built the taupe stucco building on a cul-de-sac less than three miles from Aspen's house on the west side of Fort Worth. Outside, the lawns were immaculate with flowerbeds planted in bright hues; inside, the floors had been polished to a high luster. Visiting areas were appointed in restful Wedgwood colors with matching sofas, a baby grand piano in one corner, plenty of fake Ficus trees positioned near the windows and Oriental rugs to break up large areas into smaller ones.

Then came the individual rooms, plain and unadorned for the most part, with hospital beds for those who needed nursing care and regular twin beds for those who only required minor assistance during their daily routine. Each room had a small closet, a bathroom and a picture window overlooking a central courtyard that served as an additional visiting area during bouts of mild weather.

Aspen spotted her father in the main area watching Monday night football with a bunch of elderly ladies. Groupies came in all ages, she decided, and the man was still attractive despite the fact he had trouble remembering things that happened yesterday or that morning or even five minutes ago.

After signing in at the front desk, she walked toward him with pep in her step.

"Wexford," said a nurse, holding the remote control and powering down the volume, "your daughter, Aspen, is here to see you. You do want to see your daughter, Aspen, don't you?" Enthusiastic head bob. "Sure you do. Aspen's here. Come on over, Aspen."

She realized this was one of those times when Wexford Wicklow's memory needed jogging and she didn't hold the repetition of her name against the woman for trying.

"Hi, Daddy." One of the women got up from the couch. Aspen slid into the empty space next to her father.

"Who're you?" He did a little eye squint, removed his glasses and pulled out the tail of his shirt to wipe the lenses.

"I'm your daughter. I'm Aspen. Remember?" Her chin quivered as Wexford returned his eyeglasses to his face and seated them into the little pink dents on the bridge of his nose.

"Mr. Wicklow's had a big day today, haven't you, Mr. Wicklow?" prompted the nurse.

Aspen wished she'd go away. Instead, the attendant prattled on about how he'd eaten a linebacker's breakfast of eggs and bacon with a slice of ham and a dish of peaches-and-cream oatmeal. And coffee. Wexford Wicklow loved his coffee.

Aspen gave the woman a patronizing smile and turned to her father. "I got a job, Daddy. At a TV station. I'm going to be on television."

"Who're you?"

"I'm Aspen. I got an investigative reporter job at WBFD Channel Eighteen, Daddy. If you can remember to watch the *Public Defender* spot on Thursdays, I'll be on every other week starting ten days from now."

He wouldn't remember.

But the nurse could note it in his chart and remind him.

She looked to the woman for help, but she'd already padded off, squeegee-ing the floor beneath the weight on her rubber-soled shoes.

"You're a movie star?" Wexford reared back, impressed, as if trying to recall the films she'd starred in. "I like Marilyn Monroe. Always had a thing for blondes."

"I have to go now, Daddy. I'll come see you again soon, okay? Take care of yourself." She gave the groupies a perfunctory nod, then rose from the couch in time to glimpse her mother shuffling down the hall in a silk kimono and house slippers.

She broke into a trot, intercepting Jillian Wicklow in the foyer before she had a chance to stumble upon her ex-husband.

What the hell was wrong with these people? Oh sure, doctors predicted the short-term memory loss resulting from her mom's head trauma would improve with time, but until that happened, the poor woman was vulnerable to the charms of her ex. She'd warned them to keep her parents in separate wings. The director of the facility promised neither would ever find out that the other one lived there. Now her mother was flitting around the room like a social butterfly. And Wexford Wicklow was the net.

"Momma, guess what?" Aspen took her by the arm and steered her back to her quarters. She shot a wicked glare at the front desk staff and redirected her mother's attention by mentioning the investigative reporter job.

"I'll be on every other Thursday night," she added with conviction.

The entire story was a waste of breath. As soon as she left, her mother wouldn't even recall their visit, much less have the wherewithal to remember when to tune in the TV.

She left the nurses with a brusque reminder. If they wanted to keep the tranquility in Tranquility Villas, they'd best keep the Wicklows separated.

She hurried out to her Honda, excited by the prospect of meeting a nice man who might take her mind off Roger. She wondered whether her online date actually resembled any part of the grainy photo he'd e-mailed her during the *get-to-know-me* phase . . . that period following the *your-profiles-match* stage . . . which occurred shortly after the initial *somebody-wants-to-meet-you* part.

At seven o'clock sharp, she wheeled the aging Accord into the parking lot of Chica Tica's, a premier Mexican restaurant in the heart of downtown Fort Worth. After settling a mint-flavored breath chip on her tongue, she killed the engine and checked her make-up against her reflection in the rearview mirror. She darkened her cinnamon-colored lashes with a fresh swipe of mascara and shadowed her lids with a pale shade of lilac that brightened her emerald eyes. Short on time, she moistened

her full lips with a neutral gloss and pro-
nounced herself acceptable.

She deftly adjusted her push-up bra, shim-
mying just enough to repackage the goods.
Then she opened her silk charmeuse blouse
down to the third button. With spirits
buoyed, she left the Kelly green jacket in
the car and hurried across the parking lot.

Inside the restaurant, she paused beside
the *Please Wait to be Seated* sign, near a
podium where the wait staff penciled-in the
seating chart. A swatch of fabric whisking
through a side exit snared her attention. Her
mind barely had time to register it as the
back flap of a man's overcoat when a chubby
girl wearing the Chica Tica uniform —
black skirt, white shirt — stepped into the
space behind the pedestal.

The hostess spoke in the thick Mexican
accent of an illegal immigrant. "How
meenie? One? Two?"

In a soft, hypnotic voice, Aspen informed
the waitress that she was meeting a blind
date.

"He ees tall, thees man you're looking
for?"

"Yes."

"And the hair ees *color de plata?* Silver?"

"A little on the sides, yes." She touched
the hair at her temples by way of reference.

"*Muy guapo?* Thees man, he ees berry handsome?"

"I think so." Aspen felt her face flush. She looked past the girl's shoulder and scanned the dining room expectantly. Nobody fit the description. When she refocused on the waitress, the girl's exuberant expression had dulled.

The head bobbing stopped. Her mouth hardened. "Ees — how you say? —" she fumbled, fluttering her hands to make herself understood — "he saw you coming. Took off." She thumbed at the side door. "So . . . *comida para una?* Dinner for one?"

CHAPTER FIVE

Aspen arrived at WBFD at four-fifteen Tuesday morning dressed in celery green slacks, matching pumps, a celery green jacket and paprika knit top that brought out the fire in her hair. She did a cursory scan of the parking lot looking for Tig's metallic bronze Hummer. When she didn't see it in its reserved space, she indulged a victory grin.

Inside, the anchors were preparing to break away from the national affiliate to deliver the local newscast. Make-up artists hovered around the real luminaries of WBFD: Bill Wallace, Steve Lennox and Misty Knight.

The studio buzzed with concern for an investigative reporter from a rival TV station, injured on the job. The man had gotten cold-cocked in the middle of his broadcast by a crazed Mexican couple, the focus of his identity theft ring investigation.

Bill Wallace, looking pale and sickly until the make-up artist bronzed his face and feathered a spot of color onto his cheeks with a blush brush, swiveled his chair toward Steve Lennox. "Did you see when she belted him in the nose with her plastic water bottle?" He scrunched his face. "Yow. Blood everywhere. That had to hurt."

Lennox, a younger, leaner, healthier version of Bill Wallace, said, "What about when her husband came out, tackled him and broke the poor guy's ribs?" He took a deep breath and shook his head. "Noble bastard."

Misty Knight, perky and presentable in a bright tailored suit, chimed in. "Wait until Gordon hears about it. He'll go through the roof. He'll probably assign Tig or the new girl to stand in the middle of five o'clock traffic just to shore up our ratings."

Everyone shared a good laugh while Aspen stood in the wings, pawing through the latest batch of news tips for the *Public Defender* spot. She picked up a fax and let her eyes drift over the page.

Without warning, a hand reached over her shoulder and plucked the sheet from her grasp. She whipped around and found herself looking up the nose hairs of Tig Welder.

"Maybe nobody told you, but I'm the

senior reporter, so I get first pick."

With her sweetest smile, Aspen turned to him, hand on hip. "What I was told is *first come, first served.* I was here. You weren't. I'll take that back now." She jutted her chin in defiance.

"Too bad." He grabbed the rest of the tips, a fistful of phone messages, and sauntered down the hall, calling back over one shoulder. "Sometimes it's chicken; sometimes it's feathers. When I'm finished, feel free to sort through what's left."

She stood, dumbstruck, in the sort of hurling confusion a sunbather might face on a balmy day at the lake while reaching for a Mai Tai, only to discover, too late, that it rested beside the gaping mouth of an alligator.

Aspen spent the next hour in the studio watching the anchors do the local broadcast. First, they gave the up-to-date news. Next, Misty predicted the highs and lows of the day's weather forecast. She appeared to be standing in front of a blank chartreuse screen that the technical people referred to as the chroma key wall. The way it worked, everywhere the camera registered the display screen's green color, a keying circuit would substitute another piece of video in its place — in Misty's case, what popped up behind her on the television monitor was a satellite view of the Metroplex and beyond. As she pointed out various spots on the vacant display, the monitor gave a clear picture of a French-manicured hand gesturing to different towns as she recapped their temperatures with the panache of a pro.

Looking radiant in a peacock blue suit with her honey-colored hair cascading over the lapels, Misty wooed the viewers. "What does the work week have in store for you? Let's take a look, shall we?"

A video segment with the pollen count flashed across the monitor, abruptly replaced by a soundless tract of the station's helicopter pilot, Chopper Deke, scaring the crap out of Traffic Monitor Joey as the light utility aircraft swooped close to the ground and buzzed a herd of cattle. Then Deke leaned into the dash-cam mounted inside the helicopter and viewers were treated to a deranged close-up of a gray-green eyeball with the white showing all around it. As the pilot pulled back and the camera captured Joey's mouth contorted into an inaudible scream, Misty happened to glance over at the monitor.

The sultry-voiced meteorologist did a double take.

After shooting the photographer a withering look, she quickly composed herself. "If you're worried about catching the flu this season, here's an idea for you — move. Shun other people. Become Amish. Oh, for Pete's sake — wash your filthy hands. Didn't your mother ever teach you anything? What — were you raised in a barn?" Huge blue doe eyes widened in alarm. "What the heck just happened? I disappeared off the screen. You make it look like I'm talking to myself. Which one of you idiots pushed the wrong button?" she asked of the room at large. Her hands dropped to her side in frustration.

Then Misty stormed off the set.

Aspen's eyes widened. Talk about a mood swing — she suspected she'd just witnessed a person in the manic phase of bipolar disorder plummet directly into depression without any transition in between.

"That's pretty cool, huh? Today's forecast is bright and sunny with an eighty percent chance she's wrong."

The voice came from behind and to the right.

Aspen spun around. She took in the tall, sturdy man in stages: nicely clipped mustache and goatee, blue jeans, navy T-shirt with the Dallas Cowboys logo on the front breast pocket and . . . *Birkenstocks with socks.*

Realization jolted her — in the short time they'd spent together, had Margo's snobbery already rubbed off on her?

She shook off a scowl and looked up expectantly. "What just happened?"

He smiled down at her. "You're referring to the tantrum? Today's weather girl is frightening and moody with a ninety-five percent chance she's off her meds."

"Where'd she go?"

"Hopefully to the pharmacy to pick up a prescription," he said. "I'm Max. You're the new girl."

"Aspen Wicklow." She held out her hand and he returned a hearty shake. "What do you do here?"

"Photographer."

"Maybe we'll have a chance to work together," she said hopefully.

"That'd be nice. Let me know if you need anything," he added before hurrying off down the hall to Production.

After Aspen settled into her office, she pulled out a stack of accordion file folders and withdrew a black felt-tip marker from the top drawer of the desk. Suspecting Tig might be reluctant to invade her privacy if she printed *Early Menopause and How to*

Beat It on the first cover, she labeled the rest of the flaps with *Tips for a Cleaner Litter Box, Cooking for Twelve, Using Coupons to Shrink Your Grocery Bill,* and *Desert Hiking Trails.*

Then she removed the tip sheet on prison overcrowding from her purse and scanned it for interesting tidbits. Prison overcrowding didn't seem like the stuff breaking news was made of, but she checked the wall clock, decided cops probably got to work earlier than regular people and dialed the contact number anyway. As she waited for an answer, she wrote *PMS* on a folder and stuck the tip sheet inside of it. Now she'd see whether pixies messed with her stuff.

The Johnson County Sheriff took her call while seated behind his desk, grimly re-reading the letter he'd received the day before from the Texas Department of Criminal Justice. The longer he read, the more his jaw flexed.

He told her this, and his disgruntled voice set the tone for the conversation.

According to the formal notice, the number of convicts officially exceeded the inmate-to-guard ratio. Effective immediately, the sheriffs of two hundred fifty-four counties could no longer bring inmates into the prison system until overcrowding ceased. Or the TDCJ got money to hire more guards. Or built more penitentiaries.

In other words, when hell froze.

"We're not lawdogs," groused Sheriff Samuel "Spike" Granger. "We're plumbers. Poorly paid plumbers."

Aspen grabbed a pen. She admired the passion coming from this crusty lawman. He might make a good lead-in.

Granger broke the problem down in simpleton terms.

"Think of the prison system as one giant toilet. When it backs up, there's no place for the human waste to go. Sewage swirls around inside the county jails until we can get rid of it. I'm talking about criminals," he said, dispelling any ambiguity. "We're giving these turds six days of good time credit for every day they spend here. One inmate only got fifteen years and one day for killing that crazy wife of his. At this rate, by the time we drive him down to the Walls Unit, he'll have already done his time. He'll stay long enough to swagger into Diagnostic, get his picture taken and out he goes. This is turning into a catch-and-release program."

"How can I help you?"

"Put the word out."

Aspen tapped her pen against the blotter.

She needed an angle if she planned to feature him during sweeps month, still a couple of weeks away.

"Excuse me, Sheriff, but this appears to be a statewide problem. How's Johnson County different from the rest of the two hundred fifty-three other counties?"

"What makes us different is we're mad as hell and we're not gonna take it anymore."

Aspen laughed until her face hurt. He had a sense of humor, this Spike Granger guy. And to paraphrase Rochelle, one could never tell where the next good lead-in might come from.

"Will you be in your office this afternoon?"

"Got nowhere else to go. Can't move prisoners. Come on down and I'll buy you a cup."

"Deal. I'll see you at one. Should I bring my photographer?"

"Not today. Tomorrow. When you come back."

"What makes you think I'll be coming back?"

He gave her an Arizona chuckle — a half laugh, half cough. "Oh, you'll be back. I'd bet my paycheck on it."

CHAPTER SIX

Before Aspen left the building, she poked
her head into Tig Welder's office in an effort to be friendly. Big egos like Tig's
needed stroking.

"Quick question. How do you know when
to take along a photographer?"

"Why? Are you working a good lead?"

"It's a generic question." She held his gaze
with a look of practiced innocence. "I'm
new here, remember? So how do you
know?"

"If something's brewing, take him along."

"But how —"

Tig's sneer suggested he half-expected her
to shed her human form, invade his body
and use it as a host. "You may not be working a good lead, but I am. So run along,
Barbie. If you need anything else, run it by
Rochelle."

Stunned into silence, Aspen retreated to
her office and made a to-do list.

She mapped out the location of Pop's Auto Salvage and Repair. Next, she plugged the address for the Johnson County Sheriff's Office into the computer and printed out directions. Then she stopped by Max's cubicle, couldn't find him and went to Rochelle for guidance.

She caught the secretary on the telephone, speaking into the mouthpiece in hushed tones.

"It's a surprise party. You'll need to arrive by seven-thirty. Do you work alone or do you have someone else you can bring with you?" Rochelle drew in a sharp intake of air. "You work with a python? How much does it weigh?" Long pause. "Don't get smart with me — it makes a difference. A skinny, whippy snake will only piss him off. He'd like a big, substantial snake. Seventy-five pounds — are you serious? How can you strip for someone with a big, fat snake draped around your neck? Oh . . . you put it down. On the floor? Does it move around? It coils? So let me ask you . . . this snake of yours, is it big enough to squeeze a man until he suffocates? Uh-huh, I see. If he pays extra, can you not feed it before you bring it over to his house? Right . . . it'll be in a bad mood. Can you keep it just a little bit hungry because I think he'd get a kick out of feeding it?" Another pause. "What's my name? It's Inga."

Aspen cleared her throat, *A-hem.*

Rochelle whipped around. Her eyes widened in alarm. "Call you back," she said in a raspy whisper. She batted her heavily smudged lashes and slipped into the efficient persona of a station manager's assistant. "May I help you?"

"What do I do if I need a cameraman to come along with me?"

"If you need a photographer for live, on-air, local news, take one of the ENG vans," Rochelle said, pointing toward the key box mounted on the inside door of a closet. "If you're just running down a lead, take a sedan from the company pool."

"I'm driving out to see that mechanic to scope out whether there's story potential. If I show up in a company car, it'll be a dead giveaway. I need to take my own in order for this to work." Aspen picked at her cuticles. Embarrassment made her break eye contact. "Trouble is, I'm driving around on 'E'. Do we have a petty cash fund?"

Rochelle leaned over and dug around in her purse. She pulled out a twenty and handed it over.

"Oh, no. No-no-no. I don't want your money."

"Don't worry, kid —" Rochelle winked "— I'll get it back."

Pop's turned out to be an uninviting sprawl. A twelve-foot wall of corrugated sheet metal, similar to that used for roofing, shielded the eyesore from the highway. The main office was nothing more than a portable building attached to a four-vehicle bay area with hydraulic lifts and mechanic's tools scattered about. Dead cars surrounded the remaining property.

Inside, the office reeked of cigarette smoke and petroleum toxins. No one waited behind the counter, but she realized she'd set off a buzzer when a slim young man with wheat-colored hair sauntered in. He wore drab green coveralls, had a crooked smile and acne scars that could be seen from a hot-air balloon.

"Can we help ya?"

"I'm looking for Darwin Leggett. The owner."

"Pop's my uncle. He's seventy-five. He's on oxygen, so he only shows up a few days each month. I run the shop when he's out. Can we help ya?"

"I've been having car trouble. I'm pricing repair places, looking for a fair deal."

"You came to the right place."

"So how much would it cost to fix a ten-year-old Honda?"

"Depends on what it's doing."

Aspen thought fast. "It makes a terrible noise when I shift into drive." She imitated the sound, *clunk.*

"I'll get you an estimate. But first I need to drive it up the road and back. Got your keys?"

She hadn't expected this.

She should've expected it, but she didn't.

"I'll have to come back. I was on my way to an appointment when I saw your sign."

His eyes narrowed. "Then how'd you know to ask for Darwin Leggett?"

He was testing her. Aspen thought fast.

"Some old fellow up the road recommended the place. Said he used to trade with Mr. Leggett and told me I should speak to him. So will he be in tomorrow?"

"Nope."

"Then I'll be back to talk to you."

Heart pounding, she climbed into her car. She barely slid the key into the ignition when a man around her own age jumped out of nowhere and grabbed the doorpost. Binoculars hung from a strap around his neck. In her rearview mirror, she glimpsed a white, late-model pickup that could've been his. In those first few seconds of panic, she tried to memorize the license plate while simultaneously attempting to slam the car door shut.

"I didn't mean to scare you. I just need to ask a few questions," he said, his voice weary and falling.

She chanted the truck's tag number in her head, in case the police had to be called. If she lived, she could provide it. If he planned to rob or kill her, she was wasting time memorizing his LP when she should've been positioning herself to stomp his groin.

"Let go of my door."

"Okay, but you've got to help me."

"I'm not giving you money. There's a law against panhandling." Now *that* sounded stupid. What happened to her coping skills? She should've been leaning on the horn or ripping out the keys to gouge his eyes.

"I'm not after money. I need information. I want to know the layout of this place."

She committed his facial features to memory: dark hair, stylish cut; intense blue irises the shade of old china; strong jaw, cleft chin; straight nose listing slightly to the left; lips that were neither too full nor too thin; unblemished olive complexion. He didn't look like the type to be casing the joint but one never knew. "Why not go inside and have a look around?"

"Can't. I tried to get my girlfriend's car

back and the mechanic called the cops on me. They wrote me a criminal trespass warning and told me they'd jail me if I set foot on the property again. Help me. Please."

"Is the car registered in your name?"

"No. It's registered to Gabrielle."

Realization dawned. This was the man Margo Sommervel told her about. "Look, even I'm not dumb enough to think they'd give it to you if it's not registered in your name."

"Gabrielle's out of state. She had a message on the machine saying the car was ready, and if she didn't pick it up by Friday they'd sell it for scrap. I can't let that happen."

"Call her. Have her fax you a Power of Attorney and get it legally."

"She doesn't answer her phone," he said miserably.

Aspen looked at him squinty-eyed. "You're planning to steal it back, aren't you?"

He shifted his gaze. "I tried to settle the bill. He wouldn't accept my check. Said he didn't know me. I tried to put it on my credit card but he said I couldn't take the vehicle without a release from Gabby."

"Sounds reasonable."

"He demanded cash. He said he didn't

want to fool with the credit card people in case Gabby decided to dispute the bill later. He said he'd lost a lot of money because of disgruntled people trying to rip him off."

He hadn't gone to the ATM to withdraw the cash because payday wasn't until Friday. If he wrote a check, it wouldn't clear until after his job made the direct deposit.

"Sounds to me like you were planning to write a hot check," Aspen said.

"I'm desperate."

"I'm sorry. I can't help you."

His hand dropped away from the door. Crestfallen, his gaze dipped to the ground. "I wouldn't help me either. It sounds lame, but it's the truth." He looked up expectantly. "If you could just tell me whether you saw a dark blue BMW back there, that would help."

Aspen did a one-shoulder shrug. "Sorry. I didn't know to look for one." She scrawled out the number of her business line and handed it over. "Look, if you learn anything you'd like to share about this place or these people, I'm willing to listen. I hope you hear from your girlfriend, I really do."

But deep down, she suspected the poor guy was spinning his wheels. That Gabrielle had left town with a new love interest without telling him, and even managed to dupe him into caring for her cat.

CHAPTER SEVEN

Johnson County was thirty miles away from Fort Worth and thirty years behind. As Aspen entered Sheriff Granger's digs, she inconspicuously eyed him up. She had no idea what she'd get from this rugged lawman of indeterminate age, with his elephant-hide boots, bottle-thick lenses and eyes the color of old nickels. But when he walked in larger than life with a gunfighter gaze, he definitely got her attention. He wore a double rig — two gun belts — strapped on his hips, with holsters that held identical Colt .45 Lightweight Commanders sporting ivory grips inlaid with gold longhorns. In a way that transcended self-assurance, he extended his hand, shaking hers as if they'd just sealed a multi-million dollar deal. When he removed the big white ten-x beaver cowboy hat and hung it on a peg inside his office, she noted the bald spot on top of his head. As he unbuttoned his black Frontiercut vest, the outline of body armor revealed itself beneath his crisp, white shirt.

His face creased into a broad smile.

"I'm usually on time," he said, "but this is *'Who's your daddy?'* day down at the courthouse. I went through school with Buster Root, one of the inmates, and decided to drive him to the square myself so we could catch up. See — Buster's an escape risk and I'm up for re-election. Wouldn't do to have that rascal break out of my jail. Gave me an opportunity to have a little sit-to with him."

She nodded politely and took in her surroundings in a glance. Peace officer certificates, college diploma with the graduation date in a font too small to read and a twelve-point buck mounted on the wall presiding over the room with its glassy-eyed stare; a photograph of Granger standing near a grizzly bear, a picture of him shaking hands with President Bush and an eight-by-ten glossy of a young boy — probably Granger — standing next to John Wayne with the Duke's arm slung across his thin shoulders. A rusty old Wells Fargo safe . . . and next to it, a photo of Johnson County's first hanging.

Her hand went reflexively to her throat. Staring uncomfortably at the bulging eyes and protruding tongue of the deceased, she swallowed hard.

"Call off the transport down to Huntsville," the sheriff hollered to a passing deputy.

"The chain gang's already left," came the reply.

"Then radio the men to return with the prisoners." He turned to Aspen and gave her the once-over. "You look like trouble." He flashed a wry grin.

She liked his easy manner and the way he touched her elbow as he ushered her to a guest chair, a few feet away from what looked like an automatic shoeshine machine.

"How do you take your coffee?"

"In a bottle of Big Red." After drinking a cup of the vile brew one of the photographers tried to pass off as dark roast that morning, she didn't need any more caffeine speeding through her system.

"Never trust a person who doesn't drink coffee." He eased into the leather wingback behind his desk and punched the intercom on his phone. "Lucinda, bring this young lady a Big Red." Then he said, "What're you looking at?"

"Your badge." She hadn't seen a police shield quite like that before.

"It's patterned after the Texas Ranger

badge. It's silver, made from a 1948 Mexican *cinco peso.* The coin can't be any later than that because the silver content drops and they tarnish. Care to have a look?" He pulled out the clip-on badge holder and flashed a boyish but deadly smile.

She did a quick lean-in and whiffed the faint scent of new leather. He manipulated the badge and extended it close enough for her to read the words *Estados Unidos Mexicanos* and observe the remnants of a die-struck Mexican eagle on the back. The front had pieces cut away to form a five-point star, with the seal of the state of Texas enameled in the center, flanked by an olive branch to symbolize peace and a stem of oak leaves to represent strength.

Aspen didn't know what to think as he returned the badge to its clamshell holder and clamped it back onto the pocket of his leather vest. On the one hand, he seemed nice enough. On the other hand, he looked like the kind of guy who could set his own leg. Or yank out an abscessed tooth with a pair of pliers and no scorpion mezcal.

And he was still sizing her up, measuring her with those eyes. She glanced away, but the pull of his magnetic gaze reeled her back in. Amusement crinkled the corners of his eyes. He seemed to be fighting a smile.

Probably figured out I'm new at this.
He's thinking I'm a tenderfoot.

Spike Granger leaned back in his chair. He rested his forearms on the frame, letting his hands hang limp. He appraised her with a long stare. After pulling off his wire-rim glasses, he set them on the blotter and ran a meaty hand over a weather beaten face the color and texture of old leather.

He reseated the heavy lenses into the dents on the bridge of his nose and picked up the letter that had started this mess. Then he pitched it across the desk in disgust. It sailed a couple of feet before dropping.

Without waiting for her to read it, he ran down the information in angry, abbreviated strokes. "The prisons are overcrowded. TDCJ says we can't bring in any more inmates. That means we have to house the inmates here. In the county jail. Until beds open up," Granger added in a voice laced with impatience.

Aspen pulled out her notebook, flipped to a clean page and let the pen hover above the lines. "How long will that be?"

"Until further notice."

She glanced up. "How long is that?"

"When Hell freezes."

To reinforce just how bad the situation

had gotten, he gave her a tour of the jail. They started at the booking desk, where one of Granger's lieutenants delivered the bad news. The county jail had reached capacity the day before. Now for every offender they booked in, they'd have to turn a criminal loose.

"We're coming up on the weekend, Sheriff, and you know how that goes," said the lieutenant as he slid off the bar stool and walked around the counter. "If the Fletchers get likkered up again and go to fighting, we'll need at least two more beds."

"Maybe they'll kill each other," Granger deadpanned. "They'd be doing a public service. If nobody dies, maybe we'll write them tickets for disorderly conduct."

Aspen's eyes went wide. She jotted this on her field notebook.

"That was off the record," Granger warned good-naturedly.

"Next time tell me before you say it or it won't be. Fair warning. I'm a reporter. This is what I do."

"Sassy lady, aren't you?"

His words seemed harsh but she liked what he said. And she liked the way he said it, with a grin angling up one side of his mouth and those nickel-colored eyes darkening like lead slugs.

Granger's lieutenant ventured forth with an unpleasant metaphor. "It's like packing too many chickens in the same crate, Sheriff. To keep 'em from pecking each other to death, you have to snip off their beaks. Only these ain't chickens and we can't go cutting off body parts. We don't have enough jailers to watch anybody else. It's tighter than a tick in there. We need relief and we need it yesterday."

"You can quote him on that," Granger said with a wink.

The lingering question became *What do we do now?*

Aspen asked if neighboring jails had space. If so, could another county house the Johnson County excess until the jail population thinned out?

"I contacted a friend and colleague over in Ellis County. No such luck. All Texas sheriffs are feeling the pinch."

"So what's the plan to ease the congestion?"

Sheriff Granger didn't say.

"I have to be candid with you." Aspen packed up her pen and stowed her notebook in her handbag. "Without an angle, you're story's no different than the other sheriffs."

"Even uneducated farm boys like yours truly possess a certain amount of rural cunning. And when your 'nads are on the chopping block, rural cunning beats book-smarts, hands down." He gave her a wide grin. "Care to have dinner with me?"

She remembered seeing the college diploma. Who was he kidding?

Her eyes flickered to his ring finger. He didn't wear a wedding band. Better still, he didn't have one of those telltale white circles where a ring should've been.

"I have to get back to the TV station. And I have an appointment."

He seemed genuinely disappointed. She wasn't about to confess that she'd resorted to online dating a month ago and had most recently signed up for the five-minute date, an innovative new program similar to musical chairs, started by a group of singles who'd experienced their fair share of bad blind dates. She wasn't about to admit that tonight was the first time she'd experience leaving a potential match when the timer chimed, only to move on to the next table for another speed date with a new bachelor.

"Come back tomorrow morning," Granger said. His eyes took on a speculative gleam. "And bring your cameraman."

His confidence unnerved her. "You're not going to do anything to make me lose my job, are you?"

"Don't really know about that, but I can guarantee you a story that'll make it worth your while if you're brave enough to handle it." He winked. "You might even win some kind of award once we're done."

Chapter Eight

For a fleeting moment, Aspen thought the five-minute date concept had promise, right up until a leggy runner-up from the Miss Texas pageant signed in behind her. Every man she met seemed to stare right past her, ogling the brunette and losing track of the conversation. Eventually, she figured out they weren't actually studying the competition as much as they were checking out the televisions mounted in the corners. After all, this was a sports bar. Just because it was ladies' night didn't mean women commandeered all the attention.

The first match on her scorecard called himself Lonely Kelvin. Not bad looking, with white-blonde hair and shocking blue eyes. But he was visiting from South Africa; and unless he had a penis eight thousand miles long, developing an actual relationship held about the same odds as a centerfold model keeping her clothes on.

The second five-minute date turned out worse.

As she sat across the table from Freddie-the-fat-Samoan, she realized it wasn't his weight that bothered her. Or the ancestry. When Freddie disclosed that he'd be living with his adult children while looking for employment, warning bells clanged inside her head. Not only did she not want a man without a job, she hadn't bargained for a ready-made family, either.

She left early, reflecting on the third five-minute date. Bachelor number three killed any possibility of renewing her membership. Brad from Benbrook was easy on the eyes with lush salt-and-pepper hair and a Padre Island suntan. But when he abruptly zoned out in the middle of the conversation and fixed his stare on some distant point in space, Aspen wasn't sure whether he was having a petit mal seizure or responding to internal stimuli. In retrospect, she hoped it was the latter. At least there were prescription drugs to control the hallucinations. She drove home, eager to shower and sleep until the alarm went off at three.

As she slid her key into the doorknob, Midnight, the lean black street kitty, hopped effortlessly onto the porch. Half slinking, half stalking, he gained entry to the house

84

like a home invader, following her inside and taking over in the kitchen. Allowing Midnight access to the house was like inviting U.S. Customs inside to have a look around.

She filled a small saucer with cat food, made herself a bologna sandwich with a leaf of lettuce, slice of tomato and a generous swipe of mayo, and sat at the Formica breakfast table, nibbling, while the stray gorged himself to capacity. With a chopping meow, he stood by the kitchen door until she let him out. He slinked into the abyss with his stomach distended and one of those eternal cat smiles riding on his face.

The alarm went off way too soon. She tried to incorporate the bleating annoyance into her dream, but it didn't work. Pushing herself up on one elbow, she reminded herself she needed to beat Tig Welder to the studio.

Besides, she should be excited about today.

On Wednesdays, J. Gordon Pfeiffer held weekly staffings. Promptly at nine, the news team assembled in the conference room to bat around ideas for Gordon to either accept or veto.

She selected a pair of knit slacks and top in a deep shade of paprika that brought out the fire in her hair. Instead of a jacket, she layered it with a matching silk shirt. By the time she reached the office, the electric blue digits on the Honda's dashboard clock flashed ten minutes after four. Tig Welder's Hummer was parked in the lot with a coat of dew still on it. Beads of moisture still clung to the windshield. It appeared he'd spent the night here.

Maybe he'd slept on the sofa in the break room.

Perhaps he bunked on the couch in Gordon's office.

Hell — for all she knew he lived there. She'd read Melville's *Bartleby the Scrivener* in college. The deranged Bartleby refused to vacate the office once his employer discovered he'd moved in for keeps.

When she rounded the corner to her office, Aspen hauled up short.

The last thing she expected was to catch Tig rummaging through her desk drawers. Her eyes shifted to the fake files she'd stacked on the bookshelf. They didn't appear to have been monkeyed with. The tiny scrap of paper she'd tucked into the flap of each one was still there.

"Can I help you?" She flashed a smile. Not an electric, full frontal beauty-pageant smile; more like the shrewd-eyed, *got-your-*

number smirk generally associated with cops running a search warrant.

"Where's the information on Pop's Auto and Salvage?"

"I'm sorry," she said, pretending to search her memory. "Are you referring to the story I'm working on?"

"It's not your story anymore, Barbie. I'm taking over. Give me your notes."

"The name's Aspen." She tapped a finger to her temple. "I keep my notes in my head."

It took a several seconds for her meaning to register. He set his jaw and tried to stare her down. Silence stretched between them.

"You can't steal my story. I've been working on this for two days."

"I'm senior. I can take anything I want. Get back to work on the food gig at the prep school cafeteria and give me the mechanic tip."

"You didn't want it. You'd already picked through the good stuff and gave me the leftovers. It's mine." Frustration constricted her lungs. "You can't take my story."

She didn't realize how loud they'd gotten until Rochelle materialized in the doorway. She pinched a pink phone message between her fingernails as if holding a rat by the tail.

"This just in. Looks like you may've hit pay dirt, Aspen. The caller says she knows for a fact the headmaster's getting a kick-back from the meat people who deliver at the school; that's how he's paying for his million-dollar house. She had compelling details. Here." She handed over the slip with a "You'll want to follow up on this," and a hearty "Congratulations."

Aspen glanced down expecting to read a phone number. Only the word *SUCKER!* had been printed on the slip. She wilted. Was the entire staff a pack of cutthroats? Tears blistered behind her eyeballs. She clamped her jaw to still the quiver in her chin.

Tig alerted like a dog having to choose between two T-bones. She could tell by the strange look on his face he was trying to decide which bone had the most meat on it.

"Give it to me." He held his palm out in demand.

She crumpled it protectively into her fist.

Then Gordon walked past at a fast clip.

Rochelle reached out and snagged him by the sleeve. "Looks like you'll have to settle this dogfight. Seems like Tig wants Aspen's story on the mechanic. Only now that a lead came in that'll break the cafeteria scandal wide open, Tig wants that one instead." She stepped aside, leaving enough room for the boss to enter.

He leveled a double-barrelled stare at Aspen. "What are you working on? More importantly, will it be ready to air next Thursday?"

"I'm investigating a salvage yard mechanic ripping off gullible women."

"Been done before. Not that interesting. Happens all the time. Maybe instead of whining about it, boo-hoo, the message in your spot should be for women to take an automotive course so they'll become more informed." His condescending attitude shifted to Tig. "Which do you want to report? The cafeteria or the mechanic? Pick one and let's get back to work."

"I'll take the cafeteria." In three strides, he relieved Aspen of the note, pocketed it and stalked out.

Gordon bellowed, "Good. Then it's settled." To Rochelle, he said, "See? No reason to squabble like brats on the play-ground. People can learn to play nice." He disappeared out the door and ambled down the hall in the direction of his office.

"See?" Rochelle mocked him, "not all station managers are annoying. Some of them are dead."

Dumbfounded, Aspen looked at her. "What just happened in here?"

"Once again, it's Tig biting the hand that

feeds him. He was such an ungrateful baby his mother had to feed him with a slingshot."

Aspen gave a jerky headshake, enough to clear the cobwebs. "Why would you go out on a limb for me?"

"We girls have to stick together."

A coyote wail echoed through Tig's workspace.

Rochelle's peaceful smile turned into a smirk. "The problem with Tig is that he's a selfish, narcissistic know-it-all. He needs to be taught a valuable lesson. I'd like to think you're the one who can do that."

Aspen still waited with the confounded expression of someone who'd just been told her baby had been kidnapped, only to learn that the infant in question wasn't hers after all.

"So there's no lead in the cafeteria scandal?"

"None whatsoever."

"And the headmaster's not really on the take?"

"I certainly hope not."

Aspen' eyes darted around the room. "So you just made that up about kickbacks from the meat delivery people?"

Rochelle gave her a flat stare.

A slow grin spread across Aspen's face.

Chills raced up her arms. "Why would you jeopardize your standing here to help me?"

"Things aren't always what they appear to be, hon. You have your reasons for doing things and I have mine. Tig has his, too, but ours are more noble. Let's just say you owe me one and leave it at that. For now. I'll decide when to collect."

Aspen wanted to burst into tears. "I caught him rifling through my office like a common burglar."

"Kid, you have to understand . . . Tig and Steve have the combined maturity of a twelve-year old. If you factor Misty into the equation, it's more like fourteen. Did he swipe anything?"

"I think he was snooping — trying to find out what I'm working on."

"I'll handle it."

"Please don't say anything. I don't want people thinking I'm a snitch."

Rochelle stuck out her index finger and crossed her heart. "I have other ways of taking care of Tig when he gets out of line." She did a conspiratorial lean-in. "He's juggling five women and they're all paranoid. The one named Inga's a raving psycho. She speaks three languages — all unintelligible. He lets her answer his phone like she's his personal receptionist."

She launched into an affected imitation of the girlfriend. " 'Dis iss Inga. Tig iss not available to take your call. I vill give him da message. Hold please, vile I find a pen.' " She resumed her own persona. "Next time Inga spends the night, I'll call and pretend I'm one of those hoopty-hooptys down on Hemphill Street. 'Uh, yeah, this is Feather . . . does Tig still want me to come over and blow him?' "

Aspen gasped. Men had been murdered by jealous females over less provocation than this. "Isn't that kind of rash?"

Rochelle touched a fingernail to her teeth, pondering the notion. "Unfortunately for Tig, these things often escalate until somebody dies. I used to watch out for Stinger. The last time I paid Tig back for stabbing Stinger in the back, I found out who Tig's neighbors were and impersonated them. I called nine-one-one from a pay phone and told them I'd seen him carrying a body through the backyard."

Aspen stared with rapt attention. "What happened?"

"He never said. But I drove by around two in the morning and there were backhoes, front-end loaders and floodlights all over the place." She stared at a point in space and chuckled in happy remembrance. "Tig's so plastic. He wants everybody to think he's got this perfect life and we're not good enough to be part of it. Well, I've got news for him — some of us are. But let's keep it between us, shall we?"

CHAPTER NINE

The nine o'clock staff meeting was standing room only. Four female interns from Southern Methodist University hovered around each other like Saturn's moons. Their interest on this particular morning seemed focused on whether a Beverly Hills manicure was superior to a French manicure rather than what they could learn about the television industry. They appeared Voguish in their beautiful clothes, especially the coed wearing the sensational blue silk suit with a shocking pink lining that looked good enough to lick. Much like the Drummond sisters, their common philosophy seemed to be *Shop 'til you're diagnosed.*

The news anchors formed a separate clique. They whispered among themselves while the photographers tried to drum up interest from the interns. Aspen sat by herself and attempted to ignore Tig, marinating in cologne, glaring at her across the table. When Gordon and Rochelle walked in, all businesslike, the investigative superstar flashed his veneers and put on the game face of a team player.

"Do we have meat?" Gordon asked of the room at large.

Anyone who wasn't standing sat at attention.

Steve Lennox flashed an endearing grin. "We have meat, boss."

"Glad to hear it. Listen up." Gordon glanced around. "For you interns who've been wondering what to do when it ices over, our inclement weather policy is this: Come to work. I don't care how you get here . . . ice skates, sled dogs, toboggan . . . strap tennis rackets on your feet. The point is this — if Hell freezes over, then Hell is closed but you're still coming to work. Any questions?"

The coeds exchanged bovine stares.

Gordon set his jaw.

"Swear to God." Rochelle sighed. "Some days it's just not worth chewing through the restraints to get out of bed."

When riled, Rochelle's cheeks reddened like a bad case of rosacea. At the moment, her face blazed as bright as a prairie fire.

Each member of the WBFD team shared what they were working on. When Tig's turn rolled around, he reported findings in the prep-school cafeteria scam that appeared way more grandiose than Aspen had originally thought. He'd also run down information on an illegal casino tip that came from one of the adjacent counties. According to what Tig had found out, the District Attorney wouldn't prosecute because his brother owned an eight-liner joint that also harbored a floating poker game.

When Aspen's turn came, she downplayed the mechanic investigation. After all, Tig might still be able to use his pull to con Gordon into taking it away from her.

"Are you going to be ready to run with it a week from tomorrow?"

"I'll do my dead-level best."

"No, Aspen." His eyes narrowed. "The answer is either 'Yes, Gordon,' or 'No, Gordon.' If it's 'Yes,' then I say, 'Mazel tov.' If it's 'No,' —" he shot condescending looks at the SMU girls "— then get one of our husband-hunting interns to assist you. Don't be afraid to ask for help. The only one here who'll steal from you is Tig. Isn't that right, Tig?"

"That's right, Gordon."

The room erupted in laughter.

"All right, everyone. Back to work. Tig, don't be getting into any fights. I don't want to see any one-upmanship between you and the guy from Channel Eleven. Max, if Tig dukes it out with anyone, it'll be Aspen. I want you there to video it. If she wins, we'll run it on the six o'clock news." He gave her a wry smile and clapped her on the back. "Welcome aboard, kid."

Then the room emptied out.

Rochelle intercepted her before she could clear the door. "There's a caller holding for you. Said his name was Mike. I told him it'd be a minute but he said he'd wait."

Aspen hurried to her office and punched her straight line.

"This is Mike Henson."

"Okay." The name didn't ring a bell and her lack of recognition seemed to telegraph itself through the receiver.

"I met you yesterday. Pop's Salvage and Auto? I was trying to get my girlfriend's BMW back?"

Irritation set in. She wanted to tell him he should try out that new singles bar in Sundance Square. Maybe put himself out there and find a new girlfriend in time for the cheating Gabrielle's return. A thread of anguish in his voice warned her not to.

"Did you get your friend's car back?" she asked politely.

"No."

She inhaled deeply.

J. Gordon Pfeiffer had handed her this investigation on a silver platter, with a deadline to match. The last thing she needed was to pretend to be a master at couples' counseling. The station aired a Wednesday show called "Ask Lindsey" for that kind of hoopla. A sarcastic *Ann Landers–meets–Rosie O'Donnell–meets–Saturday Night Live* kind of program that bordered on abuse. It occurred to her that Lindsey, with her tough-love, snap-out-of-it, buck-up-don't-muck-up attitude, might help him see the light.

She infused cheer into her voice. "How can I help you, Mike?"

"I was going through her things. Not spying on her," he added hurriedly, "just trying to make sense of why she'd leave in such a hurry and not tell me."

"Look, I'm sorry things aren't going well for you —"

"Please." Urgency permeated his tone. "Just listen. There's something fishy going on. I need someone to run interference for me. I know you don't know me from Adam but there's nobody else who'll lift one damned finger to help me. I'm asking you." His voice cracked. "Please. You're a reporter.

If I could get into her car and nose around, there might be information that would help me find her."

"I thought you said she went to visit her sick aunt," Aspen said with a tinge of exasperation, then wondered why she'd committed such a mundane detail to memory when Mike Henson and his cheating girlfriend Gabrielle were none of her business.

"That's just it. I found her Bible. There's a family tree. There's no aunt. There's an uncle, but there's no aunt."

Lord, Mike was thick-skulled. At least when Roger's phone calls tapered off, she took the hint. She didn't hire the television show *Cheaters* to dog him all over town, pull surveillance and then present her with tawdry video evidence of his indiscretions. He'd found her replacement and there wasn't much she could do about it.

Aspen played devil's advocate. "Maybe the uncle's married and she's referring to her aunt by marriage."

"I grew up next door to Gabby. I've met the guy. He's not married."

"Okay, so she lied. She played you."

And there you have it, she wanted to add.

Huge cat. Out of bag. Banking off walls. Running around all over the place.

"I met the people down the road from Pop's. They said during the last couple of weeks, they've heard all kinds of weird noises coming from inside the salvage yard."

"I didn't notice anything out of the ordinary."

"They said it happens at night. They said it sounds like whining. Whining coming from Pop's place."

"Maybe it's one of those grinding tools." Lickety split, her mind grasped for logical explanations. "Don't mechanics occasionally have to grind corrosion off metal and engines and stuff?"

"At three in the morning?"

"Hey," she said, unexpectedly irritable, "I don't know anything about cars. Maybe it's a dog. Show me a junkyard that doesn't come with a dog and I'll show you a nun that doesn't come with underpants."

Mike seconded the notion. "Oh, they have them all right. Two of them. Big, ugly, square-headed monsters on chains attached to those big metal corkscrews twisted into the dirt. They come about two inches from the chain link fence when they lunge at you. Believe me, I know."

She recalled seeing a couple of nasty puncture wounds on Henson's ankle. Injuries that seemed to go with the lacerations on his arm, probably from the razor wire lining the top of the cyclone fence.

She slumped into the nearest chair. It was five minutes before ten and she'd promised to be at Sheriff Granger's office with a photographer by eleven.

"I have to go. We can talk about it later this afternoon. Feel free to call me back."

"You're blowing me off."

"I have an appointment and I'm going to be late as it is. Like I said, call me back and I'll see what I can do."

Without waiting for a reply, she hung up the telephone and went hunting for Max.

CHAPTER TEN

Aspen rode shotgun with Max in the ENG
van, WBFD's electronic news-gathering
vehicle. With a microwave beam capable of
transmitting news, live on the air, for up to
sixty miles, the ENG van came with spools
of cable, an input-output panel with connectors, an *editor* — two tape machines
joined together so scenes of video filler
known as *B-roll* could be edited into a news
package to be shown in conjunction with
the live reporter — and an extendable mast
to raise the transmitting antenna in order to
send the video signal back to the receiver
located in Fort Worth.

Down in Johnson County, Granger had
assembled his men — and one woman — in
a small conference room down the hall from
his office, and his deputies were pinballing
off each other trying to get out the door
when Aspen and Max arrived for the eleven
o'clock appointment.

As they headed for Granger's office, Aspen made small talk. "Is that the only female officer who works here?"

"Who? Crazy Sheila?" He gnat-swatted the air with a wrist flick. "I only hired her to get the EEO prick over in Personnel off my butt."

"I beg your pardon?"

"That was off the record. So is this." Granger snorted in disgust. "I personally don't care what the woman does as long as she doesn't cap any of my men, wreck her patrol car or take a job as a stripper on her days off."

"You're not exactly progressive, are you, Sheriff?"

"I don't have to be. I do what's right, not what's politically correct." He slid her a sideways glance. "Now we're back on the record. You can quote me on that." He led them into his office and waved them into chairs. "Sit."

"You promised me a story." She dug in her purse and pulled out her notebook. "Let's have it."

"Put that away and help yourselves to a cup of sludge." He motioned toward the credenza where a pot of coffee sat warming on its burner. Then he punched out a number on the telephone keypad. "You'll get your story, little lady. And you don't have to write anything down, either."

Aspen dropped, unsmiling, into her seat.

"You're my witnesses. Feel free to film this part."

Max cut the camcorder on. The light beacon brightened the room. Granger's balding head went suddenly shiny.

Aspen said, "What are you doing?"

"Calling the diagnostic unit in Huntsville. I'm a sportsmanlike fellow so I thought I'd give them one last chance to come around to my way of thinking." He halted his speech and held up a finger to command quiet. "Give me the warden." Short pause. "Sheriff Spike Granger, Johnson County," he said with authority. "I want to know if he got my fax."

He slid a meaty hand over the mouthpiece and spoke in a hushed whisper.

"I faxed the warden a bill for the upkeep of one of our inmates." His expression abruptly changed, as if a light bulb idea had come on inside his head. "Tell you what . . . I'll let you two listen in."

He activated the speakerphone with a touch of a button and returned the receiver to its cradle. Then he sat back in his chair with his fingers threaded behind his neck like he'd just survived the best sex in his life.

Everyone waited for the warden to come on the line. An audible click sounded, followed by the greeting of an irritated man.

"This is Warden Baker."

"Howdy, Warden. Spike Granger here. Johnson County Sheriff." He flashed the knowing grin of a showman. "I'm calling to see if you received my fax." He gave a little bobblehead shake.

"What fax?"

Granger's smile collapsed. His playful demeanor took an ominous downturn. "Don't play dumb with me. I faxed you a bill for Harlon Verle's food. I have a court order commanding me to take Verle to your facility —"

"You're not bringing him here."

"The hell you say." Booted feet banged to the floor. The sheriff snapped fully upright. "He's supposed to be in the pen. I'm not keeping him in my jail any longer unless you pay for his upkeep."

"The gates are closed. No guards, no beds."

The veins in Granger's neck plumped like garden hoses. "Let's just shuck right down to the tamale, Warden. I warned you if I had to keep him here, I'd be billing you for his food."

"I don't give a damn if you fax us bills

until the sky turns polka-dot pink. Hell will freeze before we pay it."

The call ended with the echo of a buzzing dial tone.

Infuriated, Granger's face heated up. Gray irises flashed dark as bullets. Fury hardened the corners of his mouth. This was no longer funny; he was no longer playing.

He rose and snatched his Stetson off the hat peg, then seated it on his head and adjusted the brim low on his forehead. His pupils dilated like spent slugs. Through narrowed eyes, he leveled a double-barrelled stare directly into the camera.

"We're taking a road trip, folks. Finish your coffee and I'll pull 'Victimless Verle' out of holdover. Huntsville doesn't know it yet, but Hell's about to freeze."

Max cut the light beacon and lowered the camcorder. "We're going to Huntsville?"

"Yep." Said in the deadpan of a gunslinger.

The photographer's jaw tightened. "I'll have to go back to the station and swap out vehicles. The ENG van's only good for live broadcasts up to sixty miles."

"Then I'd get a move-on if I were you."

Max turned to Aspen. "Coming?"

"If it's all the same to you," Granger said, "I'd just as soon she stayed here."

■ ■ ■ ■

An hour later, Max returned from Fort Worth.

Even after Aspen climbed into the SNG truck and seat-belted herself in, he was still grousing about all the wasted time it took to trade out the ENG van for WBFD's SNG satellite news-gathering truck. The station's million-dollar SNG vehicle came outfitted with the same basic equipment as the ENG van — spools of cable, input-output panels and connectors, an *editor* and an antenna with an extendable mast that raised up as high as forty-two feet — but the SNG had a larger antenna that spanned seven feet across as well as a tiltable microwave dish that collapsed and nested during drive time. Designed for transmitting live broadcasts from great distances, the SNG truck had the capability to send a signal to a geosynchronous satellite twenty-two thousand miles above the Earth, where it would then be relayed back to the receiver in downtown Fort Worth.

"I'm not sure if this guy has kryptonite balls or if he's just plain crazy." Max fired up the engine and the SNG slumped heavily onto the road. Up ahead, Granger's brake lights flickered on as he slowed to enter the ramp leading onto the highway.

"Seems pretty brave to me," Aspen ventured.

"Insane people often come across as fearless, at first glance." Max kept his eyes on the road, darting an occasional glance in her direction. "Like the time Stinger Baldwin was trying to interview a teenager balanced on one of those cement dividers on top of Loop 820. The kid claimed he could fly. When Stinger took a step forward, the guy swan-dived off the overpass — *splat!* Turned out he didn't have super powers. He wasn't fearless; he was schizophrenic."

"You think Granger's crazy enough to pick a fight?"

"Already did," Max said, following the patrol car through the bluebonnet-dotted countryside. "In a way, I can see his point. Why should the costs for feeding and housing a habitual criminal come out of the county's budget? The judge decided fifty-two arrests for so-called victimless crimes were enough. The court order says this guy, Verle, should do pen time."

"What do you think Granger will do?"

"Beats me. But he seems like a real *'get yore bidness straight'* kind of guy, so I don't figure we're wasting a trip. Even if we are, I know a good barbeque place the church ladies have right smack-dab in the middle of town." He did a halfway decent job mocking Granger's country ways.

She wondered if Max was suggesting the sheriff was too stubborn to back down. "You think he's a train wreck?"

His expression told her he didn't know what to make of the lawman. "Man scares the hell outta me, you want to know the truth. But I'd want him on my side in a bar fight." He slid her a sideways glance.

"You think he'll make an ass out of himself?"

"If he does, I'll capture it on camera."

One hundred ninety-four miles later, the Byrd Unit, a large compound made up of red brick buildings, came into view. Aspen pulled down the visor. She flipped up the mirror and reapplied a thin layer of lip balm.

"How do I look?"

Max shrugged. "Better than Britney Spears . . ."

She smiled.

". . . not as hot as Angelina Jolie."

Her lips took a downward turn.

Without looking in her direction, he said, "Better not be wearing any jewelry unless Gordon approved it."

Reflexively, she reached for her claddagh necklace, then remembered she'd taken it off.

Max slowly braked until they were riding Granger's bumper.

He turned to Aspen. "Call him on the cell phone."

Max wanted her to prompt the sheriff to switch on the microphone he'd outfitted him with before leaving the SO. Aspen punched out the number and listened for a connection.

When the lawman answered, she said, "Turn on your mike so we can get a reading."

"Ten-four."

The phone went dead in her hand. The mike came on and they heard a devilish chuckle.

"Testing one-two-three. There once was a girl from Nantucket . . ."

Max powered down the window and gave him the OK sign.

The sheriff wheeled the patrol car up to the first of two checkpoint stations. He'd already forewarned them about the tower just outside the razor-wire fence. Cops called it "the picket" and it housed a prison guard armed with a high-powered rifle. The guard lowered a bucket and Sheriff Granger dropped in his gun, ammo and mobile phone.

Max slowed and deposited their phones.

At the second checkpoint, a gate groaned open enough for Granger to pull in a couple of car lengths. Before Max could follow him inside, the gate crawled across its track like a mouth closing over food.

"We'll have to video from here," he said, jamming the gearshift into park. "If I give you the cutthroat gesture, stop talking so you don't drown Granger out." Max worked fast. He unspooled cable and strung it out, then hooked the connecters to the input-output panel. He slapped at a couple of buttons and up went the mast. In a full scramble, he hoisted up the forty-five thousand dollar camcorder and barked orders. "Go stand next to the cyclone fence and look alive."

She bailed out and trotted over to the mesh barrier, where coils of razor wire stretched the length of the enclosure. Max did a finger countdown, *Three-two-one*. Aspen stood tall, breathing in gulps of crisp, afternoon breeze to calm herself.

This was it.

Feeling her pulse thud in her throat, she stared into the camera. "We're standing outside the Byrd Unit in Huntsville, where small-town sheriff, Spike Granger, says he's *mad as hell and he's not going to take it anymore.* The Johnson County lawman says the Texas Department of Criminal Justice will *take no prisoners* so he's come down to Huntsville bringing a message: *'Go ahead, make my day.'* "

Max did a heavy eye roll and slit his neck from ear to ear with a finger. Aspen faltered. He shifted the camera and zoomed-in on the activity behind her. Aspen turned to look.

Two prison guards approached the patrol car, eyeing Granger and his captive through wraparound sunshades. The sheriff powered down the window and rattled Harlon Verle's paperwork at them.

"What the hell?" said the burly one. He bent at the waist and peered into the vehicle. "We aren't accepting inmates. We're full. Did you not get the memo or can you just not read?"

Laughter erupted from the back seat of the patrol car. Verle's taunts came in loud and clear. "The screws ain't gonna take me, boss."

Granger conjured up a death ray glare sure to penetrate the wire mesh cage. He spoke to the guards in an even, metered tone. "I'm dropping him off and that's that."

112

The guards unsnapped their holsters.

"Holy smoke." Aspen's throat closed around her words.

The prison guards ordered the sheriff to turn the car around and get on down the road.

Granger shifted into reverse. The gate groaned open and he floored the accelerator enough to churn up a choking dust cloud. He curbed the patrol car in front of the closed gate, alighted from the vehicle and yanked open the back door.

He jerked "Victimless Verle" off the seat and marched him over to the fence. Then he reached around to the small of his back and pulled out the pair of handcuffs he'd looped over his belt.

Aspen watched, dumbstruck.

With the camera still rolling, the Sheriff of Johnson County shackled the inmate to the chain link fence, stuffed the prisoner's papers down the front of his jail greens, gave the guards a palsied, over-the-shoulder salute and got back into his car and sped off.

Back at the Johnson County SO, Max was inside the SNG truck editing the story, putting together filler pieces of video from the B-roll to use in the ten o'clock broadcast.

When he finished, he came outside and activated the camcorder so Aspen could introduce the news package.

Her heart thudded as she shoved a mike in Granger's face and asked the million-dollar question.

"Why'd you do it?"

The sheriff cleared his throat. Adjusted the brim of his Stetson and leveled a no-nonsense stare directly into Max's camera lens. His eyes turned flinty and his mouth feral. "I sent them a bill for the cost of feeding and housing their inmate. The warden said they'd pay it when Hell freezes over. Well, guess what? Hell froze."

Aspen turned to the camera. "And there you have it. One man, one county, taking on the Texas Department of Criminal Justice one step at a time. I'm Aspen Wicklow, WBFD News."

CHAPTER ELEVEN

With her shoes kicked off and the telephone pressed to her ear, WBFD's newest investigative reporter lounged in a waiting area outside the studio where she could watch the anchors deliver the late-night news on the TV monitor.

Mike Henson was on the line again, trying to convince her to take another look at Pop's Auto Salvage and Repair. While he ticked off reasons why consumers should be warned against doing business with Pop's, Aspen waited for the ten o'clock news to air so she could watch what amounted to Granger's publicity stunt. The anchors had already taken their seats. They were bantering insults and joking around when one of the runners assigned to monitor the police scanners slipped Steve Lennox a note.

"Jeepers creepers," Lennox yelled. "Get a crew out there — now."

Aspen sat bolt upright. "I have to go. Call

back later."

"You're giving me the bum's rush?"

"No time to explain." She hung up, squeezed her swollen feet back into her shoes and ventured toward the studio to get the lowdown.

"Where's Tig?" Lennox shouted. "How come we don't have any frickin' reporters here? It's a news station for God's sake," he called up to the acoustical ceiling. "We report the news and we don't have any reporters? What the hell?"

Aspen thumbed at her lapels. "I'm a reporter."

Lennox gave her a condescending once-over. He shouted to the room at large. "Where's Tig? Where's Gordon?" He checked himself. "What the hell am I saying? Gordon's eating dinner with his wife at the frickin' Petroleum Club. Stinger Baldwin would've been here." He shook his head in disgust. "Management fires the only employee who practically lived here and now we don't have anyone to cover this . . ." he rattled a sheet of paper ". . . *breaking news.* Somebody page Tig. Tell him to get his ass back down here."

"I'm a reporter." Aspen sauntered into the studio, approached the anchors and braced her palms against the desk. "Use me. I'm here. I can do it."

Lennox looked at her slitty-eyed. "You're the chick from the staff meeting . . . the one who replaced Stinger?"

Aspen swallowed. "I am."

"Fine. This is just frickin' fine. Biggest story this week . . . hell, maybe this year . . . and we're about to get scooped."

"Give it to me." She plucked the paper from his grasp. He snatched it back. "I'm not twelve. You want a job done, I'll do it." She scanned the room. "Where's my photographer?"

Lennox bellowed for Max. He twisted in his seat enough to direct a comment to Misty Knight. "You should do it."

"Why not?" the meteorologist answered, incredulous. The image moving across the station's Doppler radar had gone from the amoeba that ate the Metroplex to looking like a Western omelet at an all-night diner, heavy on the salsa. "And while I'm out in the field, you can figure out which of these swirly things are tornadoes. Without a teleprompter. Rotsa ruck, Rooby Doo."

Lennox's shoulders slumped. "Biggest frickin' story and it goes to a newbie who looks like she's still in grade school."

"I'm still standing here. I'm not deaf. I can hear you," Aspen warned. Max rushed up with his shoulders slumped under the weight of his gear. He grabbed the news sheet from Lennox and thrust it at her.

Aspen's eyes drifted over the page. No wonder Lennox was upset.

This was big.

Very big.

"Let's do it," she said almost breathless, and they raced outside to the nearest ENG van.

The decomposed body of a female had been found in a drainage ditch less than five miles from the home of Caramel Janine Drummond.

CHAPTER TWELVE

Emergency lights lit up the night. In the scramble to set up his gear before the rival stations rolled up, Max looked over at Aspen and barked instructions.

"Don't be scared." He yanked off the red bandana twisted loosely into a headband and handed it to her. "Dry your eyes. Your nose looks like a stoplight. You'll never make it at W-Big-Fucking-Deal if you turn into a sniveling, hysterical heap every time you see a dead body."

She wrung her clammy hands, drying her palms against the fabric of her slacks. "This is horrible."

The victim's pained face had hardened into a grotesque mask but Aspen had no doubt the corpse was that of Candy Drummond. Her stomach went squishy as she breathed in air so gauzy and stale that each breath left a bad taste in her mouth.

She averted her eyes. "I can't help it. She

was a person."

"And now she's not."

I knew her. We pledged the same sorority. She wasn't nice to me but no one should die like this.

A grizzled sergeant from the Tarrant County Sheriff's Office sauntered up with a scowl on his face, mud on his boots and purpose in his step.

"Where's Welder?" he demanded in a thorny baritone, scouring the perimeter with furtive glances as if WBFD's lead investigative reporter had slipped past the cordoned-off area.

Max said, "He's not here. This is the new girl — Aspen Winslow —"

"Wicklow."

Max did a sheepish head duck. "She took Stinger's place."

Aspen did a quick lean-in, enough to read the sergeant's nametag: *Barrington.* She extended her hand for a shake.

Sgt. Barrington made no move to take it. He stood in a typical cop stance — legs apart, massive forearms braced across his chest — and intimidated her with a menacing look.

"We'll get along fine, long as you stay behind the crime scene tape." To Max, he growled, "Don't film the body. If you so much as aim that camera in the direction of that corpse, I'll make that bar brawl your station reported on last week's newscast look like a slow dance at the Jewel Charity Ball." Then he stomped into the darkness, meandering around obstacles in his path, disappearing and reappearing in the beacon of a brother officer's flashlight.

A few feet behind the crime scene tape, Max switched on the spotlight.

Aspen's curls glowed like campfire embers. Steve Lennox's voice boomed in her ear fob. "We interrupt this program to bring you breaking news."

Max counted her down, three-two-one. "You're on the air."

The fledgling reporter stared into the camera lens and pretended she was talking to a friend.

"Steve, this is a sad situation out here. The decomposed body of a young female was found in a drainage ditch just outside the Fort Worth city limits in southwest Tarrant County earlier this evening by a man and his dog who stopped to change the tire of a stranded motorist."

Max grimaced.

Well hell. No wonder he sneered. Made it sound like the dog changed the tire.

She regained her composure.

"The motorist, who asked not to be identified, stated when she got out of her car, she smelled a foul odor . . ."

A middle-aged woman, lacking in poise and sophistication, stood next to a horse trailer with Flying W Ranch written across the back panel in loopy, lazy script.

"It's that Drummond girl, isn't it? Caramel Janine Drummond." Grabbing Aspen's hand, she jerked the mike close. "I'll tell you what you want to know but you've gotta put those fuzzy little blocks over my face. I don't want no trouble with whoever did this, you hear?"

Aspen reclaimed her hand, and along with it, the mike. "What did you do after you saw the body beside the road?"

"Puked."

Aspen inwardly winced. "Did you call the police?"

"Actually, I phoned my husband and told him to quit swillin' down beer and get over here and get these Appaloosas back to the barn."

"What caused you to look in the ditch?"

Aspen's cell phone shrilled. In her haste to cover the story, she'd neglected to disable it. She slid her free hand into the pocket in a frantic attempt to shut it off.

The maneuver didn't work. The mobile

phone trilled again. In a fluid move, she pulled out the wireless, opened the clamshell and hit the off-switch. Instead, the phone activated in her hand.

Now she had a call.

She motioned Max to pan the camera in on the witness as she took a backward step.

"Aspen Wicklow," she hissed into the cellular. "I'll call you back."

"It's her, isn't it, Aspen?" The thin, pitiful voice of Margo Sommervel vibrated through the wireless phone, followed by a moaning, keening wail of despair. "Tell me the truth."

"Can't talk." Said in a harsh whisper.

Can't hang up, either.

The witness kept talking and Max kept shooting video.

"The smell just about made me keel over. When I looked down in the ravine and saw her all purple and gray and mangled up, I puked. Takes a lot to upset my stomach, even after a spicy supper at Taco Loco — hey Enrique; hey Pancho." The woman waved at the camera. "I remembered to give your place a plug, now how 'bout one of those free dinners you're always giving away to the po-lice?"

Aspen steered her back on track. "Did you check to see if she was still alive?"

"Lord no. Are you addled? It stank worse

than a thousand buffalo butts. I'm not crazy. I live on a ranch. I know when something's dead. The only thing missing out here is buzzards. It's that Drummond girl, isn't it? The one that's been missing?"

In a voice choked with emotion, Aspen hurried on. "Deputies will continue their investigation. Coming to you live, I'm Aspen Wicklow, WBFD news. Back to you, Steve."

She pressed the phone to her ear.

Margo Sommervel's shriek slid down her ear canal and ricocheted off her eardrum. "Is it Candy? Is it my sister? You have to tell me, Aspen. I can't stand it any longer."

Aspen burst into tears. "I'm not aware of a positive ID being made. The police aren't saying anything."

"But do you think it's her? You know what she looks like. Is it her? Please talk to me."

Tears degenerated into sobs. "I'm sorry, Margo. I'm so sorry. I'd give anything not to be the one to tell you this." She did a quick hand-swipe across her eyes. When she looked over at Max, the red recording dot on his camcorder shone brighter than the Queen's ruby.

"Are we still on the air?" Realizing the gravity of the situation, she snapped, "Oh, for God's sake, Max, turn the damned thing off. I'm on the phone with the victim's sister. Can't you see we're having a crisis?"

In a daring move, Max disregarded the sergeant's orders and "sprayed" the crime scene with the camera, panning from side to side in an effort to record as many images as he could before the lead officer took notice. Then the photographer switched off the beacon, leaving them bathed in the eerie blue shadows of nighttime.

"I have to hang up now, Margo. I'll swing by later," Aspen said miserably. "You can go now, Mrs. Williams."

"I just hope I helped."

Helped get me fired, you mean.

CHAPTER THIRTEEN

When Aspen and Max rolled into WBFD's parking lot, they glimpsed Gordon through his office windows pacing along the broad expanse of glass. From the flailing hand gestures and the way he kept grabbing his head, he appeared to be hopping mad.

She thought back to her internship at the University channel, when she fell asleep during *Night of the Iguana* and snoozed through the second reel. Thirty minutes and a black screen later, the night manager came in screaming like he'd witnessed a massacre. No wonder she got reassigned.

While Max unloaded his gear, Tig intercepted her in the foyer. She didn't need him to tell her the Spam had hit the fan.

"You screwed up big time. Gordon wants to see you in his office."

Her jaw torqued. She'd had a gutful of Tig Welder. "I'm warning you — don't make me take off my earrings."

She stared into impenetrable eyes, predatory and flat. If justice prevailed, there would someday be a reptile slithering around wearing Tig as a belt.

Rounding the corner, she saw Gordon filling the doorframe with a scary expression on his face. She felt an unpleasant lurch in her stomach as he swept her inside. This had fast deteriorated into one of those moments where she should probably pull out garlic and a cross. If he'd turned into a bat and flown away, it wouldn't surprise her.

She stood, marooned, as he lit into her.

"What the hell's wrong with you? We never ever mention the names of the dead until their identity has been confirmed and the next of kin notified. That's day one, Journalism 101." As she moved toward him, he thrust sausage-sized digits in her face. "Give me three good reasons why I shouldn't fire you."

Aspen mirrored Gordon's outstretched hand with an upraised finger of her own. She needed this job, but these unpleasant intervals with Tig were enough to turn a normal person into a cutter. If she didn't develop a cast iron stomach and freon nerves, she was as good as gone.

"First, let's get something straight. I'm not the one who identified the body as

Candy Drummond. Mrs. Williams did."

"Should've wood-shedded that hillbilly before you put her on camera."

"There wasn't time. I had to use what I had."

"Two more reasons," Gordon yelled. "Give me two and make them good."

Aspen spread her fingers into a "V". "I was the only reporter available when the information came across the police scanner. You take what you can get. Like Mrs. Williams. If I hadn't gone out there, we'd have been scooped."

"You'd better believe heads will roll for that little oversight." He was looking for more. "And?"

"And . . ." She crossed her fingers behind her back and hoped for a reprieve. ". . . I did the best I could considering what I had to work with."

"What the hell's that supposed to mean?"

Her voice trembled with the effort of speech. "It means you could have the story the way I delivered it or not have the story at all. The way it worked out, we got on the air first. If the other stations went out there, they couldn't have shown anything until tomorrow. Which would you prefer?"

"Oh, now you're the one asking questions? I don't much cotton to smart-ass-y attitudes."

"I have a question for you." She studied him in earnest. "Instead of yelling at me, why don't you tell me three things I did right so I'll be motivated to do better next time?"

"Maybe there won't be a next time."

"Three things."

J. Gordon harrumphed. He lifted a bratwurst-sized finger, letting it hover in the air between them. "Your hair photographs well."

"Thank you. My friends all warned me I should go blonde but I —"

"Silence." He flexed his meaty jaw. "You came across as sincere on camera. That's a good thing because most reporters I know are jaded motherfuckers who'd just as soon step over a live body as a dead one. But you'll never be anchor material if you don't suck it up and deliver the story. This is no place for crybabies."

She felt a sudden prickle in her nose. Her eyes misted. He'd probably fire her.

Wait a minute — did he say "anchor material"?

"Still, it's important that people think you're trustworthy. For a station to hang onto their ratings the public must have trust in the person bringing them the news."

Could it be . . . nooooooo . . . surely he wasn't considering her to replace the outgoing talent? Was he?

"I'm trustworthy."

"Remains to be seen," he cautioned her. "You may be trustworthy but you looked like a sot. Red eyes, red nose, red cheeks. All you needed was a bottle of wine and a bad case of the hiccoughs. You can't crack up on camera just because the subject matter bothers you."

"And the third thing I did right?"

"Can't think of one. Go home and get some rest. You've made a big enough mess for one day."

Wednesday night dissolved into Thursday morning. After only four hours of sleep, Aspen padded to the kitchen with her fuzzy slippers on the wrong feet and put salt in her coffee. By the time she arrived at the studio and checked the assignments desk, she knew from the slim pickings that Tig had beaten her to the draw.

She was about to tuck her tail and slink to her office when Gordon's door yanked open. He ordered her front-and-center and pointed to a chair. She sank into the cushion like a rag doll.

"Let's go over it one more time: Never get involved in your story. Get everything pre-approved. And don't break the law."

"I haven't."

"Just so you know, I saw the footage on your little caper with the Johnson County sheriff. You ask me, it came damned close."

"But did you like it? That's the real question."

A light knuckle-rap on the doorframe sheared their attention. The station manager snarled, "What?"

Rochelle cracked the door open a sliver. "Oh, good," she said cheerily and strolled on in uninvited. "You're both here. The phones are ringing off the hook. It's all I can do to keep up." Looking stylish and attractive in a cobalt blue silk suit, she wiped invisible sweat off her forehead and flicked it into the air. "People are calling about Miss Wicklow."

Gordon whirled on her. "For Chrissakes. I *knew* it." He practically spat the words. "This is what I've been preaching to you about. If you give a perfect delivery and a lock of hair falls across your face, the public doesn't give a tinker's damn about the time and research you put into the news because all they remember is the flaw."

"Actually, the calls are mostly good, Gordon." Rochelle shot Aspen a sidelong glance. "Ninety-nine out of a hundred were positive."

"We didn't get a hundred call-ins." The unspoken part of his sentence could be read in his face: *Did we?*

"More like two hundred. The switchboard stayed jammed most of the morning. Callers wanting to know if Aspen's a local girl. I broke these down into categories. Want to hear?"

Gordon Pfeiffer gave her a raptor-eyed stare. Rochelle apparently took it as a sign to proceed.

She consulted her list. "One hundred twenty-five found her compassion for the Drummond girl's sister uplifting. Thirty-four wanted to know if she's single. Twenty-one asked where they could send flowers and trinkets. Fourteen asked for her home phone number. Three talk-show hosts want to book her on their respective radio stations, one caller wants to marry her and two were religious crackpots who suggested Caramel Janine Drummond brought this on herself because of her lifestyle — whatever that's supposed to mean. Two hundred calls, Gordon, and nobody said anything negative about Aspen. One old lady even referred to her as 'a breath of fresh air.' " She flashed a quick smile. "Just thought you should know."

Inwardly, Aspen smiled, victorious.

Now Pfeiffer didn't need to think of a third reason. He had more than enough to chew on. He snatched a fax off his desk and handed it to her.

"I saved this for you. Don't say I never gave you anything."

Another assignment?

She flirted with the idea he wasn't going to fire her. Not today, anyway.

As she read it over, Gordon filled in the blanks. "Fort Worth businessmen are up in arms about the number of vandalism incidents occurring outside their shops. Look into it."

"Isn't that a job for the cops?"

"I won't do your job for you, kid. But I'll toss you a bone since you're still green as a gourd. Ever since Hurricane Katrina, we've got all these evacuees hanging around downtown Fort Worth. They've assimilated into the homeless population and they're causing problems. People around the courthouse have complained about panhandlers, thefts, burglaries and even a few armed robberies. Figure out if the Katrina people are behind this. Now get back to work — both of you."

He cast the ladies off with a quick wrist flick. They skulked toward their respective workspaces while members of the news crew pretended to look busy.

Tig strolled by.

Rochelle dangled a pink message slip in his direction. "Your friend Inga just called. She said for you to pick up your clothes before she sets fire to them."

The secretary and the new reporter exchanged knowing looks while the veteran reporter ad-libbed a flimsy explanation.

"She's talking about the dry cleaning. She wants me to take my things to the dry cleaners. Last night at dinner, the clumsy waiter spilled shrimp remoulade on my pants and now they smell."

Tig made a poor liar.

In the sanctuary of her office, Aspen contemplated what to do with this new information, considering that solving crimes happened to be a job for the police. She closed the door behind her but that didn't stop Tig from barging in.

"What are you working on?" he said.

"I just walked in."

"What are you working on?"

"Mr. Welder —"

"Please," he patronized her with his tone, "call me Tig."

"Tig, when I speak, what do you hear? Do you hear the back-masking needle-scratch of an Iron Maiden record, or do you hear the high-pitch frequency of dolphins talking?"

"You're holding out on me, aren't you?"

"To quote one of my mentors, we're colleagues but we're also competitors."

His face turned beet red. He backed out of her office and slithered out of sight.

Aspen hurried out the door looking for Max. When she didn't find him in the studio, she stopped by Rochelle's desk to relive the glory.

"Two hundred people really jammed the switchboard?" she asked, bewildered by her instant popularity.

One perfectly plucked eyebrow shot up. "Sister, you've gotta be kidding. Nobody ever calls this fucking dump to say they like anything. Only to complain."

"So there were no calls from people saying they liked me?"

"Not a one, shug, except for this. Only from the sound of things, I don't think the caller much likes you." She picked up a pink phone message slip and handed it over. Before Aspen had a chance to glance at it, Rochelle went on with her take on the matter. "Someone from Tranquility Villas phoned bitching to high heaven. She said it's important and if you don't call back soon, there'll be hell to pay. I told that loudmouth this *was* Hell and I only accept cash, money orders, cashier's checks or gift cards. She slammed the phone down in my ear."

The sheriff of Johnson County had left a message, too.

He wanted her to come straight down to his office.

And he wanted her to bring the SNG vehicle and a cameraman.

CHAPTER FOURTEEN

While Max waited outside Tranquility Villas in the SNG truck, Aspen consulted with director Harriet Ramsey, a tall, hatchet-nosed woman with graying hair and a no-nonsense attitude.

"It's your father, Miss Wicklow." Anger pinched the corners of her mouth. "He's out of control."

"What's he doing?"

"We caught him crawling into bed with several of our female patients. Not just once. Bunches of times."

Aspen gnawed her bottom lip. So far, Tranquility Villas had come through with flying colors. They'd promised that life for Wexford Wicklow would be exactly like it was when he was married and living at home. Apparently it was since he still hadn't stopped screwing around.

"Can't you tell him to go to his room?"

"We don't have the staff members to

watch him around the clock. Besides, he says they sneak him in so it's consensual. Look, Miss Wicklow, I know what you're thinking . . ."

"Really?" She gave the director a pleasant smile. "What am I thinking, Mrs. Ramsey?" She felt her spirits buoy knowing Tranquility Villas had a clairvoyant on staff. One never knew when such services would be necessary.

"You're thinking we're not doing enough but I assure you we are."

Actually, she was contemplating putting her father under a guardianship. The last thing she needed was for him to slip out and marry one of these gullible, dementia-diagnosed women. Convincing Wexford Wicklow to stop dipping his biscuit in the company gravy was like using a foreign language to try and talk a jumper off the top of the roof.

"Why don't I speak to him before I leave?"

"Mind you, he needs a harsh talking-to. Our efforts have fallen on deaf ears."

"I'll see what I can do."

She found her father in the piano room crooning Sinatra tunes to a love-struck dement and pulled him aside.

"Daddy, we need to talk."

Wexford blinked. "Who're you looking for?"

"You."

"I'm not your daddy. I'm not even married."

"I know you're not married anymore. But I'm still your daughter."

"No, you're my teacher."

Fine. If he wanted her to be his teacher, he'd get the lecture.

"Stop screwing around."

Confusion lined his face.

"As your teacher, I'm telling you to stay away from these women. They can be your friends but you can't go slipping into their rooms. It's forbidden."

He stared, crestfallen. "A man has needs."

She wanted to ram her fingers into her ears until the tips touched. To flick her tongue back and forth between her teeth moaning *"addle-addle-addle-addle-addle"* until he stopped talking. Imagining her father, unclothed, doing *anything* sexual was an ugly visual she wanted to drive from her mind.

"Knock it off or you'll receive an 'F' this semester. And you know what that means." Her voice turned ominous. "It'll go on your permanent record."

He took his hangdog expression and

returned to the piano.

She followed him. "Did you see me on TV last night?"

Befuddled, he squinted as if trying to place her. "Are you a movie star?"

"Investigative reporter. I told you I got on with WBFD. Don't you remember?"

"I saw Maureen O'Hara crying over a dead girl but I didn't see you. Of course . . ." he looked down at his shoes, suddenly bashful ". . . gentlemen prefer blondes. Marilyn's my favorite."

She left with a sinking gut and a promise to Mrs. Ramsey that she'd come by more often and try to whip Wexford into shape. The only promise she exacted in return was for Mrs. Ramsey and the staff to keep her parents from finding out the other one lived there.

Granger thought he looked pretty good on the six-and-ten the previous night and he told Aspen so when she and Max arrived at his office.

Today, he'd gotten up early enough to eat breakfast at the café on the courthouse square, where at least ten people congratulated him for his fiscal responsibility. A dozen commented on his brass balls.

Aspen said, "So what's next? Why're we

down here?" She sneaked a glance at Max.

A light knuckle rap sounded at the door. The secretary poked her head through and said, "The Bluebird's ready, Sheriff."

Bluebird?

Granger explained about the ugly white bus parked at the vehicle barn. Slowly, it sank in. He intended to transport the Huntsville chain.

Aspen gave him a dedicated eye blink. "You're not really . . ."

"I thought you'd like to be there when the ship hits the sand."

She shifted her gaze to Max. "Start the video."

He flicked on the light and started the camcorder rolling, then signaled Sheriff Granger with a pointed finger, *You're on.*

"I'm transporting twenty of our worst offenders, and don't forget our debutantes." He ticked off names using his fingers. "Hilda 'Two-Bit' Horvath, John 'Needle-Dick' Larkin, 'Home-Invasion' Harold — anyone convicted of burglary, arson, robbery, rape or kidnapping is going on that bus."

Aspen grimaced. "You do realize they won't open the gate this time, don't you?"

He appeared genuinely disturbed by the notion; yet she sensed excitement mounting behind the frown.

"Guess I'll have to resort to guerilla tactics."

Granger gave Aspen and Max time to gas up the SNG truck. When they arrived at the bus barn ten minutes late, the sheriff was already behind the wheel warming up the Bluebird. She didn't hear what he yelled at the prisoners, but whatever he said stirred a resounding chorus of, "Yes, boss."

Twenty inmates fell silent.

Granger grabbed the lever and banged the door flaps open. He tilted the brim of his Stetson. "What're you smiling about?"

Aspen stepped onto the bus with Max in tow. She gave him a knowing headshake. "They're not going to open the gate."

"Doesn't matter. Ready?"

Her eyes slewed to the prisoners. Each inmate had a ball-and-chain attached above the ankle.

"You're scary." She turned to Max. "Roll tape. Zoom in on those medieval restraints."

Granger grinned. "Want to ride along?"

"You're single-handedly trying to get me fired, aren't you?"

"Hell, no. I want you to win an award for excellence in broadcasting. What kind of awards do they have in your line of work?"

The Peabody, the Scripps Howard, Alfred I.

DuPont . . . the Pulitzer . . .

Acrylic obelisks and silver trophies with money prizes attached to them raced through her mind. If this gutsy maniac was about to do what she thought he was about to do . . . if she did her job right . . . she might actually win one of these.

Euphoria turned to dread.

The award she'd most likely be up for probably looked like a troll doll with its butchered hair combed over to resemble Donald Trump's, and the words "You're Fired" branded onto a little wooden stand. As for the money prize, it would go to the featured subject of the piece in the form of an out-of-court settlement.

Her last face-to-face moments with Roger flashed into mind, his words still echoing with the stinging reason he didn't want to be with her anymore. *"You're just not that interesting."*

She appealed to Max. "Mind if I ride along."

"I don't like this."

"Show me how to operate the camcorder and I'll record the trip while you follow in the SNG truck. I want to get some quotes from the inmates."

"This is a forty-five thousand dollar piece of equipment. You might as well ask me to

143

part with a kidney."

"I'd give you one of mine."

Max sighed heavily, clearly resigned to impending disaster. "Oh, well. Maybe if we live through this Gordon won't have to actually know you were traveling on the bus."

"Do me a favor," Granger remarked, not necessarily in jest, "if I'm shot dead at the prison gate, make sure you zoom in for a good close-up. I hear sucking chest wounds boost ratings."

Hands trembling, Aspen grabbed the mike. The sheriff's words triggered second thoughts and she didn't want to lose her momentum.

"This is Aspen Wicklow, WBFD-TV, reporting from the Johnson County Sheriff's Office, where Sheriff Spike Granger says he's going to empty convicted felons out of his jail today in protest against the Texas Department of Criminal Justice's current freeze on inmates."

"Sheriff, what's your plan?" She tilted the mike at him.

"Don't have one. I'll make it up as I go along."

"And there you have it. One angry sheriff just doing the right thing."

Max cut off the camera and slumped onto

a bench as she carved out a hollow next to Granger's windbreaker. She sank onto the uncomfortable metal surface and momentarily relaxed. The photographer commandeered the seat across the aisle for his gear. Then he turned on the camcorder and shot footage of inmates in the caged area of the bus. "Leroy the Abductor" groaned out the first of several haunting spirituals. He ended his repertoire with a Death Row tune guaranteed to sober the rowdiest of thugs, all documented on the camcorder.

Aspen sneaked a peek at Granger.

She liked this crusty lawdog, she really did. And what the hell? She'd look killer in her lime green silk pantsuit with the lime-and-aqua silk shell next to her face. Nobody could ever say she didn't look positively dynamite on the Bataan death crawl to the soup line.

Max packed up and headed to the SNG truck, alone.

Sunlight gilded the fields as they made the rest of the trip to Huntsville in relative silence. Banter that started out so loud Aspen wanted to drive a spike through her head soon gave way to the hum of tires against the pavement. By the time they rolled into town, the air reeked of an unsavory combination of the inmates' fear and body odor. Dragging in air that felt unbreathable, she wondered how the sheriff could stomach driving a bus that smelled of imminent death and decay. When Granger turned off the freeway and onto the main road to the penitentiary's HQ, he cut his eyes in her direction.

"And what does *Mister* Wicklow think about you being an investigative reporter?"

"If you're referring to my father, let's just say it hasn't sunk in and leave it at that. If you're talking about a husband, there's no Mr. Wicklow. There's not even a Mr. Wrong. There's no Mr. Anybody."

He's trying to interview me.

She cut him off at the pass, dropping her gaze to the out-of-date inspection sticker. "By the way, when's the last time this bus was serviced?"

"I have no idea."

"Did you know your Motor Vehicle Inspection sticker expired?"

"Let's hope the Highway Patrol doesn't stop us. Then again, there are probably other things wrong with the bus, too."

"Such as?"

He gave her a one-shoulder shrug. "You never know. Might need an oil change." His eyes turned dark. "Or the brakes could fail."

They chugged up to the picket.

This time, instead of the guard lowering the bucket from the tower, he pulled out a hand-held radio and appeared to be speaking into it.

Granger gave a half-baked salute and rolled the bus on through. Inside the closed gate, two guards stepped out of the kiosk and took passive-aggressive stances. They braced their arms in front of their chests and gave the Johnson County transport a couple of slow headshakes, *No damned way.*

Max had already sprung into action and was stringing out cable. He hooked up to the input-output panel with precision timing.

Without taking her eyes off Granger, Aspen sent her photographer a telepathic message. *Are you getting this?* Her eyes flickered to the camcorder and back. She knew by the red glow from the *record* light they were rolling. When Max formed the OK signal with his free hand, she knew he could hear Granger's amplified instructions to the prisoners through the mike.

"I'd better not hear a peep out of you. If you so much as whisper The Lord's Prayer, I'll see to it any good time you've earned is taken away."

He gave the door lever a yank. The flaps swung open and let out a prolonged squeak.

He seated the Stetson on top of his head and stepped off the bus.

Max trotted closer. He readied the camcorder and zoomed in.

Granger cupped his hands to his mouth. "I have twenty prisoners from Johnson County."

Stone-faced, they held their positions. Granger's neck veins corrugated. He gave a derisive grunt and climbed back onto the bus. Max started to follow him aboard but Granger's upraised hand signaled him to wait.

"Told you so," Aspen said, leaning forward to catch a breath of fresh air. "Told you they wouldn't let you in." After all the bluster and bravado, she was embarrassed for him. How humiliating — having to return with the chain gang. "Now what?"

"Get off the bus." His eyes sparked with flashes of anger.

"You're ditching me?" Her voice crescendoed to a high-pitched squeak.

"You told me your boss said he'd fire you if you became part of the story. So get out."

Aspen reeled off the Bluebird with the grace of a drunken sailor.

Granger was crazy. She'd been riding with a florid psychotic.

She sprinted toward Max for guidance.

When she came panting up, the photographer kept the lens focused on the sheriff. "What gives?"

"He wants us to wait out here. Just keep shooting footage. I think we've got ourselves a dement." If the video didn't get her an award, perhaps the DA could subpoena it as evidence to use in Granger's mental commitment trial.

Granger shifted the Bluebird into reverse. He backed out of the drive enough to snarl traffic. With the gearshift in neutral, he revved the RPMs. Black exhaust boiled out of the tailpipe.

Max whipped out his cell phone and dialed. He whipped the wireless to his ear and started talking.

"Oh, no." Aspen's mouth gaped. Chills ran the length of her torso. "You don't suppose . . ."

They shared a simultaneous thought — *Oh shit!*

Granger's voice reverberated through the bus. "Sit down, shut up and brace yourselves."

"Holy guacamole," Max said. "This guy's batshit crazy."

But Aspen was thinking despite the inherent danger lurking underneath, Spike Granger had to be the most interesting person she'd met in her whole life. If she stuck by him, some of it just might rub off on her.

The sheriff pulled down the visor and barked orders at the mirror. "Prisoners — hang onto your balls." The inmates exchanged awkward glances. Half of them steadied the cast iron spheres. The other half grabbed their crotches. "When we come to a complete stop, pick up your ball-and-chains and step off the bus in an orderly fashion."

"Okay, boss," they chorused.

Max said, "I've got contact with the blow-dries at the station. We're going live — brush the hair back from your face. Gordon hates that. You've got expressive eyes. Let everyone see them. They're running this as breaking news. Ready?" He cued her. "Three-two-one, you're on the air."

She stood tall, lifting the mike inches from her face.

"Hello viewers, I'm Aspen Wicklow, WBFD-TV, reporting live from the Byrd Unit in Huntsville, where Sheriff Spike Granger of Johnson County has a busload of twenty convicted felons to deliver despite the ban on transports attributed to prison overcrowding. Granger, who's incensed by the Texas Department of Criminal Justice's *take no prisoners* attitude, has started a grassroots campaign to rid his jail of inmates who he says should be housed in the penitentiary."

Granger got a white-knuckled grip on the steering wheel. He showed her a ghost of a smile and gunned the engine.

Nostrils flared.

He stomped the accelerator.

The bus shot forward and crashed through the gate, filling the air with the demon shrieks of twisted metal and screaming inmates.

CHAPTER FIFTEEN

Aspen derived such an adrenaline rush watching Spike Granger plow through the penitentiary gate that she'd almost convinced herself she didn't give a hoot if Gordon fired her.

She'd just witnessed the experience of a lifetime, seeing twenty convicts hoist their ball-and-chains up enough to get off the bus and drop them on the lawn of the Byrd Unit. When the guard in the picket finally lowered his rifle and gave them a power salute, Aspen felt the lightheaded rush of a survivor.

As Granger backed out through the wreckage, she ran toward the bus, arms flailing. As it slumped heavily onto the roadway, Granger pulled the door lever and the flaps swung open. She jumped onto the bus with her heart in her throat.

Max was still shooting video outside the chain link, concertina-wire fence when she scooched up behind Granger.

Convicts receded in the Bluebird's side mirrors.

"Off the record — are you on any kind of psychoactive medication?" she asked with a warble.

"I make my own medicine. Care to have a drink later?"

"Looking for a new job might be a wiser use of my time. Do you act this way in front of Mrs. Granger?" Her pulse thudded in her throat.

According to the sheriff, if she meant his mother, the woman — God rest her soul — was dead. If she meant his wife, *that* Mrs. Granger was now the ex Mrs. Granger. He claimed, straight-faced, that he'd divorced her once he figured out she was a raving lunatic. Now, all he wanted out of life was a boring woman who didn't mind staying home to tend house.

Aspen suspected he was pulling her leg.

More than thirty television reporters had camped out at the Johnson County SO waiting for the sheriff's return. When the Bluebird rolled up with the grillwork smashed in, they ran toward the bus with cameras rolling.

Reporters from rival stations pelted him with questions.

"Did you really leave twenty inmates on the lawn wearing ball-and-chains?"

"Who drove the bus through the prison gates?"

"Were you aware CNN's sending a crew down to interview you?"

"What's next, Sheriff?"

Granger grasped the nearest mike. Lucky for Aspen, it was hers.

He migrated over to WBFD's SNG truck and framed himself next to the logo. She wasn't aware she was smiling until it dawned on her — this was Granger's way of ensuring that WBFD got free advertising at the expense of their rival stations.

This lawdog was wily like a coyote.

At the impromptu press conference, he promoted an idea certain to inspire the rest of the Texas sheriffs. "We're going to requisition tents for the prisoners."

The reporter didn't get it. "You're setting up tents in back of the jail?"

"To pitch on the Capitol grounds," he said, and slid Aspen a sideways glance. Then he called a halt to the melee with a brusque, "Stay tuned," and swept her into the building with him.

Locked in the sanctuary of his office with Aspen, Max and WBFD's rolling camcorder, Granger removed his Stetson and smoothed his thinning hair with the flat of his palm.

"Did you notice you stopped in front of our truck? Now WBFD will be on every newscast that airs," Aspen said. "That's funny."

"Some people believe in serendipity. Or chance. Or random acts. I happen to believe there are no accidents. I make my own luck."

She did a double take. Maybe he'd been serious about wanting her to win an award. "You're not really planning to start a tent city for criminals on the Capitol steps, are you?"

"Nah." But his eyes sparked flashes of mischief that suggested otherwise.

She remembered seeing a news feature where an Arizona sheriff came under scrutiny for housing prisoners in tents. He made them wear stripes and pink underwear. Granger might be ballsy enough to do the same. She could only hope.

The sheriff went on to explain. "We'd never get away with it. Too many cops. Can we go off the record?"

Aspen looked at Max. She gave him a nod and he shut off the camcorder.

"What I need," he drawled, "is a stunt that'll bring this crisis to a head."

"If you come up with anything good, will you give us an exclusive?" she asked wide-eyed and breathless.

"Yep. I'll wait a few days to see if TDCJ tries to bring any of these som-bitches back. Heaven help them if they do," he said in an offhand manner. "I'll pull 'Dysentery Gary' and 'Rappin' Rodney' out of their cells and start an *Adopt-A-Con* program."

Plotting aloud must've given Granger a *Eureka!* moment.

His mouth gaped.

A huge grin split his face.

Suddenly inspired, he made up the plan as he went along and gave them the run-down on how it'd work. He'd pair up several obnoxious criminals with influential people. Kind of like providing each thug with a mentor.

Only this newfound idea wouldn't be a rehab program.

Far from it.

Back at WBFD, Gordon bolted out of his office. He intercepted Aspen and Max as they entered into the foyer.

"Great story. The guy's a psycho. Next week we'll be in the middle of sweeps so I want you to put together a dynamite news package for the investigative report. We'll move Tig's story to the week after. Meantime, how's the vandalism piece coming?"

"There's no piece — yet. But Max and I are going out tonight. Aren't we, Max?"

She scanned the area but the photographer had already slipped off to edit the footage for the six o'clock news.

The way Aspen had it figured, she had three choices. She could return to Pop's Salvage and pump the acne-scarred mechanic for information. She could find Max and check out Gordon's lead on the Katrina people. Or she could go home, make herself a bologna sandwich and get a good night's sleep.

The magnetic pull of home won out.

Before she left for the evening, she poked her head inside Gordon's office to say goodnight.

Tig was on the sofa flailing his arms like a turtle on its back.

"Nice work, Wicklow." Gordon waved her off. "See you in the morning."

Tig shot her a lethal glare.

She checked her in-box and found a pink message slip from Mike Henson. Whatever he wanted, it'd have to wait. She crumpled it into a ball and shoved it into her pocket. Happy to finally call it a day, she headed for her car beneath a sky that looked like melted Crayolas dripping down the horizon.

CHAPTER SIXTEEN

Friday morning dawned in a brilliant shade of tangerine.

Aspen decided not to return Mike Henson's phone call until after she drove back out to Pop's Salvage and had a look around. Wearing Bass Weejuns, blue jeans and a thermal pajama top layered with a dark blue T-shirt, she tucked her hair up into a backwards ball cap. Then she sauntered into the shop without a stitch of makeup on, chewing bubble gum and looking for Pop.

The same mechanic with the pockmarked face ambled up to the counter wiping grease off his hands with a rag. He had on clean overalls with permanent stains and an oval nametag above the left side of his chest that had *Jacob* stitched in red thread.

"I need to speak to Pop."

"Not in. Whatcha need?"

"I was here the other day. My car's making this weird noise."

A flicker of recognition shone on his face. "You're that reporter. I remember you now. You found that dead girl." He held out his hand, palm-up. "Keys."

"You must be mistaken."

"You look like her."

Aspen slipped into panic mode. "I work in a shoe store."

He still had his hand out. "Before I can quote you a price, I need your keys. I have to drive your car up the road so I can figure out what's wrong with it."

Without thinking, she rummaged through her purse, pulled out her key fob and handed it over. Keys to the station. Her house. The car. A safe deposit box at the bank. A feeling of unease gripped her. Before she could ask for them back, he'd slipped out a side door.

Aspen swept the room in a glance, looking for mounted cameras and two-way mirrors. Confident that there were none, she took a blank invoice from a stack next to the telephone and stuffed it into her purse.

She checked her watch. He'd been gone so long she started to suspect he'd stolen her car.

Yeah, right. Who'd want a ten-year-old Honda?

When the mechanic finally returned, she

was fit to be tied. "I have an appointment. I have to leave. What took so long?"

"I put your Honda on the diagnostic machine. You've got a lot of problems with that car. Lucky for you we're running a special on half of them."

"What's wrong with it?"

He gave her a rundown, delivering the bad news with such confidence that she almost believed him. "Front end's out of alignment. Brakes are bad. You need new tires and a new muffler or your car won't pass inspection."

"How much?"

The estimate sucked the breath out of her.

"I can't come back until payday."

When she got into the Accord and thumbed through the key ring, an odd sensation made her neck hairs prickle. She studied the keys, holding her breath until they were all accounted for. As she sat behind the wheel, meditating on why they seemed out of order, a hand smacked her window.

Aspen came up off the seat.

Like a bad horror flick, she'd arrived in time for *The Return of Mike Henson.* She could almost hear creepy strains of organ music in the background. Binoculars hung from his neck by a leather strap. Sweat beaded his forehead.

She powered down the window. "If you want my help, you have to stop scaring the crap out of me."

"Gabby's house was burglarized."

"Did you report it to the police?"

"No. My fingerprints are all over the place. I don't want them to suspect me."

"What was stolen?"

"I don't know."

"Then how do you know there was even a burglary?"

"Her stuff's been rearranged. I hadn't noticed it before. But when I was feeding the cat last night, I . . ." He looked away. "I looked through her drawers."

On instinct she fingered Mike Henson for a pervert.

"It's not what you think," he rushed on. "It started in the kitchen. I was looking for a fork to scoop cat food out of the can. Only they were all dirty. So I opened the drawer where she keeps the sterling. It was gone.

"I started looking around. There were other things out of place but I haven't been over in awhile and she could've repositioned stuff. Then I checked her bedroom. Some of her lingerie was missing."

"Maybe she packed it when she left to visit her aunt."

Henson scowled. "Don't ask me how I know, I just know. Her car's missing. She doesn't answer the phone. She hasn't reported in and her house has been burglarized."

"How'd they get in? Did you find any broken windows? Pry marks?"

"That's just it. There was nothing. It's like they had a key."

She wanted to tell him to give it up. To find another girl and move on. It was the healthy thing to do.

"I have an appointment. I have to go."

"You're not going to check this guy out, are you?"

"What do you think I'm doing here? Investigations don't happen overnight. I'll call you when I have something. If I get anything." She rammed the key into the ignition, fired up the car and watched Mike Henson shrink in her rearview mirror until he dwindled to the size of an army ant.

She swung by the house to change clothes.

After disrobing, she selected the plain black dress she saved for funerals, fastened a double strand of her mother's pearls around her neck and squeezed her feet into a pair of black pumps. She drove in rush hour traffic, hitting every red light until she arrived on Margo Sommervel's street.

The block was cluttered with cars and Margo's driveway was packed.

Aspen found curb space at the end of the next block. She parked the Honda and strolled along the sidewalk leading up to the Sommervel house. On impulse, she paused before ringing the bell and tried the handle instead. The door gave way and she stepped into a foyer buzzing with the sounds of family and friends.

After signing a guest book near a centerpiece of fresh flowers, she wandered into the den. Her eyes widened when she saw the ladies flanking Margo.

Sorority sisters.

She knew them on sight — more people who'd low-rated her because she couldn't keep up with them financially. They'd been seniors the year Aspen pledged. And they weren't inclined to have anything to do with freshmen.

She found herself standing in front of Margo.

The women glanced up expectantly.

Margo wore the flat affect of someone shot with an animal tranquilizer. The others had the look of remedial math students, stumped by a simple equation.

"Aspen," Margo mumbled dully, "how nice of you to come." She lifted her hand

and gave a sluggish wave toward the dining room. "There's food. Help yourself to coffee."

"Thank you; I'm fine. How're you holding up?"

"She's managing, aren't you, Mar-Mar?" The long-necked brunette patted Margo's hand, then did a double take. "Don't I know you from somewhere?" She gave an eye squint.

"I'm Aspen Wicklow. We were in the same sorority."

"I remember you," said their friend, a highlighted honey blonde with a breast augmentation two cup sizes too big. "You're Asprin."

"Aspen."

"Right." Big head bob. "Aspen Winston. I remember you."

"It's Wicklow. Aspen Wicklow." She forced a smile. They were the mean girls the Drummond sisters ran with. The ones who made fun of her clothes and her haircut.

"Are y'all friends?" A dubious wrinkle formed between the brunette's thinly arched brows.

"Aspen's helping me track down Candy's car. She's with WBFD-TV now. She's a reporter."

"Investigative reporter," Aspen said firmly,

proudly. "Look, Margo . . . could I talk to you for a moment?"

"Sure," Margo said, her reaction delayed.

"In private." She took the grieving woman by the hand and helped her to her feet, ignoring Margo's friends. They traveled the length of the hall, arms linked, to the bedroom, where Aspen helped Margo into a chair. "I apologize for the bad timing but I need to ask you a few questions about your sister."

"About Candy," Margo said airily.

"After Pop's Salvage exercised a mechanic's lien on Candy's car, was her house burglarized?"

"I don't know. I don't think so." She shook her head. "No. I'd know something like that, wouldn't I?"

"I'm sorry to have bothered you," Aspen said dully. "I shouldn't have intruded. I thought I might be onto something but . . . clearly, I was wrong."

"Is that all you wanted to know?"

"For now. I'll be going so you can get back to your friends."

"Okay. You'll come to the funeral, though." It was more of a demand than a question.

"I'll be there."

"Good." Margo spoke with the slurred speech of a drunk. "They tortured her. Did you know?"

Aspen stood speechless. She didn't know the particulars and didn't want to know. The brief impression she'd gotten when she glimpsed Candy Drummond's blue-gray corpse would stay with her the rest of her life.

"I'm so sorry. We don't have to talk about it if you don't want to." Aspen pleaded with her eyes. *Please don't want to.*

"The police told us. Our family doctor came right away. He practically used rhino darts to medicate my mother," she said in the slow, colorless tone of a zombie. "Candy had so many marks on her neck they said he must've choked her, revived her, tortured her, choked her again . . . until finally . . ." She gave a violent shudder. The dreamlike haze cleared. Her eyes came alive, focused on the here and now as they walked back down the hallway to the front door.

Margo looked over at her friends, who were saying their good-byes and air-kissing each other's cheeks with a *mwah, mwah.* "I'm sorry about Fain and Veronica. They didn't mean it. We were all such brats."

"Take care."

Aspen paced herself on the walk to the door even though she wanted to sprint out the foyer and into the fresh air and break free of the stifling memories of those awkward days.

"But I thought you wanted to know about the burglary," Margo called out after her.

Aspen halted in her tracks. "You said there wasn't a burglary."

"No. You asked if my sister's house was burglarized *after* that mechanic took her car. It was burglarized *before.*"

CHAPTER SEVENTEEN

Gordon must've lost his mind.

After changing back into jeans and a Texas Ranger jersey for casual Friday, Aspen found herself a captive audience trapped in the station manager's office. Trying hard not to yawn, she listened to his commentary on the footage shot on Sheriff Spike Granger's wild ride to Huntsville.

Abruptly, he said, "I've come up with a new slogan. I'd like to try it out on you."

It made her feel good, him taking her into his confidence. She said, "Sure," and settled back into the chair as if she actually belonged at WBFD.

"Picture this." He shaped the thumb and index finger of his left hand into an "L" and the right hand's correlating finger and thumb into an inverted "L". Then he framed his porcine face with the "Ls" and assumed the voice of a TV announcer. "This is Aspen Wicklow, coming to you live from WBFD-

TV. We want to get you in bed. You won't regret it in the morning."

She sat up, board-straight. "What? I'm not going to say that."

"Then come up with a catchphrase of your own. I've decided the station needs a new teaser and it's not in the budget to hire a consultant. So Rochelle said I should award a prize to the employee who came up with the best idea. I said I'd pay for dinner for two at the most expensive steakhouse in the Metroplex but Rochelle called me a cheapskate and talked me into springing for one of those four-day cruises to the Bahamas."

It was as if Rochelle had bat radar for ears. She rapped on the door before inviting herself inside. "Max is looking for you." She turned to the boss and rattled a cylinder of rolled-up papers. "Gordon, here are the programs scheduled for sweeps month."

When Aspen didn't find Max, she returned to Rochelle's desk like a homing pigeon. She found the secretary standing in the break room, in front of a small refrigerator with her head stuck inside and one arm propped against the open door. She appeared dazed and confused.

"Looking for something?"

Rochelle turned, flush-faced. "Why yes. I

am." Sarcasm dripped. "I'm looking for my youth."

"Pardon?"

"It will happen to you," she added miserably. "There's no escape. I'm thinking of getting one of those little Igloo coolers and putting a block of ice in it and shoving it under my desk. I realize you're probably getting an ugly picture in your head but there's no other way around it. A woman's gotta do what a woman's gotta do. It's either that or kill somebody."

"Pardon?"

"Hot flashes. I have this overwhelming urge to commit murder. I think it should be Tig." Abruptly she slammed the fridge shut and returned to her desk with Aspen following in her wake. "What do you want? I'm about to go into the ladies room and stick my head under the cold water faucet. Chop-chop. Do I look like I have all day?"

"How am I supposed to figure out who's behind the vandalism and break-ins downtown? That's a job for the cops."

She tapped a manicured fingernail to her temple. "Think smart."

"I don't understand."

"You'll have to be clever."

"Are you suggesting I get an unmarked car and go set up on that area for the night?"

Max, who'd been working inside the studio, hollered over his shoulder. "Don't call me unless you've got something worthwhile to video."

"Another dedicated employee at WBFD," Rochelle snarled as she took a paper towel and patted the moisture on her forehead dry.

"Why don't the store owners just call the cops?"

"Oldest reason in the book." Rochelle pulled a skinny cigarette from a pack and stared longingly at it. WBFD was a non-smoking building, so she caressed it with her fingers instead. "They're never around when you need one. Besides, I had a burglary a few years ago. The young lady they sent out to take the report was fine but the crime scene detective they sent wasn't worth the powder it'd take to blow him up."

Aspen gave her a quizzical eye squint.

"He fluffed a little fingerprint powder around, enough to dirty my walls, and then announced there wasn't sufficient ridge detail in the prints to be able to lift them. I wanted to yell, 'How do you know if you don't try?' but the bottom line is, he took one look around, passed up taking a picture of the chair with muddy footprints on it; ignored photographing the two footpaths leading to my next door neighbor's house; blew off the blood trail of crystals dropped from the chandelier those slimy bastards cut down from my ceiling; and he hopped into his van and took off like a bat outta hell. Need I say more?" She let the skinny cigarette hover near her nose and, for a few seconds, closed her lids and inhaled its menthol fragrance.

"I didn't know you smoked."

"I quit." Her eyes popped open. "But we're coming up on sweeps month and this place has me keyed up; yesterday, I lit up two at the same time. Tig called me a walrus. I've decided to kill him."

"Am I supposed to get a car and sit downtown all night waiting for something to happen?"

"Wouldn't that be fun?" Rochelle said impassively.

"No really, I want your opinion."

"My opinion—" she slid the unlit cigarette back into the pack, "—is that nothing will happen if you park down there. In a situation like this, a good reporter should blend in with the scenery so nobody knows they're reporting the news."

"You've gotta be kidding me. The only people downtown after two in the morning are drunks and homeless people."

"You might enjoy impersonating a barfly."

"That's like asking to get raped."

"Then go as a homeless person."

Before Aspen could protest, Rochelle's idea washed over her. "Hey, that might work."

Rochelle pushed back from her desk. "Come here, shug. Let's play."

"What?"

"First, we have to see what's available in WBFD's toy box."

She took Aspen to a supply room full of briefcases, microphones, pin cameras — anything you could want to put a hidden camera in. Rochelle selected a fountain pen from a small box.

"See this? Pin camera." She fished around for a wire. "Here. Wrap this around your body, under your clothes and secure the mike to the inside of your shirt. Max will be listening on the other end if you come across anything."

"I'm not coming out unless you have something interesting to film," came Max's disembodied voice.

"Is he listening to us?"

Rochelle leaned in close. Her voice dropped to a whisper. "I've long suspected this place is bugged. Let's test my theory, shall we?" In *voce fuerzo,* she said, "Don't even waste your time trying to date Max. I heard Tig talking the other day." She paused for effect. "He said Max is so gay he could burst into flames any minute. It's because of the ponytail."

"I heard that," Max yelled. "I'm having his kneecaps busted."

Rochelle cupped her hands to her mouth. "Call if you need help."

Aspen turned serious. She placed a tentative hand on the woman's sleeve. "What if I get jumped?"

"Hon, if you go as a homeless woman, that'll be a given. Dress up as a man."

"You're kidding."

But Rochelle didn't look like she was kidding. "Get those Katrina evacuees on tape and you'll have a good story."

"Or end up dead."

"Then Tig will have a good story," she said with put on sweetness.

Aspen spent the rest of the afternoon mapping out her assignment for that night. She spoke to two downtown businessmen about the problems, scribbling notes until she felt the force field of a fast food restaurant pulling at her. After a quick run to the drive-thru for a hamburger Kid's Meal, she experienced familial obligation sucking at her and made a quick detour to Tranquility Villas.

Harriet Ramsey met her at the information desk. "He's doing it again."

Aspen took a deep breath. In her mind, she counted to five. "Doing what?"

"It's this morbid fascination with widow women. We're thinking of putting him on Depo Provera."

"Wait — isn't that what they use to chemically castrate sex offenders in prison?"

The director responded with a satisfied smirk.

She knew Mrs. Ramsey couldn't be serious. But the woman had clearly reached the end of her rope, so if Wexford wanted to avoid neutering . . .

"I'll talk to him. Where is he?"

"Last time I saw him he was in the green room."

Wexford Wicklow wasn't in the green room. She didn't find him in the piano lounge either. He was probably in the dining room, surrounded by seventy-year-old groupies, so she struck out for the west wing for a quick hello to her mother.

The door to Jillian Wicklow's room was closed. When she twisted the knob and pushed, the heft of a chair prevented her from entering. She knocked hard enough to bruise her knuckles. When her mother didn't respond, she forced her shoulder against the wood and heard chair legs grating along the floor.

What the hell?

"Mom? Mom, are you in there? Is everything all right?"

She heard a fleshy thud and the rustle of fabric. When she pushed the door the rest of the way in, two silhouettes cropped up in her field of vision. She flipped on the light and did a double take.

"Mom?" Her eyelids fluttered in astonishment. "Dad?"

A naked Jillian Wicklow ducked under the sheet. Wexford Wicklow picked himself up off the floor. He stood, nude, in all his withered splendor, with a chow-hound grin cracking his face.

The room swam in front of her. She'd been dreading this so much that she hyperventilated. When she couldn't find a paper bag to wheeze into, she emptied out a box of tissues and huffed into the cardboard opening.

Wexford snatched his pants from a pile of clothes by the bed. "I'll call you," he said, hopping on one foot as he tried to jam a toe into the trouser leg. When it didn't work, he pressed a kiss into his ex-wife's hair and hurried out the door, buck-naked, with his ass jiggling.

It was an assault on four out of five senses.

Aspen's yell rent the air. "What the hell are you doing?"

"He's a very nice man. You'd like him," Jillian said with a pout of defensiveness.

"I'd like him? Do you know even know who he is?"

"He didn't say. I'll introduce you next time you're here."

She took her mother's arm confidentially and applied a crippling grip. "Listen to me, Mother. He's the devil."

"He's a lovely man. You shouldn't say such things about people you've never met."

"The frickin' devil. Devil with a hard-on. Sex devil."

"Well, all I can say is, he sure screwed the hell out of me."

CHAPTER EIGHTEEN

Around eleven o'clock that night, Aspen returned to WBFD. She locked herself in her office and put her head on her arm to cushion it against the desktop. Sleep came quickly.

A loud knuckle rap woke her up. She rose on unsteady legs and felt her way to the door. At the wall, she flicked on the light switch and wiped crusty drool from her mouth. Then she opened the door and blinked Max into focus. He was holding a half-eaten chili dog.

"Yowza. What happened?" he said. "That's some high-voltage hair. Where'd you have it done, *Styles-by-Stun-Gun?*"

"Don't mess with me or you'll be wearing that dog like an Easter hat."

"I thought you were changing clothes."

"Where's your stuff?"

"Already loaded in the van."

She bought herself fifteen minutes to

change clothes before meeting her photographer in the parking lot.

At two o'clock in the morning, after the bars stopped serving alcohol and the drunks spilled out onto the streets, Max parked the company van at the airport shuttle, a fenced location within walking distance of downtown. Aspen removed a shopping cart on loan from a nearby grocery store. To help her look the part, Max had filled it with aluminum cans from the office garbage and even attached a spy cam to the front of it.

As he pulled a sci-fi book out of the back pocket of his jeans and flicked on the dome light, Aspen announced, "I'm ready."

"Good. Have fun." He leafed through the pages until he found the dog-ear marking his place.

"Is that all you have to say?"

"Be careful." He slouched against the seat back, nestling his shoulders into the upholstery.

Realization dawned. "Wait a minute. You're not coming with me?"

"Call if you stumble onto anything."

"Call you?" she repeated. "You're leaving me out here?"

"No, you're leaving me in here."

Panic set in. Tiny hairs on her arms stood straight up, piercing the fabric of her shirt.

"So I'm just supposed to go out there by myself?" Her eyes darted around like pinballs.

A lightning bolt idea seemed to hit Max squarely in the jaw. He came up out of his resting position, leaned in and removed two walkie-talkies from the van's glove compartment.

"Here. Take this. If you get in a bind, holler."

But she was thinking if she got into a bind Max would be of little use. Oh sure, he might get there in time to zoom-in on her cold, dead body with blood pooling beneath her head, but that was about it. Max made an unlikely superhero — unless one's idea of a superhero was to blend in by wearing long hair pulled back in a ponytail, ratty jeans, a Star Wars T-shirt with the caption "I'm not from here," carrying a Kryptonite paperback he could throw at the villain should the need arise.

She placed the walkie-talkie in the child seat of her metal shopping cart. "You suck."

"Hey, you're the one getting paid big bucks."

She huffed in contempt. "So you're throwing me to the wolves?"

"All part of the job. You're the one who wanted to be an investigative reporter."

"Why're you being so nasty to me?"

"You almost had me fooled." Max rested the book on his lap. His eyes narrowed. "Gordon thinks having a female reporter is a great idea. The rest of us think it bites. I thought you might be different and decided to give you the benefit of the doubt. But now I realize — you're one of *them*."

"You don't think a woman can pull her own weight?"

He heaved a contemptuous sigh. "I'm talking from experience. We had twelve interns come through here last year, all females. None of them were hungry enough. They all came from SMU and they all drove Porsches and other high-end sports cars. Why would they want to give that up to go slogging around in an unmarked vehicle trying to get a story? It's easier to live on Daddy's money." He went back to his book. Held it up to the light and feigned reading.

"Hold your horses — you think you know me? You don't know anything about me."

"I know you're good-looking, so it's pretty much a given that you're spoiled rotten."

The back of her neck tingled with the thrill of Max's compliment.

He thought she was hot.

Wait — he'd just insulted her.

"Let me set you straight. I'm living off

Ramen noodles and bologna until payday. I haven't even established enough credit to finance a Happy Meal. I drive a ten-year-old Honda. I'm so broke I'm what poor wants to be when it grows up." She didn't want to add that the biggest difference between her and the SMU interns was that those divas probably didn't have enough candlepower to sense imminent danger, and this wee-hour fishing expedition she was about to embark on scared the living daylights out of her.

"Congratulations."

"I'm not like those other girls." The truth. The rent was due. The electric bill was overdue. The refrigerator had precious little food in it. If Daddy had any money to give her, he'd forgotten where he put it.

"Mazel tov."

"You have no right to be contemptuous of me. You don't even know me." Tears blistered behind her eyeballs.

Max lowered the book. "No, I don't know you. And I don't want to know you. As far as I'm concerned, you're just like all the rest of the society babes parading through WBFD."

"You're mistaken." She clamped her jaw to stop the quiver in her chin.

"Let me clue you in." Max slapped the

book facedown on the passenger seat. He gave her a look capable of withering a hothouse orchid. Then he unloaded on her. "If the station ever did get a gung-ho female investigative reporter, she'd be popular. She could write her own ticket. Go straight to the top."

Heart thudding, she waited for more.

"Sure, it's tough for a woman. I never saw any of those chicks dress up like a queer —"

Excuse me?

"— and schlep around with a shopping cart, so I've gotta hand you that much. But women have it made . . . the ones who want to work, that is. Know why?"

His eyes demanded a response so she gave him a shoulder shrug.

"Because men tell women secrets." He sat back triumphant. As if he'd given her the key that unlocked the box containing all knowledge.

"Thanks for the tip. I owe you."

He tossed out an idea — a scary one. "What're you going to do if some homo bushwhacks you?"

Her eyes went wide. Goosebumps cropped up on her arms. In her own naïve way, she'd assumed Max would stick beside her. It hadn't occurred to her when they left the station and rolled out of the parking lot that she might be in real danger.

Lambs led to the slaughter didn't make a sound. Pigs and cows pitched walleyed fits.

Fear siphoned off her breath. She wanted to high-tail it out of there, only now she was stuck.

"God, you're dumb." Max leaned over and dug around under the seat. When he sat upright, he'd pulled out two unopened bottles of Thunderbird. "Take these. If anybody tries to putz around with you, offer them a swig."

Her mouth gaped.

"When you're down to the last swallow, you can always bash them over the head with the empties."

"Thanks." She backed up warily, holding the wine bottles by their throats as if they were Molotov cocktails waiting to be thrown.

"Don't mention it. I don't much like you but I'll be damned if I'll let you check out on my watch."

Shrouded in baggy jeans, a T-shirt and an ancient long-sleeve, plaid flannel from the men's clothing section at the Salvation Army store, Aspen wheeled her cart up the sidewalk, past old buildings wearing the patina of neglect, toward the granite courthouse. She'd remembered to tuck a plastic container of bottled water into the basket along with a brown bag that contained a bologna and Swiss cheese sandwich and two plums. And she carried no money, not even enough to drop down the chute of a pay phone.

By day, the temperature had been a scorcher. By sunset, the climate had cooled dramatically. Texas weather changed more often than a debutante updating her wardrobe. Ten minutes into exploring the night, Aspen wished she'd worn a light jacket.

This was the reason to watch the weather broadcast.

Although she wouldn't have chosen WBFD's, that's for sure.

She'd catch Stormy Rainbolt's forecast.

Five years ago, WBFD had an opportunity to hire Stormy away from KODE Channel 12's *Good Morning Four States* program in Joplin, Missouri. Only Gordon refused to meet the drop-dead gorgeous meteorologist's salary demands. So "Openly-gay José," with his wispy little mustache and thick horn rim glasses, continued to broadcast the weather in his dark gray suit. No one could be certain how Openly-gay José got the nickname. He was neither homosexual nor Hispanic. But during one big hiring push for minorities, Gordon suggested Joe Martin become the on-air meteorological talent known as José Martinez. Since none of the other sexually ambiguous employees wanted to own up to being gay, the station manager left the role to the family man with six children.

When Openly-gay José retired, Gordon took leave of his senses and hired Joe's daughter — Misty Knight. These days, anyone with half a brain would watch Stormy Rainbolt on Channel 15 for accuracy; or catch moody Misty's act on Channel 18 and plan for the opposite to happen.

Aspen saw movement at the limits of her vision. The distant tree line took on eerie shapes, like the silhouettes of a hundred Kokopellis traveling in a conga line. She shuddered.

Four blocks up the road, human shadows moved behind a stand of oaks. Her heart picked up its pace. Two ghostly specters ambled out and started her way.

She keyed her walkie-talkie. "Max. You copy?"

A low squelch broke in the night. "Ten-four."

"I've got activity. Two men. Headed my way."

"Don't forget to take down their names if you get anything good."

"Take down their names? *Take down their names?*" Her voice shrilled. "Are you kidding? They'll probably gut me like a deer and leave me for dead."

"Roger. The police will need the names if you want your murder solved."

She covered the walkie-talkie with her sack lunch. Seconds later, two rangy-smelling black men sauntered up and flanked her.

"Got any coins?"

Aspen deepened her voice. "No."

"Got any grub?" A meaty hand plucked out her sack lunch. "Thanks." He rifled through the bag and pulled out the bologna and Swiss. With dirty fingers, he halved it, shoving the smaller section toward his buddy.

She thought of the wine bottles and hoped they wouldn't dig through the cans. Unable to move past these men, she fell into step as they munched bites of sandwich.

"Where'd you get the chow?" one asked.

Aspen thought fast. "Church ladies. They came to the Mission."

"You's kinda young to be living on the streets. How you make yo' money?" Both men leered.

She wasn't about to let these derelicts

manhandle her. She invented a reason that might hold them at bay.

"Got no money." She spoke in the low-down, bluesy voice of a ne'er do well. "Family turned me out. I've got AIDS."

Like the Blue Angels peeling off from their formation, the two men split away and took flight in opposite directions. They rejoined each other and slunk toward the stand of trees, blending back into the indigo night.

Aspen's heart raced. She thought of Max's comment about the SMU girls. Then she questioned whether she'd make it at WBFD.

By three o'clock that morning, she'd given one of the wine bottles to a camp of Katrina evacuees, a small but decidedly creepy bunch of people now living on the streets of Fort Worth. Their illegal campsite had a sinister feel, orbited by stray pit bulls and mongrels whose body parts seemed to be cannibalized from different dogs of indeterminate pedigrees. They had bits of rope or grimy bandanas knotted around their necks and roamed the encampment with low growls resonating from their throats. A few people lit up cigarettes and passed them around. It wasn't long before the smell of marijuana, mingled with the odor of dirty clothes, permeated the air.

They offered to ladle up a scoop of pinto

beans with a slice of bread toasted over the small campfire, but she declined. When they gave her flinty-eyed looks, she explained that Hepatitis-C did that to a person . . . dulled their appetite.

A light wind ruffled the treetops. They spoke of woes and hard times — the inability to find work or to keep it once they'd been lucky enough to land jobs. According to one old black sage, only two evacuees traveling on the same bus from Louisiana had managed to stay employed. They'd found the American dream and were living happily ever after.

Unlike the rest of them.

Before leaving, she presented the other bottle of wine to the group. Not exactly an altruistic move on her part. She'd gotten the disturbing feeling that a couple of the men might follow her down the road and jump her if they thought she had anything left of value in the grocery basket.

She pushed her cart up Calhoun Street, past two of the businesses that had been burglarized the previous weekend.

All's well.

She moved quietly through the night using her cart as a shield, creating contingency plans in her mind in the event scary people popped out of nowhere and wanted a piece of her. Rounding the corner, she noticed six patrol cars behind the row of buildings that fronted on Calhoun.

She lifted one hand and gave them a weak wave. Nobody responded.

No one even looked her way.

They were either fast asleep or had become victims of carbon monoxide poisoning.

"Holy smoke," she whispered into the breeze. "Is this for real? I think I just stumbled onto a factor contributing to the burglaries."

She called for Max immediately.

A half block away, her photographer coasted up in the van. He hit the electronic button and the window rolled halfway down.

"Take a look at these lazy bums. They're asleep. Every damned one of them," Aspen said. "I want you to video this."

"Won't make you very popular with the police," Max said, hopping out of the vehicle, quietly pushing the door until the lock snapped.

Aspen jammed her hand on one hip. "I didn't go to SMU. I'm not entering a popularity contest. It is what it is and I want it captured on video."

"You're the boss."

They crept within twenty feet of the patrol cars. With heads tilted back and mouths wide open, Aspen could almost hear the snores of Fort Worth's finest vibrating off the windows.

"Can you get a good picture without lighting them up?" Aspen whispered.

"Infra-red," Max said, and hit the record button. From the angle of the camcorder, she watched him feature each officer. "Have you figured out how to package your story?"

Had she ever.

"I'm calling it *Asleep at the Wheel.*"

CHAPTER NINETEEN

In the safety of the ENG van, they traveled down Interstate Thirty back to the station. Staring out the windshield, with the glow of the moon silvering the asphalt, Aspen reflected on her unlikely accomplishment. Adrenaline still coursed through her veins — she could've been beaten, maimed and killed undertaking such an assignment. Instead, she'd developed one amazing story. Chills crawled over her body. Meeting the Katrina evacuees under such dangerous conditions, dressed as an imposter, turned out to be her most exciting experience in the past ten years. Well, that, and riding out the horrible tornado that sprang up out of nowhere and tore up downtown Fort Worth and the entire west side.

But tonight had been different.

During the tornado, she didn't have a choice other than to hunker down in the bathroom with a sofa cushion clutched against her body because the warning sirens didn't go off in time to get outta Dodge. By the time they activated, the sky had already turned black and a horrible, freight-train roar descended on her quiet neighborhood. When the rumble finally subsided and deafening silence took its place, she staggered outdoors to find the houses on both sides of hers flattened, and nothing but a thin pecan tree branch, stripped of its leaves, on top of the Wicklow family garage.

Looking back on the event, she wondered if the Drummond sisters thought tornados were God's way of telling them to go out and buy all new stuff.

She shook off the reverie and concentrated on this new facet of her personality.

What made tonight's terrifying adventure so important was that she didn't have to go undercover to get Gordon's story. She could've played it safe, interviewed burglary victims and gotten quotes from the NPOs — neighborhood police officers. Instead, she'd pulled off a coup.

Maybe she wasn't such a scared-y cat after all.

Never mind that it didn't turn out to be the story she started out investigating. Hadn't Rochelle suggested that consumer tips had the capacity to morph into totally different topics?

Tires droned on the asphalt. She peeled off the baseball cap and shook out her matted hat hair. In an effort to regain a semblance of femininity, she fluffed her limp waves. While threading her fingers through dampened coils, she posed a burning question to her photographer.

"So what's your secret?"

"What secret?" Max stared through the windshield as if monitoring the traffic. But his meaty hands, tightening around the steering wheel, did not go unnoticed.

"You said men tell women secrets. So what's yours?"

"I don't know you well enough."

She studied his profile. Square jaw, Roman nose and sturdy bone structure. With a Mediterranean skin tone, salt-and-pepper hair and Caribbean-blue eyes, Max was a man of indeterminate ancestry. Handsome in a goofy sort of way — if one could get past the Bohemian style of dress — she could imagine him in a tux at the annual Awards banquet. If he'd cut that ponytail, shed the Birkenstocks and get a good haircut, he might actually be someone she could invite to escort her to the Peabody Awards — whenever she received one. Even if achieving such a lofty goal was so far off in the future they'd be attending the ceremony in his-and-hers wheelchairs.

"No, really," she pressed. "What's your secret? Are you rich? Here to prove to your family that you can earn a decent living before you take over Daddy's company?"

"Touché."

She leaned in close enough for him to smell the mint chip dissolving on her tongue. "What's your secret, Max? I want to know."

"Why?"

"Because I've noticed Gordon doesn't treat you with a lot of respect. He doesn't treat me well, either. I just thought . . ."

"You just thought because we have something in common that I should spill my guts to you?"

She gave him an answer brimming with honesty. "I'm testing out your theory that men tell women secrets. I want to know yours. I won't tell anyone."

Without a preamble, Max detoured to an all-night restaurant. In a corner booth, over a cup of hot coffee, he confided in her.

"Little known fact . . . I restore old houses."

"Sounds interesting. Why do you keep that a secret?"

Max took a deep breath. "My twin brother

was killed by a DWI a few years ago." Steam coiled up from his decaf. "His wife, Cerise, my sister-in-law, was devastated. They'd bought this old Victorian re-do and they'd only completed half of the restoration. She didn't have the money to move and nobody wanted to buy the place un-restored. She decided the only way to market the house was to finish the cosmetic details herself. One evening, she called me crying. She'd tried to hang wallpaper on the ceiling. It kept falling down on top of her."

Aspen gave a slow head-bob. "I can see where that'd be a two-person job."

He nodded into the vapors of his mug. "I did what any good brother-in-law would've done. I went over to help. The room was a disaster. Cerise was sitting, cross-legged, on the floor with globs of wallpaper paste in her hair, sobbing into her hands. My first mistake was helping her to her feet."

Aspen gave him a blank stare.

"My second mistake was steering her into the shower. My third mistake was helping her —"

"Into bed." Aspen finished the thought. She drew in a sharp intake of air. "You're sleeping with your dead brother's wife."

Max grimaced. "Can you say it any louder? Maybe you'd like a microphone? I don't think the people in the smoking section heard you," he said miserably.

"I'm not judging you. I've never met anybody who hasn't had a one-night stand."

"That's the problem. It wasn't just one night. It's been going on for a year and I don't know how to end it."

"Take it from me, women like to get bad news over with fast. Other than that pearl of wisdom, I decline to give advice on anyone's love life. Maybe you should go on the 'Ask Lindsey' show."

"That'd be like dabbing perfume on a pig." The smirk on Max's face faded away. "Cerise doesn't want it to stop. She says it's like having her husband back." The coffee had cooled enough for him to gulp it down. "So," he said, reseating the cup in its saucer, "what's *your* secret?"

"I'm scared of the dark," she said, and then laughed as if she didn't mean it.

Once they'd returned to the TV station, Aspen went straight to her office. She'd been feeling invisible cooties inside her clothes for the past hour and was itching to peel off the rest of her disguise. She pushed the door closed for privacy and shucked off the baggy jeans. As she unbuttoned the oversized flannel shirt, a gentle knuckle rap sounded against the doorframe.

Aspen kicked the jeans aside, smoothed a crease from the front of her top and said, "Come in."

Max pushed the door open until half of his face showed. "If you're through with me for the night, I'll take off."

For the sister-in-law's.

He seemed to read her mind. "Not for Cerise's. I've decided not to do that anymore. It's not healthy."

"I'm not judging you."

He backed away. "We shot some great footage tonight. I'll catch a couple hours' sleep and come back to package it. If you want to put on something a little nicer than that —" he scrunched his face at the sight of the flannel shirt grazing her knees "— I'll shoot the lead-in for your story when I come back."

"Thanks for all your hard work. And for the wine. That saved my bacon."

He gave her one of those *Not a problem* head nods and pulled the door to until only a sliver of light slanted in from the studio. "A word of advice," he added. "Watch out for Rochelle."

The warning jarred her. "How so?"

"Like I said earlier, men tell women secrets. Women guard theirs with a vengeance." He gave her the visual once-over.

She wanted to ask more about the secrets Rochelle hid, but the door clicked shut, effectively closing Max off from view.

Aspen retreated behind her desk. With an outstretched arm on the blotter, she rested her head against a pillow of flesh, longing for the reinvigorating results of a quick power nap that would leave her clear-headed enough to drive home and catch a few hours of dead-to-the-world slumber.

Dog tired and ready to drop in her tracks, the last thing she expected was a restless night's sleep.

Then Sheriff Spike Granger gate-crashed her dreams.

CHAPTER TWENTY

Aspen rolled over in bed and peeled off the black satin sleep mask. She slitted her eyes open, wanting to pull the covers over her head and drift back to the part of her dream where she'd left off.

She hadn't finished the best part — the part where she publicly humiliated Roger by dumping him at the altar. Sleep had been deep, filled with Technicolor images; now the digital readout on the clock radio flashed nine o'clock in electric blue numbers. Caramel Janine Drummond's funeral would start at eleven on that sad Saturday morning.

She considered skipping the service and showing up at the gravesite, then reconsidered. It would be rude and she'd probably get caught. She decided instead to make a cameo appearance, sign the guest book and run like hell back to her car before anyone she knew ratted her out.

After a quick shower, she toweled off and put on the same black dress she'd worn to Margo's house the day before. She had access to a black hat that her mother owned and made a decision to wear it, pulling the net veil down to her nose. Topping off the outfit, she shoved on a pair of dark sunglasses and complimented herself for looking very Jackie-O.

The funeral was being held at the First Methodist Church in downtown Fort Worth. The parking lots were packed with cars, limos — and a WBFD ENG van. Other TV stations were on the scene, too. But it was the WBFD van, looking like a huge albino cockroach with its various antennae poking out, that raised the hairs on Aspen's neck. She walked across the lot and found the vehicle locked.

That could only mean one thing.

Whoever came to cover the Drummond service had already set up inside the church.

An usher threw open one of several massive Gothic doors and stepped outside to light up a cigarette. She climbed the steps, sidestepped a plume of smoke, entered the red-carpeted foyer and glimpsed Max with his back to her. As she circled around with the skill of an Indian warrior, she spied Tig scanning his notes.

The light beacon came on and Max counted him down.

"Three —"

"What's going on here?"

"— two." Max turned to look. "Hey, Aspen. How's it going?"

She carefully modulated her voice to conceal her anger. "This is my story. What do you think you're doing?"

"Tig asked if you were covering it. You said you didn't need me for anything else so I told him I didn't think so."

"You snooze, you lose," Tig said through a grin. His nefarious wink siphoned the rest of the oxygen out of her lungs.

Heat rose to her cheeks. Her face clenched, along with her fists. "I can see how we might have to battle the competition for a story," she hissed. "I just didn't realize I'd have to duke it out with you."

"That's a little harsh, don't you think?" Tig kept his tone suave and debonair, as if he'd just invited her to jet off with him in the company plane, but his mouth seemed feral.

A throng of mourners pushed past, eyeing the three of them as if they were looking at sheep-killing dogs. Even Aspen had to agree — coming into the church to do a follow-up story while the other stations waited a polite distance outside was a little too *"get the widow on the set"* for her taste.

"What'd you do, put on a little Don Henley and crank up the volume to *Dirty Laundry* on the ride over?" She lowered her voice. "Here's what I think: Ask no quarter, give no quarter. If these are your rules, I can play by them. Just don't go whining to Gordon when I rip off one of your stories."

But Tig had already tuned her out. He primped his hair with the flat of his hand. "Count me down, Max."

With tears rimming her eyes and an ink pen poised like a dagger, she practically carved her name into the guest book. After slapping the pen against the pedestal, she yanked open the second set of doors and picked her way through a pew packed with mourners.

Aspen skipped the graveside service and drove straight to Tranquility Villas. More than ever, she needed to talk to her mother. Before the horrible accident that left her brain-damaged, Jillian Wicklow had always dispensed sound advice. Maybe, in a lucid moment, she could still work her magic.

Mrs. Ramsey was off for the weekend but Mrs. Hendrix had arrived in her place. At first glance, Loquita Hendrix cut a grandmotherly figure the envy of Norman Rockwell painting. With a hefty bosom and a pale, doughy face dusted in a thin layer of talcum powder, she appeared to be a pleasant sort.

She wasn't.

When she looked up from the accounting ledger and saw Aspen, she slammed down her pen and pushed back from the desk.

"I want to talk to you about your parents." Dark eyes thinned into slits, glinting like onyx beads.

"Good. Because I want to talk to you about my parents."

"My office." Mrs. Hendrix hooked a finger in the air and pulled it toward her.

Aspen closed the door behind them. She took a seat and waited.

"They're incorrigible." Mrs. Hendrix braced her arms across her chest. "Both of them."

"This isn't my mother's fault."

"I'm holding them both responsible for what happened in the courtyard last night."

"The courtyard?"

"They practically had an orgy going. Your father talked these gullible women into playing strip poker and before you know it, they were all naked. Except for your father. I guess I don't have to tell you who won."

"I know what you're going to say, but I'm not moving either of them. If they can't be at the same address, then I can't look in on them as often as I need to."

"I wasn't going to say anything of the sort. Married people can stay together. We don't have a rule against that."

"But they're not married anymore. They're divorced."

"They're about to get married. The wedding's a week from today."

Aspen stared with the dumbfounded expression of someone who'd realized, too late, that the man springing up from the floorboard of her back seat looked strikingly similar to one of the armed robbers from the bank heist she'd just witnessed.

"They can't get married. They're functionally retarded." Panic turned to a mysterious blend of euphoria and dread as she carefully sorted out the dilemma in her head. "They're like those apes that have to work in pairs in order to groom each other. They couldn't pick fleas off themselves without help." She tapped a finger to her temple by way of illustration. "They don't have enough wattage left between them to get a preacher here."

Mrs. Hendrix crushed her hopes.

"We have a chaplain on staff. He usually

comes here when people are dying, but he's been known to show up for an occasional wedding. It's all very legal."

"*Ha.* You don't know them the way I do. Her mind erases as soon as you turn your back. He can't remember anything that happened after the Korean War. These people behave like very bad children. Tell them if they don't knock it off, you're going to put them in time-out. And then do it."

"Lucky you got here when you did. The only reason they didn't tie the knot last night was because he insisted on inviting his teacher."

Aspen's eyes fell to half-mast.

When the news fully soaked in, she came up out of her chair and headed down the hall looking for Wexford, spoiling for a fight. She didn't find either parent. And since the people in charge of Tranquility Villas didn't think two missing lunatics were serious enough to put out an All Points Bulletin, Aspen headed back to the station to catch up on leads for the next story.

When she stormed inside WBFD, one of the runners intercepted her on the way to the assignments desk.

"Oh, you're here," he said. "I didn't know you'd be working today." He sauntered on over to the message cubby hole that still had Stinger Baldwin's brass nameplate on it and retrieved her messages. The pink slip on top had come in from Mike Henson within the previous five minutes. "He said it was urgent. He wanted your home phone number but we don't give those out."

"Thanks. I'll be in my office."

She didn't want to call Henson back. He'd become a pest during her first week at WBFD and she saw no point in encouraging bad behavior. The kindest thing she could do for him, she decided, was to furnish him the name of a good mental health professional. One who could help him get over Gabrielle's rejection. She seated herself in the swivel chair, fished out the Yellow Pages from the bottom drawer and looked up Psychologists. She selected a couple that specialized in relationship counseling and scrutinized the ones with photographs in their ads.

As she copied down phone numbers for three different doctors — one older man with a kind smile, a younger man with a confident expression and a middle-aged female that looked remarkably like Rochelle — her office line rang.

She picked it up and sing-songed, "Aspen Wicklow."

"It's Mike Henson. I have to talk to you."

Damn it.

"I was just about to call you."

"She got fired."

"What?" It took a few seconds for his words to soak in.

"Gabby. She got a termination letter in the mail today."

"You're opening her mail? Isn't that an invasion of privacy?"

"The return address was from her job. I had to," he said miserably. "It was a formal notice since she hadn't gotten approval to take leave. She's been gone over a week and hasn't called in. So they fired her."

A small throb in Aspen's throat became a pounding sensation that moved up behind her eyeballs. What started in the studio as a low-level hum turned into a rumble of excitement rippling down the corridor. The runner who'd intercepted her as she came into the building now framed himself in her doorway, sucking air.

"Get off the phone. Lennox needs you now."

She slipped her hand over the mouthpiece. "Steve Lennox asked for me?"

"No, not specifically for you. He wants a reporter, fast. Since you're the only one here, tag, you're it. Now hang up and come with me."

She told Mike Henson she'd call him back, slamming down the receiver before he could mount a protest. As she trailed the runner down the hallway to the studio, voices increased in volume and frenzy.

"What's going on?" She hustled to keep up. Catching him by the shirtsleeve, she pulled herself up even with him.

"Dead girl. Just came over the scanner. Lennox needs a reporter to cover it. Tig's covering the Drummond girl's funeral with Max so you'll have to take Reggie."

"Who's Reggie?"

"Photographer. Yo, Steve," he yelled, peeling her hand off without so much as a downward glance. "I got you a reporter."

"Astor." Lennox glanced her way. "The new girl."

"The name's Aspen." She walked toward the anchor desk, nervously fingering her pearl choker.

"Whatever. I'll just call you 'New Girl' for now." He tore a sheet from a pad. "Get on this. Reggie's outside waiting in the van. And don't screw up."

"Fill me in. I don't even know what's going on."

"Dead girl. Been missing for a week. Employer hasn't seen her. Boyfriend making a pest of himself down at the police department. Everything else you need to know is right there." He flicked the paper with his fingernail. "When you arrive at the location, get as close to the crime scene as you can get without contaminating it — or getting arrested. Grab a cop and see if he'll add anything to what we already know. Then go live. Now hurry."

"Do I have time to —"

"No. Hustle. And take off those pearls. Gordon hates jewelry. If it isn't real, he gets annoyed."

CHAPTER
TWENTY-ONE

Aspen climbed into the ENG van and took in Reggie's presence in one dismissive glance. He sported hair that looked like it'd been cut with a hacksaw and had the gangly, uncoordinated movements of a geek. With worn sneakers, frayed shoestrings, tattered jeans and a rangy smell that came from wearing the same clothes several days in a row, her photographer made Max look like a fashion plate. She powered open the window a crack, introduced herself and got a bored eye blink for her trouble.

As soon as the door snapped shut, Reggie gunned the big V-8 engine. Tires squealed against the pavement, propelling the van forward like an eight ball. Leaving tire smoke vanishing in their wake, they bounced over a concrete divider bolted to the asphalt, rocketed out of the parking lot and careened the wrong way down a one-way before Reggie jumped the curb in a frightening, midblock U-turn.

He reached into the door's side pocket and pulled out a can of Red Bull. Using his elbow to steer, he popped the aluminum pull-tab and sucked down the energy drink. When he finished, he crumpled it in his hand and reached for another.

Aspen grabbed her seatbelt. She fastened it before giving it a good, hard yank.

"Do you know where we're going?" She glanced over expectantly. The cold depths of his dark-lashed eyes could freeze salt water. "Because if you don't know," she added helpfully, "I have the address." She consulted the paper. "It says to take Interstate-30 until we reach — *for the love of God, watch out.*" She clapped a hand to her mouth to squelch a hysterical scream.

He whipped into the fast lane and powered up her window using the controls embedded near the door handle on his side of the van. While her nose clamped down in self-defense, Reggie's window hummed down. He stuck out his arm, shot the finger at the driver behind him, snaked his hand back in and powered up the glass.

Aspen leaned over enough to check his speed. From her vantage point, it appeared he'd exceeded the limit by thirty miles per hour. Which meant they were going ninety in a sixty zone. On a Saturday afternoon. While twenty traffic cops funded by a new Federal grant were out in full force. Her gaze dipped and she was treated to a sneak preview of Reggie scratching his privates.

He reached for the Red Bull nestled in the van's cup holder and swigged it dry. Crushing the can in his fist, he tossed the empty aside and reached into the map pocket where he'd stashed a third drink.

"I'm not sure those are good for you." Aspen's mouth curled into a grimace. "You just swilled down enough energy to power a small electrical plant."

"Keeps me from overeating. In case I have to fall back on my career as an underwear model."

Her eyes flickered to the speedometer. They were pushing a hundred.

A lance of fear shot through her. "What happens if you get a ticket?"

She was glad she could see the clock mounted in the dash. That way, she could take an accurate pulse check before stroking out.

"You want to get there before the competition, or not?"

"Yes. Preferably alive." She grabbed the overhead handgrip and braced herself, then spent the next few seconds contemplating the raspy, two-pack a day voice. Reggie didn't smell like cigarettes. But he bore the remnants of an old scar that ran from his Adam's apple up to his jaw. Go figure.

She decided making small talk would take her mind off imminent death. "So how long have you worked at WBFD?"

He lifted one shoulder.

"I guess you've seen a lot of excitement. Has anyone ever been hurt on the job?"

He cut his eyes in her direction and pointed to his scar. "Where do you think I got this?" he said. Recrimination swam in his eyes.

"What happened?"

He stared at her with a degree of censure. Intuition warned her to stop probing.

She shifted her gaze to the speedometer. The needle vibrated above one hundred. With a white-knuckled grip on the armrest and fingertips digging into the door padding, she made a request. "Could you slow down to maybe about eighty?"

"Tig probably heard the call by now. I imagine he's headed our way."

"Well, what're you waiting for?" Aspen yelled over the road noise. "Floor this tin can."

What the hell? They'd need a dragline to pick up all the pieces. But scooping Tig on a story would almost be worth it. Besides, her skin was pulling Gs and the high-voltage adrenaline current pumping through her body like a high-performance engine's fuel-injection system made it practically impossible to scream.

At the Loop-820 exit, Reggie locked up the brakes and veered right. Aspen was convinced that his side of the van lifted off the pavement. She made a mad grab at his seat to redistribute her weight in the scant hope it would keep them from flipping like a roll of the dice. Her hand closed firmly around his wrist and she tightened her fingers on him painfully.

"What's your problem?" Reggie fixed her with a bored look.

He was a mangy Doberman, off his chain. But the clench in her chest caused her more concern for the heart attack she was probably having.

"You don't look so good," he said.

"Do you think you could get us there in one piece?"

"Don't like my driving? Suppose you could do better?" Eyes that hid a universe of pain took on a speculative gleam.

It occurred to her that he might just jam on the brakes, wrench the column shift into park and toss her the keys. She gave him a big head shake, pantomimed an invisible lip-zip, locked it and tossed the invisible key over her shoulder. At least doing it Reggie's way, death would come quickly and without pain. She decided he should probably go faster, just to make sure they never knew what hit them.

The photographer gave a derisive grunt. Favoring her with an uninvitingly blank look, he delivered instructions. "When we get stopped, look for the nearest uniformed officer, preferably one with stripes." He drew an imaginary chevron on one sleeve with his finger to suggest she should find a ranking officer — sergeant or higher — who had the authority to give an interview quote.

"What if he won't talk to me?"

"Then I'll count you down and you wing it. Say something like, 'Police are refusing to comment on the circumstances surrounding the discovery of a body of a female found in east Fort Worth. . . .' Then tell the viewers the cops aren't commenting on whether this body is linked to the one found earlier this week. That'll let you segue into the Drummond case. Believe me, you'll have plenty of material to draw on after that."

Aspen's heart leapt to her throat. "I think I'm going to black out."

"If you do and your dress rides up, I'll record it on video so we'll have something to watch at the Christmas party."

"You're kidding."

"I'm not. Every year the photographers get together and create a short flick we like to call *Stupid Outtakes.*" Reggie stomped the brake with both feet. The van slid sideways and careened to a screaming halt. He yanked up the emergency brake and flicked open his seatbelt. "Then we sit around and make fun of the rest of you guys."

"That's cruel."

"Yeah, but it's all we have considering we don't make as much money as we deserve."

Speaking of money, Aspen balked at traipsing down a muddy incline leading to the crime scene. She didn't want to ruin her best pair of shoes, especially since she had no disposable income left from Friday's paycheck to pay for new ones.

Reggie seemed to read her thoughts. He looked up at a bank of threatening clouds hanging overhead. Then he glanced down at her feet.

"Go ahead and sacrifice the slippers, Cinderella. If it's a good story, you'll be Gordon's little darling. Besides, you're a probationary employee. If we video from up here and a rival station gets a better shot, Gordon will get the idea you're chicken."

The sound of his words went tinny and distant. The only part that stuck was the probationary employee thing. No one had bothered to tell her that when she hired on.

"What do you mean I'm on probation?"

"WBFD has an at-will doctrine. They don't pay unemployment because they don't have to keep you if they don't want to. You work at the pleasure of the station manager."

Well, screw it. She needed the job. How bad could it be?

Gauging the distance down to the crime scene turned out to be unnecessary. Two steps later, Aspen slipped. Her right hip hit the ground and she rolled twenty feet before skidding to a stop, muddy and dazed, at the bottom of the embankment.

While Reggie stood on the shoulder of the highway videoing the disaster with his camcorder, a patrolman rushed over to help.

"Are you all right?" From her place on the ground, she eyed the fleshy overhang above his gun belt. Her ribcage ached. She'd probably punctured a lung. The trees did the hula in front of her as he helped her to her feet. "Did you hurt anything?"

"Only my feelings and my self-esteem."

She blinked back tears, waiting until her spine realigned itself before trusting her shaky legs to carry her closer to the crime scene.

For no reason other than instinct, she shifted her attention to the dead woman. The guys from the Medical Examiner's Office wore emotionless stares, empty of curiosity. Realizing they wouldn't have to process her corpse next, they remembered they had work to do and went about the business of securing the body.

"I ruined my shoes, my dress looks like it came from the rag bin and I don't have the slightest clue what's going on even though I'm supposed to be out here reporting the story."

Working at WBFD was causing her to become immune to indignity. The little black dress wasn't exactly a seductive outfit, but the officer's eyes locked onto her cleavage where he carried on a polite conversation with her breasts.

"Can't do anything about the way you look, although the hair's great. Kind of wild, like a lioness. I like that in a woman. I can, however, tell you what's up as long as you don't quote me, film me or otherwise refer to me in your story. Are we off the record?"

"Deal." She swiped her hands together in

an attempt to dislodge the mud clumps.

"Her name's Gabrielle —"

"Ohmygod." Aspen blinked. "I know about this girl."

"You can't identify her until we notify next-of-kin." His eyes went dark. His face lined with the fear of someone spooked.

"I won't. I don't know her next-of-kin but I've been talking to her boyfriend for the past few days."

"What's his name?"

"Mike Henson. Are you going to call him?"

"No, ma'am. You are." He yelled to a brother officer, got his attention and motioned him over. "This is —" He looked at Aspen, blank-faced.

"Aspen Wicklow, WBFD Channel Eighteen." She extended a muddy hand, thought better of it and pulled it back.

"Tell him what you just told me."

Aspen related conversations with Mike Henson from the past few days. When she finished, she noticed the chevrons on his sleeve and sent him a wobbly smile of hope.

"One good turn deserves another, Sergeant. Can we get closer to film?"

"Long as you stay behind the yellow tape."

She waved Reggie down. He took duck-footed steps, planting each heel into the ground for stability. When he reached her level, he rearranged her ear bud and the umbilical cords that connected them back to the studio, then pulled out the hand mike he'd tucked in the waistband of his jeans.

"The sergeant says we can get as close as the crime scene tape."

"Then do it." They stopped behind the Day-Glo barrier. Aspen turned to the camera as Reggie said, "I'll count you down."

"Wait — how do I look?"

"Like a mudpack. Your face is smudged."

Her ear bud crackled to life, filling her head with Steve Lennox's voice. "Give me a reading, Astro."

"It's Aspen."

"Sounds good. Reggie, take it away."

The beacon came on. The cameraman spotlighted her. "Three —"

"Wait — I don't have my compact. You have to help me get the mud off."

"Two —"

"I'm asking you nicely. Please give me just a second. Do you have a mirror?"

"One. And . . . you're on the air."

Mortified, she held the mike inches from her lips.

"I'm Aspen Wicklow, WBFD, coming to you live from the east side of Fort Worth, where police are investigating the discovery of a second body found this week. According to sources close to the department, there may be a connection between the deceased female in this case and the murder of Caramel Janine Drummond."

A clap of thunder broke her concentration. Lightning crackled in the distance.

Aspen regained her composure. Her surroundings faded into the background and she channeled what she needed to do to deliver the news. She looked directly into the camera lens and pretended she was having an intimate conversation with the only person who still gave a tinker's damn about her — Jillian Wicklow.

"Drummond, who was buried this afternoon after a memorial service in downtown Fort Worth, had been missing at least a week before a man walking his dog discovered her body about a mile from her home. Back to you, Steve."

She paused, staring at her muddy hands. When she looked up, Reggie didn't give her the invisible throat slit to end the piece. A few raindrops pelted her head. Then the bottom fell out of the sky. With her head tilted heavenward, she felt the sting of raindrops like shards of glass against her face.

"What are the weather conditions out

there?" Steve asked.

"Well, Steve . . ." Exasperation brimmed behind her calm exterior. "As you can see, we're standing at the bottom of this muddy embankment I took a header down about two minutes ago, getting pounded by bullets of rain."

"Is it a hard shower or just a drizzle?"

"Well, Steve," she said, no longer able to keep her irritation in check, "it's like being fired on by an Uzi."

"That should make it harder for the police to do their investigation, shouldn't it?" Lennox coaxed her onto graver thoughts.

"Why, yes, Steve. The crime scene search team is trying to recover evidence and the inclement weather isn't helping."

"We understand the police have called a relative and that we may have an identification soon."

"I believe they've arranged a call to a friend of the deceased's." Raindrops sluiced down her forehead. She brushed away a lock of wet hair. Her hand came back clean, which meant her face was not.

Another thunderclap sounded loud enough to rattle teeth. Aspen experienced an epiphany.

Holy smoke — she'd just figured out Reggie's identity.

Lennox coached her on. "Do we know anything about the friend?"

"Only that the police are in contact with him to make positive ID on the young woman. I'm Aspen Wicklow, coming to you live from WBFD-TV, the station that'll go through Hell and back to bring you the news. Back to you, Steve."

Reggie killed the light and hit the off-switch. They stared at each other, making silent assessments with the rain pouring down.

"The scar." She traced a finger along her jaw and felt a tug of affection for him. "I remember hearing about you my freshman year. You got it when you did that piece on the eight-liners — slot machines — at those illegal casinos in Wise County. The reporter ran like a gazelle but your equipment weighed you down. They jumped you and cut your throat and left you for dead. You videoed them while you were bleeding out."

Reggie said nothing.

"You're my hero."

He gave her a blank stare.

She directed her thoughts to the clouds. "What kind of job is this that we're willing to break our necks or die over a paycheck? This is just plain fucked up."

"You can't complain that your job's boring."

"Look at me." He did. "I'm standing here in a shredded dress, with mud filling my best shoes, trying to be the first reporter on the scene so I can get a story that's good enough to ensure I get another paycheck next week. How messed up is that?"

"Did you have fun?"

"That's not the point," she said, trying to keep the thickening dismay out of her voice.

"But did you?" He offered his elbow. She hooked her hand through the crook of his arm and used him for balance.

When they reached the top of the hill, she shamelessly stripped off her panty hose as a concession to the mud. A butterscotch sun broke through the low-hanging clouds and the rain stopped.

Reggie nudged her. "Look what the cat dragged in . . ."

She tracked his pointed finger and finished his sentence. ". . . that the dog barfed up."

He pressed his lips together until the color blanched.

The van with Max and Tig rolled up beside them and slowed to a stop.

Tig powered the window halfway down. "Lucky the big dog got here in time."

"What's that supposed to mean?" she

demanded, fist on hip.

"It means you're a Chihuahua-mix trying to enter yourself against Kennel Club purebreds. Look at you. You can't do the news looking like that."

"Already did."

Max wore the dumbfounded expression of a man who'd just thwarted a home invasion, only to be electrocuted as he grabbed a beer from the refrigerator to celebrate.

Tig's eyes blazed like black fire. "What's that supposed to mean?"

"Rough."

She pivoted on one bare foot, making barking noises *ruff-ruff-ruff* all the way back to where Reggie now stood beside the van. When she yanked open the door, she yelled, "And I'm not a Chihuahua, you big, overgrown, story-stealing Rottweiler. I'm an Irish Terrier and I'm about to become *First in Show.*"

CHAPTER
TWENTY-TWO

"I know you think I'm a real bitch," Aspen said to Mike Henson on the way back to the station. She'd called him on her cell phone to explain why she'd been unable to finish the earlier conversation. "Did the police contact you?"

"They haven't shown any interest in talking to me since I reported Gabby missing."

She fixed her eyes on Reggie and spoke, tentatively, into the phone. "Listen, Mike, when's the last time you watched television today?"

"Haven't turned it on."

She huffed out a resigned sigh. "The police want to talk to you. There were some new developments —"

"What kind of new developments?" His voice went strident.

"There's this sergeant — wait, I have his number — he needs to talk to you." She gave him time to grab a pen and copy down the policeman's direct line. "Will you do something for me?"

"What?"

"Call me after you finish with the detectives? I'd like you to come down to WBFD so I can interview you."

Gabrielle's boyfriend became abruptly noncommittal. The most she could coax out of him was the promise of an update once he'd spoken to the cops.

Reggie turned off the interstate and got caught at the traffic light. The signal changed to green and the car behind them leaned on the horn.

"Sonofabitch." Reggie rammed the gearshift into park. He fumbled for the door handle as the car's horn continued its annoying bleat.

"What're you doing?"

"Going to kick some ass."

Low-grade anxiety turned to fear. Her stomach roiled. Her voice pitched to incredulity. "Ohmygod. You're going to get us killed, aren't you?"

Riding with Reggie was turning out to have all the characteristics of standing on the brink of a sinkhole while it gobbles up the entire village.

"Be right back." He flung open the door and bailed out with the keys in the van and the motor still idling. With arms flailing, he trundled toward the driver.

She reviewed Gordon's rules in her head: don't break the law, get everything pre-approved and never become part of the story. Street lamps flickered on around them. Her day was about to end in a body cavity search.

She twisted in her seat for a better view of her photographer and did a panicky review of her options. She could call nine-one-one on her mobile phone. She could jump out and try to charm him back into the van before he hurt somebody. Or she could do nothing.

Inertia kept her in place.

A pale arm shot out of the driver's window, curled pasty fingers into the front of Reggie's T-shirt and hauled him halfway through the window. Reggie's gangly legs kicked violently.

Aspen grabbed the door handle. She bailed out armed only with her cell phone and an aerosol can she found rolling between the seats. She ran toward the passenger side of the car, saw that it was unlocked and yanked it open.

With the spray can pointed at the driver, she poised her finger to depress the nozzle.

If anyone had been watching, they'd have

seen a dark-haired woman with cigarette smoke snaking out of her nose, sitting behind the wheel, holding Reggie by the scruff of the neck. And a redhead with a spray can of WD-40 ready to squirt through its straw. In other words, bystanders would see lunatics.

She heard her name called out.

Reggie grew impatient with her, insisting that her screams bothered passersby.

For a moment, she looked at the driver, blank-faced. Recognition kicked in.

"Rochelle?" Aspen's voice spiraled upward. She blinked, seeing where this was all heading. "What the hell?"

Rochelle unhanded Reggie's shirt and he wriggled out of the opening.

"Just having a little fun with you," said the photographer, "testing the fight or flight theory."

"I could've hosed you," she said to Rochelle.

"And then I would've had to kill you," the secretary said sweetly.

Aspen scowled at Reggie. "Did you know this was Rochelle in this car?"

Reggie nodded. "Whenever Gordon's called down to the station, Rochelle's not far behind."

"So you just set this up to see if —"

"If you'd run like the other reporter."

Her skin tingled like falling grains of sand. Still gripping the spray can, she backed out of the passenger compartment, into the lane of traffic.

"You're going to pay for this." She advanced on the photographer with projectile lubricant shooting through the straw.

Reggie took off like a turpentined cat. She caught him at the driver's door of the van and threatened to soak him.

"It was a joke." Despite the laughter, he clutched his sides as if the hysterics pained him. "King's-X."

"There's no such thing as King's-X."

"Truce. What do you want?"

"A new pair of shoes. And a new dress. You buy them for me."

"Now wait just a minute."

With an eyebrow arched, she raised the can inches from his face.

"All right. Pick them out and give me the bill."

"Deal." She lowered the oil can and hip-checked him out of the way. "That was kind of fun," she said on her way back around to the passenger side.

"Want to go out sometime?"

She sighed. "Probably not. I'm fed up with

the late night drunken phone calls and nasty emails."

He regarded her with a look of utter bewilderment. "I don't do that kind of thing."

"I'm talking about me."

But what she was really thinking was that these people at WBFD should be studied like a treatment-resistant viral strain.

When Reggie careened into the station's parking lot, Aspen noted Gordon's car in its reserved space.

"Does he ever go home?"

"He shows up when Bill or Steve or one of the scanner monitors calls him at home. You'll probably get your ass chewed for saying that about WBFD going through Hell to get the news out."

"Yeah?" She looked down at her feet. "Tell it to my shoes."

On the way inside the studio, Gordon intercepted her. *"'We'll go through Hell and back to bring you the news'?"* he greeted her in a deep, flat baritone. "I like it. Feel free to use it again until we come up with a permanent slogan."

After her eyes telescoped back into their sockets, she went looking for Steve Lennox. She found him at the anchor desk, flirting with Misty Knight.

She braced her hands against the laminated surface and leaned in. "Steve, is it?"

"Hi, Astral." He gave her a little hand wave. "Nice job."

"It's Aspen." She injected a lethal dose of syrup into her tone. "Aspen, like the tree. Aspen like the resort. Aspen like Colorado." She snapped her fingers and struck a sarcastic pose. "Hey, I know what . . . the next time you call me anything but Aspen or Ms. Wicklow on the air, I'm going to refer to you as Mr. Lummox. Do I make myself clear?"

Having made her point, she didn't pull into her driveway until after midnight.

In true serial killer fashion, Midnight the cat paced the length of the porch. When she fished out her key ring to let herself inside, she cast her gaze to the floor and saw a mouse torso displayed on the jute Welcome mat. Its feet were missing. So was its head. She winced in disgust, nudging it off the mat and into the flowerbed with the toe of her mud-crusted shoe.

She'd already let herself inside and flipped on the light switch before realizing she hadn't used her key to get in.

Midnight ducked inside, exercising the predatory instincts of a jungle cat. Without warning, he demonstrated a vertical leap and darted back out into the darkness. Aspen stood still and mute, as if she'd been pole-axed. Backing out of the house, she dialed nine-one-one on her cell phone and took off up the street in a dead run.

"Nine-one-one, what is your emergency?"

Swallowing the lump back down her throat, she struggled to keep her voice calm. "I need an officer. I think someone broke into my house."

CHAPTER
TWENTY-THREE

Once police completed the burglary report, Aspen knew she couldn't stay home by herself. The house had a creepy feel, as if the sinister residue of an unseen presence still lingered, and it poisoned any chance of her sticking around for the night.

She had no place to go — that part hurt to admit. Her college friends had scattered to the four winds after graduation. Other than her parents, the closest family members lived several hundred miles away.

She gnawed her lip and tried to figure out what to do.

Tranquility Villas could probably grudgingly put her up for the night, but she'd consider it only as a last resort. Her presence would be disruptive to both parents. And the staff frowned on guests staying past visiting hours. Margo Sommervel might be willing to put her up as long as she was still investigating Candy's missing car. But the

funeral had brought in out-of-town mourners and she had no reason to think Margo
didn't have a house full of company.

Then there was WBFD. The TV station
had plenty of couches, but she hadn't
worked there long enough to feel comfortable taking liberties or bunking over.

She didn't have enough disposable income
left from Friday's paycheck to rent a motel
room. And eventually, she'd have to return
home or move.

Random thoughts turned to Spike Granger.

She had the number to his mobile phone.
With him working in law enforcement, he'd
probably understand her reluctance to stay
put. It boiled down to calling Granger or
Rochelle. And Rochelle, with her hot
flashes, would probably be the more likely
of the two to kill her in her sleep.

She picked up the wireless and punched
out Granger's number. By the third ring,
she convinced herself he'd already gone to
bed. She was about to hang up when she
heard a roguish inflection in Granger's hello.

She laid out the problem for him like a
losing hand of five-card stud. As far as she
could tell, nothing appeared to be missing
in the burglary. But to a woman suffering
from sleep deprivation, the idea of an

interloper creepy-crawling her house was too much to deal with. She needed a favor.

"Would it be improper to ask if I could sleep on the couch at your office?" She swallowed hard. What if he thought she was flirting? What if she *was* flirting?

"I can do you one better. I have a spare bedroom. You can have it for the night."

"I wouldn't want to impose." She sensed him grinning at the other end of the line.

"No imposition at all. I'll meet you at my office in forty-five minutes. It's easier than giving you directions to my house. You can park your car and I'll pick you up."

And that was how he found her, sitting on the hood of the ten-year old Accord, shivering in the night air when he rolled up in his unmarked patrol car.

The driver's window hummed halfway down. "Got any carry-ons?"

"Make-up bag and a change of clothes." She held up a plastic grocery sack, stuffed to the gills.

He got out of the car, slipped off his jacket and whirled it across her shoulders before walking her around to the passenger side and helping her into the seat.

He excused himself, briefly disappearing inside the building. When he returned carrying two bottles of Big Red from the vending machine, he said, "I'm a little surprised you didn't call your boyfriend."

The remark hit like a stun gun to the brain.

For the next few seconds, Aspen heard white noise in her head.

Forcing cheer into her tone, she gave him the condensed version. "My breakup with Roger was so awful somebody wrote about it in a bathroom stall at the mall. I got calls from people I didn't even know wanting me to recount it."

"He must've been crazy to let you go."

"A stripper stole his heart." She barely restrained a sigh.

"Don't be so hard on strippers. If God didn't expect naked women to dance on tables, He wouldn't have created busboys to clear the empties off."

Granger's attempt at levity bombed but his smile warmed her.

"I don't mean to sound harsh," he said, stroking his chin, "but if you want a male's perspective, no woman can steal another gal's man unless he wants to be stolen. You should count your blessings. This fellow did you an unintended favor." His next question chilled her to the bone. "So why'd he dump you?"

She pretended to search her memory. This

part hurt. She probably shouldn't be disclosing such personal information, but Granger made her feel comfortable. And God only knew she felt safer now that she didn't have to return home.

Aspen fidgeted in her seat. She turned her attention out the window. Scenery flew by like bolts of charcoal fabric unfurling.

"He said I was boring."

"He told you that?"

"I assure you he did." She caught herself nodding. "I always thought I had a sweet disposition. Apparently, to certain people, that means boring." She unexpectedly experienced a real *Ah-ha* moment. Maybe she should try skydiving — yeah, like that was going to happen. Besides, she didn't relish walking around with the instructor's boot imprint on her butt. But she could do a feature piece in the alligator cage at the zoo — yeah, like clinging to the gates and screaming for Last Rites wouldn't disturb the other animals. Her mind free-associated until she realized Granger was speaking. "I'm sorry — what?"

"The way to keep from being boring is the same way you keep from being bored. Keep busy. Take up a hobby. Hell, take up several."

"I had a hobby once. I tried scrapbooking. But since I haven't done any scrapbooking in months, I think I'm probably less of a scrapbooker and more of a collector of scrapbook supplies."

The sheriff found her sarcasm howlingly funny. She couldn't remember the last time Roger had laughed at something she said.

She studied his profile in the comfort of the shadows, this rough-cut handsome guy who — in casual clothes — looked more like a pro-football quarterback than a throwback to the Old West. For at least a mile, she'd been rehearsing the same question in her head, waiting for the right time to spring it on him. Before she could work up her courage, it slipped out on its own. "So how old are you?"

"Old enough to know better," he said with a hint of laughter, "young enough not to care." He darted a quick look at her, then shifted his attention back to the ribbon of asphalt unwinding in the distance.

Granger veered off the main highway, onto a county road where the street lamps played out. Shadows formed sinister shapes under the light of a silver platter moon. In the distance, the faint glow of two incandescent bulbs flickered in the night. The car bumped over a cattle guard as he continued up a long, unpaved road.

He lived in a sprawling ranch house with a glider on the porch and two old bloodhounds stretched out on tattered blankets, folded to provide extra padding.

"That's Jake and that's Ray. If you get too close, they'll cold nose you. They're what you might call rude dogs."

Inside, he showed her to a tastefully decorated room with a simple chenille spread covering the mattress and an antique quilt folded at the foot of the bed.

"Are you hungry? I can whip up a few leftovers if you like."

She was starving. "I don't want to be any trouble. I can just crash for the night."

"I have homemade chili. I could throw in Fritos and a handful of grated cheese — and a Big Red."

That did it.

After a whirlwind supper, Granger led her to his study, a man's room with a deer antler chandelier and a wagon wheel coffee table positioned next to a small leather couch. He motioned her to the sofa and assumed his place in front of the computer. He questioned her about the burglary and seemed surprised nothing was missing.

"I have a couple of old sterling silver picture frames that are worth a small fortune. And a wall-mount high-definition TV that belongs to my father that hasn't been mounted. It had been moved, almost like the prospect of taking it was an after-thought. But the photographs are missing. At least I think they are. What do you make of that?"

"What were the pictures of?"

"Me."

She thought of the dead girls and inwardly shuddered. Pressure mounted behind her eyes. It built up in her nose like a bad sinus infection, leaving her to experience one of those brain freeze, *have-to-die-to-feel-better* sensations.

"You're not going to cry, are you? Men hate that."

"Why do they hate it?"

"Because there's no way to predict if a little sniffle's going to turn into one of those annoying *wah-wah, boo-hoo* hissy fits, or a rip-roaring, guts-out conniption fit that makes restaurant customers stop their forks in mid-bite and stare at you like you shot Bambi's mother."

She laughed in spite of her pent-up frustration. "What else don't men like?"

"They don't like it when women keep their clothes on. That stripper knew exactly what she was doing."

She almost spewed Big Red out her nose.

"And they don't like women who are mean-spirited."

"Let me get this straight. In order for me to keep a man, I have to hide my emotions, take off my clothes and act nicely, even if I want to perform the Heimlich maneuver on his neck."

Granger's head bobbed. "That about covers it."

"Might as well be alone."

The sheriff scoffed at the notion. "Oh, I don't reckon you'll be alone forever. There are probably men tripping all over themselves to get to you."

"Like who?"

He swiveled his chair away from her and resumed his computer work.

"What are you doing?" She leaned in for a closer look and inadvertently skimmed his arm with her breasts.

"Checking databases." Granger pulled off his gold wire-rims, placed them carefully on the desk and mashed his eyes. "I'm searching for influential people who can assist me in my fight with the TDCJ."

"Can you do that? Find people, I mean." She was wondering if he'd do her a favor — find the stripper who ran off with Roger. It was a crazy idea, of course. And it wasn't as if she wanted to have an actual conversation with the girl. But this longing desire to compare herself with someone who seemed — at least on the surface — to have nothing going for her but a set of augmented breasts and a willingness to flaunt them for money, had become overwhelming.

Granger's words pulled her back into the present.

"I can find anyone as long as they're alive and residing in the Great State of Texas." He spoke in a voice laced with curiosity and rural cunning. "Tell me something. Have you ever been locked up for protecting a source?"

"No."

He pressed two fingers, hard, against the bridge of his nose before putting his glasses back on. "The smell of jail and the smell of freedom are distinct. Jail reeks with the permanent odor of death and decay. It's the underlying stench of condemnation that you don't get with the smell of freedom. That's why I've decided not to tell you what's next in store for the TDCJ."

Dumbstruck, she said, "You're not going to give me an exclusive?"

"Of course I am. I already told you I think you might win an award. You'll come along because I've promised you a story. Only your boss can't accuse you of becoming part of the story if you didn't know what the story was."

She listened with rapt attention, suddenly aware of the low-voltage sexual current running through her body. Being around Granger was like un-layering an onion. The man definitely had more depth than she'd initially given him credit for.

And boy oh boy, was he hot.

It was close to one in the morning before she fell asleep in the guest room. She awoke to the smell of bacon frying, dressed quickly in the same clothes she'd worn the night before, ducked into the bathroom for the morning routine and back out again.

She found Granger towering over a couple of cast iron skillets, turning strips of bacon and grilling Texas toast.

"I don't think I've ever met a man who can cook," she said. "All the ones I know are helpless in the kitchen."

"If I didn't, Jake and Ray would be dragging road kill up to the door. You want orange juice, milk, coffee or all three?" He elbowed the air in the direction of a coffee-maker.

They ate on his back porch overlooking a field stocked with cattle. Oak trees dotted the countryside and in the middle of the land was a water tank with cows presiding over it. When they finished breakfast, Granger led her to the edge of the deck where she could enjoy the taffy-smeared sky in all its glory. He slid an arm around her shoulder in such a casual way that she hadn't even noticed until she felt its weight.

He took a deep breath. "Smell the fresh air. There's nothing quite like it when a crisp breeze blows in." Then he gave her an avuncular squeeze and his arm fell away. As they stood side by side, he scoured the pasture once more before their eyes met. "Want to see something amazing?"

"When I was in third grade a boy asked me that very same thing. He lied."

Granger chuckled, rocking his shoulder against her. "You're fun."

"No I'm not." She gave him an embarrassed chin duck and a playful swat to the arm. "Nice of you to think so, though."

"C'mon." He took her by the hand and led her down the steps. "Let's go for a walk."

They strolled down a path leading away from the house — he dressed in a red flannel shirt, khakis and boots; she in a pair of straight-legged jeans, a lilac cashmere pullover and matching ballerina-inspired flats. He stayed one step ahead, gently pulling her along by the fingers while she enjoyed the kiss of the breeze on her face.

But when she could no longer see the back door, instinct halted her in her tracks. Unable to trust her feelings, she stood perfectly still with her internal loran humming. Grass and blown leaves were the only movement. Spider webs, still glistening with dew, floated in the morning's golden glow.

Sunlight slanted through the oak trees, casting lacy patterns on his face. Granger squinted fiercely, lifting his hand to shield her against its rays. The glint from his *cinco peso* eyes was as level and unyielding as she imagined his aim would be.

"What's on your mind, little darlin'?"

More, more, more. Things were starting to get a little too "Rebel Yell" for her out here.

She closed her lids to blot out his image and the sex dream she'd had last night of him sweeping her into an endless stream of pleasure came back with a dizzying rush. This was bizarre. She'd only imagined what it would be like in his passion-rumpled bed because she was lonely. It wasn't as if she wanted to make such an overpowering seduction happen — her, rocking easily above his intent regard; him, sheathing himself deeply inside her. It wasn't as if he wanted to devour her, starting with her lips, moving to her neck, then down to her —

Granger called her name and her eyes

popped open. Instead of a hungry, smoldering look, she saw relaxed humor in his face.

Probably thinks I'm having a seizure.

Or wondering if I need CPR.

"Sorry. Out of body experience," she said in what amounted to a stage whisper. "Where are we going?"

Dream sex was one thing. Living it out was entirely different. If and when she decided she cared for the man enough to test his stamina, she certainly didn't embrace the idea of a romp in a haystack. Especially when there were beds covered with nice linens in the house.

His eyes thinned as if he'd read her thoughts. "Look, I like you. And what I want to show you is special to me. But if you don't want to see it —" he offered his upraised palms by way of an apology — "fine by me."

"It's just — I have to go. I didn't realize it was so late."

But that wasn't it at all. She didn't know Gordon's policy for dating the subject matter of her feature piece, but she was pretty sure it didn't include standing in a cow pasture, stripping the teeth off a man's zipper and showing him the true meaning of "amazing."

Images of dream sex continued to explode

in her head.

Enough already. Who was she kidding? The real reason for not letting this get out of control was because he'd eventually decide she just wasn't that interesting. And if it came down to choosing between a physical relationship and friendship, she'd rather have the friendship.

He spoke softly, without judgment. "Let's head back." With great tenderness, he placed a hand on the small of her back and guided her up the path to the house.

Oh brother. Now he thinks I'm convinced he hangs bodies on meat hooks out here.

Inside the guest bedroom, she stuffed her belongings into the plastic sack. She found Granger in the kitchen scraping off the dishes, parceling out table scraps into dog bowls full of chow. Jake and Ray were seated at the back door with their leathery noses pressed against the screen, thumping their tails in expectation. He smiled when she walked in and caught him dividing last night's Frito-dotted chili remnants, eyeballing the results to make sure each pet received the same amount, and the awkwardness she'd felt on the way back from the clearing instantly vanished.

"Just out of curiosity, what was it you wanted to show me?"

"Next time," he said, putting an end to the conversation. "Let's get you back to your car."

She didn't want to leave. But she had no business out here in the sticks when she ought to be heading back to civilization to get the jump on her nemesis, and she told him so.

"What're you doing tomorrow?" he asked with a sheepish grin, no longer looking as tough as the callous on his trigger finger.

"Running down leads for my *Public Defender* piece on Thursday."

"How about getting your cameraman and taking a road trip with me?"

"To Huntsville?"

He barked out a laugh. "Not hardly. The warden gave orders to shoot me on sight. I was thinking we'd drive down to Austin. And San Antonio. Houston."

"In one day?"

"Whatever it takes. We'll leave bright and early Monday morning. Are you on board?"

Aspen sucked air. "Does this have anything to do with what you wouldn't tell me about last night?"

Granger made no response. But the coyote smile was enough to suggest she wouldn't want to miss out.

CHAPTER
TWENTY-FOUR

Aspen left Granger's house around eleven o'clock Sunday morning with a promise to call early Monday. This time she wouldn't snag Max for Granger's publicity stunt. In her mind, Max had turned traitor. Reggie would make for much better company.

Just outside the Fort Worth city limit, an eighteen-wheeler motoring along ahead of her made a hard right. Aspen's eyes went wide. A pickup truck with a lost load of two-by-fours had limped onto the shoulder, leaving a path of splintered wood in its wake.

She slammed on the brakes.

Nothing happened.

The Honda shot forward like a hockey puck.

She hit the brakes again. The pedal went clear to the floorboard. She stomped it repeatedly, feeling every hair on her body standing on end. Lightning fast, she jerked the steering wheel hard right, veering into the middle lane, nearly sideswiping another car.

Aspen's heart beat wildly. She jammed the gearshift into neutral and winced at the engine's roar. The car lost speed, but not enough to keep her from gaining on the semi. Rear-ending it meant certain decapitation. She pumped the brakes to no avail. In a last-ditch effort to save herself, she yanked up the emergency brake. She slowed, enveloped in the smell of burning metal.

Behind her, horns blared.

She hit the hazard lights and limped the car to the right shoulder, threading the Honda through rude drivers until it coasted to a stop.

She could've been killed.

Her heart thudded so loud she could hear its echo between her ears.

She gathered her composure and reached for the cell phone. What the hell? Now that she was safe, she should look on the bright side of this near-death experience. If she'd been killed, she wouldn't have to attend her parents' wedding.

Aspen thumbed the number for the first of two phone calls.

The wrecker service answered on the second ring.

She considered having the Accord towed

to Pop's Salvage. After all, the acne-scarred mechanic had warned her the brakes needed work. Guess this was proof he knew his craft. But Pop's had fallen under a cloud of suspicion. The Honda might be ten years old and in need of repairs, but she didn't want to take a chance of having the car sold out from under her. Plus, Gordon would fire her if she became part of her own story.

She authorized the wrecker driver to take the car to a service center closer to her home and instructed him to leave it in their parking lot. When he discouraged her from riding along by telling her he wasn't bonded, she waited on the side of the road like a common hitchhiker.

Soon, a lipstick red Nissan pulled up beside her. The passenger window slid halfway down and the electric door locks snapped open.

"Hop in before somebody squashes you like a bug. And don't tempt me."

Rochelle.

Aspen climbed inside. She belted herself in and slid Gordon's assistant a bland smile. "You're a lifesaver."

The woman looked vibrant behind the wheel of the Z, as bright as the clothes she had on.

"Where to?" said Rochelle.

Aspen related the burglary incident. With reluctance, she provided her address, then dropped hints about not wanting to be alone.

"I know —" her excitement brimmed "— you could stay over with me. We could go to your place, you could pick up an overnight bag and we could have a pajama party."

Rochelle's eyes narrowed into slits. "Do I look the type to do slumber parties? As far as your little overnight soirée, I'm trying to cut back. See, I have a hard enough time keeping people from slitting my throat at work; I don't need to cut my own on my days off. This is turning into a bad horror flick, Gidget."

Aspen inwardly panicked. If Rochelle wouldn't bunk over, the options reverted to Tranquility Villas or WBFD.

"I have a better idea." The secretary smoothed over her harsh words with a bit of verbal lubricant. "Why don't we swing by your house? You can grab an overnight bag and come home with me."

"Really?" Her eyes welled.

"Fair warning: I do all of my cooking on Sunday and freeze food for the week. You'll be pressed into service, but you'll learn a skill and I can use the help."

The tears she wanted to cry instantly evaporated. Not only would she have a place to stay, she'd get decent food. Maybe Rochelle would share and she could brown bag it until payday. Which was important now that she'd be eating a car repair bill.

"This is perfect, Rochelle. You're wonderful. Thank you so much."

"That's what you say now."

Gordon's assistant lived in a spacious brick townhouse in a garden home community. Each residence had been wrapped with variegated, rose-colored brick, styled with leaded glass front doors and had plenty of undraped windows that made for a light, sumptuous feel. The lawns were similarly manicured, but Rochelle had added Grecian urns near her doorway. They bracketed the entrance and contained silk flowers that looked so real from the street Aspen actually touched a couple of petals as a test.

The home's interior contained a marriage of French and Italian provincial furniture with a few Chinese accents thrown in. Aspen could tell from the decorator pieces that her new best friend liked cinnabar, since carved lacquer vases adorned many of the flat surfaces.

"Your place is beautiful."

Rochelle gave a perfunctory nod. "It's a dump. I'm moving as soon as I can find a sucker who won't demand an inspection."

Aspen spread her palms in confusion. "But look at it. It's lovely."

"If this place were human, I'd be living inside Misty Knight — pretty on the outside, falling apart on the inside."

"I think you did a wonderful job pulling all this together. You shouldn't be so quick to run your domestic talents into the ground."

Rochelle sighed. "Where do I start? The roof leaks, nothing's square, there aren't enough electrical outlets and they didn't use treated wood for the underpinnings so the floor could cave in anytime. I wondered why I got it so cheap. At first, I considered myself incredibly lucky. Then I fancied myself a shrewd businesswoman, having scammed the old geezer selling it. *Hey — I said to myself — wasn't my fault he didn't know the value of this place. Wasn't me who decided to cut corners by not listing the house with a realtor.*"

Rochelle painstakingly told how she'd walked through the townhome admiring the appointments and period furnishings in the candlelight glow of girandoles and sconces. He'd ushered her down the halls, gently warning her not to touch the walls. Freshly painted, he'd said, and hurriedly whisked her through the various rooms with the skill of a museum docent. The scent of freshly baked cookies filled the air. When the old man and his wife seated her at the breakfast table and talked over a cup of rich Kona grind, the chocolate chips were still warm and gooey as they hit her tongue.

"Downsizing — that was their cover story. I found out later from a neighbor that they fled the states to one of those countries where there's no extradition treaty. But I'm getting ahead of myself."

The old couple had warned her about the neighbors. They told her she should keep her distance from the men living on either side unless she enjoyed the thrill of being unceremoniously dumped by serial play-boys.

"We made one of those seedy parking-lot-tailgate deals right there at the table; me, euphoric from the chocolate chip sugar high; them looking sweet and demure like kindly old grandparents."

She'd thought of going back inside to offer more money. After all, they were elderly and on a fixed income. But then one of the neighbors she'd been warned about sauntered out and wanted her to join him inside his townhome for a cup of coffee and a little chat. That didn't surprise her, being a smartly dressed, shapely woman of good breeding; but she already had a man-friend, thank you very much, so no thanks. It wasn't until later she learned the neighbor wanted to warn her not to buy the house.

"I walked away from the closing laughing my ass off because I'd stolen this great garden home right out from under them. Then guilt set in." Rochelle gave a remorseful headshake. "I should've known I'd been had as soon as I pulled out of the parking lot at the title company. I glimpsed him in the rearview mirror, driving away, laughing like a hyena."

Aspen hung on every word. Listening to Rochelle was like getting caught up in the most fascinating story, patiently awaiting the O. Henry ending.

"Once I moved in, I made all kinds of unpleasant discoveries, starting with the first painting I nailed up. I leaned against the opposite wall to admire my handiwork and left an imprint of my body in the sheetrock. It looked like a crime scene, only without the Day-Glo tape. I'm telling you the wall moved. Termites had whittled the studs down to toothpicks. My gut sank. It was like having the doctor pull back the blanket to show you your ugly baby and suddenly realizing that the man you married for his perfect bone structure and movie star good looks had his ears pinned and a nose job."

Aspen let out a belly laugh. Rochelle was a riot. She couldn't remember the last time she'd had this much fun. "Where should I put my stuff?"

"Follow me. And don't touch the walls."

A blue point Siamese slinked out from behind a chair and hissed.

"That's Attila the Hun." She gave a casual wrist flick in the cat's direction. "He talks a good game but he's really just a big pussy-cat. Do you have pets?"

"There's a stray that comes by. I named him Midnight."

"Hon, if you named him, he's not a stray. Is Midnight his first name or his middle name?"

This had never come up before and Ro-chelle picked up on it. "Kid, if you want to pass your cat off as a purebred, you'll have to give him three names."

"Then I suppose Midnight would be his middle name. Which would make his first name Dammit."

"I like you, kid."

They arrived at a small bedroom with a twin bed and a walnut desk with a desktop computer. Textured sheetrock had been painted Wedgwood blue with wood moldings in glossy white.

"Make yourself at home," Rochelle said. She swiped her hand against the desk and stealthily removed a small silver picture frame on her way out. "Do what you need to do to settle in and then meet me in the kitchen."

They started preparing lasagna and graduated to stuffing manicotti with spinach and ricotta. Rochelle preheated the oven and stuck in a frozen custard pie. While Aspen braised chicken breasts in a buttered skillet, Rochelle moved on to boiling coconut curry sauce in a pan to top off their Cantonese noodle dinner.

Aspen lifted the lid and dampened her nose with the aroma of meat and marinara sauce. The women worked in concert, with Aspen adjusting the burner to a low flame while Rochelle pulled out a sack of frozen corn and pressed it to her forehead. She wore it like an ice pack while she stirred curry. As she forked up a noodle to see if it was done, she flipped the bag over and slapped it to one side of her face. After switching sides, she tossed the sack back into the freezer and uncorked a bottle of wine.

"Feeling better?" Aspen asked.

"I never thought I'd say this, but I'm secretly glad we have gun control." Rochelle sloshed white Zinfandel into crystal stemware and handed over a glass. "Women with PMS and those in the throes of menopause — especially those working for W-Big-Fucking-Deal — definitely should not be allowed to carry guns." She raised her goblet in a toast. "Here's to hell. May we have as good a time there as we did getting there. Cheers."

Aspen lifted her flute. "Here's to heaven. May you be there a full half hour before the devil knows you're dead. *Sláinte.*"

Then she said, "Do you have a gun?"

Rochelle fixed her with a laser stare. "Certainly. I've had a permit to carry ever since Texans were allowed to apply for them. Before that, I carried one in my car on the sly and slept with one under my pillow. You'd have to be crazy in this day and age not to carry a pistol. I think everybody but babies should be allowed to carry guns."

"Do you think I need one?"

"Buy three or four. One for your purse in case you get mugged, or if the Arab down at the convenience store tries to cheat you. One for your vehicle. Carry it in the front seat in the event you get carjacked. One for underneath your pillow. You never know when that'll come in handy during a home invasion robbery . . . or if you discover your cheating boyfriend has another woman. Having the barrel of a gun poked up a man's snout is like having your own lie detector test without all the wires and needles and the need for an electrical outlet. And you should keep one in the trunk of your car in case they carjack you, toss you in the back and slam the lid on you."

"Do you carry your gun into the station?" In her mind, Aspen pictured the universal No Handguns sign posted at the door.

"For the sake of my co-workers, the answer's no. But if Tig ever makes me mad enough, I can always go fetch it from the car."

They spoke of other things that afternoon; Aspen's parents' situation for one; sweeps month, for another. And men. Especially men.

"Want to hear something weird?" Aspen asked, suppressing a loud exhale.

"The weirder the better."

"I dreamed about the Johnson County sheriff. Spike Granger." She watched Rochelle to gauge her reaction. The woman arched one brow.

"Did you have dream sex with him?"

She cast her gaze to the floor, then abruptly resumed eye contact with the coy look made famous by "Shy Di," Princess of Wales. "Let's just say I had him in my bed, gasping for breath and calling my name. What do you suppose that means?"

"Means you weren't forcing the pillow down hard enough." An ethereal expression washed over Rochelle's pale, impenetrable face. "That happened to me once," she said reflectively, fisting the sides of an invisible pillow and shoving it in a downward motion over the head of someone only she could identify. "Be certain you have a really tight grip or you'll be sitting in front of the grand jury for three hours. I should know."

Aspen let out a huge belly laugh. "No, really — I value your opinion. What do you think it means, me dreaming about Granger?"

"You mean like if you trip climbing a flight of stairs, it's supposed to represent a fear of stumbling on your way up the ladder of success? Or if your teeth fall out like Chiclets and you're scrambling to pick them up off the ground, it means you need to get laid? Or, or, or —" she infused a degree of excitement into her voice "— you dream you're falling off a cliff and it symbolizes the fear of getting fired?"

Distress puckered Aspen's lips. She'd been having that one since the day Gordon hired her. She couldn't tell whether or not Rochelle was making fun of her, so she nodded, *Go on.*

"Get real, kid. I may've been born in the dark, but I wasn't born last night." She paused over a saucepan long enough to fork a piece of squash she'd been blanching, taste-test it and turn off the burner. "It's your subconscious mind talking. You're hot for the man."

"No, no, no," Aspen declared in the face of her confession, fending off the notion with a vigorous hand wave. "He's nice enough, but I'm not interested in getting involved with anyone right now."

"Oh, good. Because I thought you might be about to say something stupid."

Aspen abandoned the topic of Granger to a scary silence. Rochelle had seen right through her. Now she needed time to digest the idea of the sheriff's unexpected influence in her life. While he marinated in her thoughts, she carried a week's worth of meals to the freezer and stacked them neatly into groups.

The woman had an opinion on everything. What kept her from being obnoxious was she didn't inflict it on you. Rochelle made you ask for advice. Then if you didn't take it and things went south, she got the satisfaction of saying *I told you so.*

Aspen poured two glasses of tea and carried them to the dining table. As she sugared hers and squeezed in a lime wedge, she thought of another question she wanted to ask. But when she returned to the kitchen, her thoughts went blank. Rochelle had a knack for doing that to people — making them feel self-conscious and all.

For several seconds, she worked up her bravery, rehearsing the line in her head. Words popped out before she realized she'd spoken.

"Have you ever loved a guy so much it hurt? And then you found out he didn't really love you back, after all?"

"You're asking me? *Ha.* My ex told me he loved me the day we got married. When I asked why he never said it anymore, he said he'd let me know if anything changed. Believe me, kid, if you have to ask, it's not there," Rochelle said as she opened a drawer, rattled around in it and disappeared out of the room with the sterling.

Silverware clattered as she set the table. When she re-entered the room empty-handed, she selected two plates from the china cabinet and dished up Cantonese for a late lunch — or an early dinner. Aspen carried in their wineglasses and they ate in silence until Rochelle blurted out a solution to the Wicklows' impending wedding.

"I should send Attila with you over to the nursing home to suffocate them — he'll put an end to this hoopla about marriage. Pick the parent you like best. Leave Attila with the other one. He'll do the rest."

Glassy-eyed, Rochelle studied some distant point in space and continued to dispense motherly advice.

"Don't date the photographers. They have a way of making their subjects look unflattering if they get it in for you." She sipped her wine and did a conspiratorial lean-in. "Once, we had this blonde SMU intern who took to flashbulbs like they were sunlight. The minute the camera lit her up, she could go from pouts and petulance to smiles and radiance. Unfortunately, they don't offer Cameras 101 as part of the curriculum at SMU, so she didn't realize it was her photographer — not her parents or her dentist or her plastic surgeon — who was responsible for her incredible on-air good looks.

"This particular young lady spurned Max's advances. Next time she reported the news, he zoomed in on her nose hairs. For the love of God, I thought I was viewing a

266

spelunker piece on cave exploration or Carlsbad Caverns.

"Then he moved down to her lips. She had bright-white teeth; straight as a picket fence teeth. For the longest time, I sat there wondering *What's so interesting about a close-up of a picket fence?*"

Rochelle wagged her finger in a "no" motion. "I know what you're thinking. You're thinking I must've been stinking drunk. I only wish I'd been plastered. I saw what I thought was a penis — it turned out to be that hangy-down thing in the back of her throat. Her gag reflex. The uvula. Max zoomed in on it.

"As for me, I couldn't rid that penis image from my head. I spent the rest of the evening charging D-cell batteries for my vibrator. As for Gordon, he fired her the day after the piece aired."

Aspen's mouth rounded into an *O.* "He should've fired Max."

"You'd think, wouldn't you?" Rochelle let out a steady chuckle that sounded a lot like an Uzi with a silencer. "The other stations are always kicking our ass because they've cornered the market with attractive, on-air talent."

"What about Misty Knight? She's pretty."

Rochelle spat the name. "She's like a

crusty patch of skin you can't exfoliate. We only got her because Openly Gay José is her father. And I'll let you in on another little secret — you think that's her real name?" A healthy swallow of Zinfandel lubricated her tongue. "*Ha*. That's the name Gordon gave her. And it's stupid. I've survived the industry long enough to meet every April Rain, Stormy Showers, Sunny Day, Whitey Snow, Wendy Winters, Summer Breeze, Misty Knight — you name it, I've met all of the people in the Lame Name club. You're lucky Gordon didn't monkey with yours. For all you know, you could've ended up broadcasting as Aspen Leaves. It's amazing what the viewers will put up with. Morons, all of them. Anyone with half a brain isn't watching WBFD; they're tuned to CNN.

Rochelle continued her rant. "But WBFD has two things everyone wants — the photographers." She went on to explain. "Most cameramen are sane. They get an assignment and shoot the footage from a safe location. Not these two. Reggie's intrepid, like one of those tunnel rats in Viet Nam. Max — who's like having a life-size Chia pet with a sweater on — is just too screwed up to give a shit."

Aspen sat there wondering how long they'd been bipolar.

According to Rochelle, dealing with Reggie and Max was a lot like watching the Flying Wallendas. Only if Reggie and Max were shooting video, they'd be right behind the performers with their toes curled around the same tightrope.

"That's why Gordon pays big bucks to keep them. I'm expendable. You're expendable. Stinger Baldwin was expendable. Everyone else at the station is expendable. Max and Reggie are not."

"I don't see you as expendable. You're very good at what you do. You're efficient —"

"Yeah-yeah-yeah." She poured herself another glass of truth serum. "There are hundreds of middle-aged women out there who aren't suffering from hot flashes who're standing in line to replace me."

Aspen soaked up Rochelle's lessons like a spa towel. As they cleared off the dishes and carried them to the sink, Aspen pumped her for more information.

"Did Tig have anything to do with Stinger leaving?"

"I love Stinger," Rochelle said wistfully. "And Tig will pay for what he did. Matter of fact, I've already planned out what to do. Next time I'm at that self-centered braggart's house for one of those monthly breakfasts he throws as a ruse to show off his latest purchase, I'm going to call the Secret Service and impersonate him. I'll threaten to kill the President and make it vague about how I'll implement my plan. That ought to prompt an urgent visit by men in trench coats."

Aspen hooted. "You won't be able to pull it off. They'll know you're a woman."

"No they won't." She smiled knowingly. "I sound like a transsexual first thing in the morning before I have my coffee."

Aspen laughed so hard her face hurt.

"You think I'm kidding? Misty called in sick the other day. She misdialed and spent five minutes talking to a man before she figured out she got the wrong number."

Aspen got a stitch in her side. Still snuffling with laughter, she tucked her feet up under her and rolled into a ball, delighted by Rochelle's wit. WBFD had all the earmarks of an insane asylum, only with cameras.

"Anyway," Rochelle went on, "if that doesn't do Tig in, the next time he goes up to Oklahoma to see his mother, I'll call in an anonymous tip to the Department of Public Safety, give the troopers his route and tell them he's trafficking in narcotics and has them well hidden in his Hummer."

"You can't do that. That could get him killed," Aspen said, suddenly serious.

"You think?" Rochelle's sarcasm conveyed hopefulness. "I put KKK stickers on his bumpers last April Fool's Day. Tig has to drive through Stop Six to get home. Can you imagine being black, sitting at a traffic light, minding your own business, when this frickin' Hummer plastered with KKK stickers comes barreling down on you? I thought that would've done it — you know, that somebody might've gotten out of their car and shot him — but it didn't happen and now we just have to live with it."

Rochelle couldn't stop talking. "Which brings us full circle to the gun issue. If even so much as one of those women Tig's juggling finds out about the others, we'll have a bloodbath on our hands. Although I don't really understand why women want to kill the other woman. They should kill the man. Remember, kid, guns don't have to be a bad thing. Guns can be God's way of saying *You've cheated for the last time*."

"Isn't that a bit harsh?"

Rochelle disagreed. "I've decided to go on the Dr. Phil show just as soon as they have a program on obnoxious co-workers," she went on. "I love that guy. Watch him every day."

"How can you watch Dr. Phil when you're at work?"

"Perhaps you haven't noticed, but I time one of my hot flashes to go off at three o'clock on weekdays."

Aspen gave an almost imperceptible nod. "Very clever." She could learn volumes from this woman. This woman was almost as good as having a mother who cared about you.

Rochelle had a light bulb idea. "Let's watch a movie."

She pulled one out from the DVD library in a cabinet under the television and slipped the disc into its drawer. The opening credits came on, followed by the title of the movie.

Fatal Attraction.

Rochelle claimed it was her favorite. She dropped a thin wool throw over her legs and cozied up against the sofa cushion. "You can learn a lot from this flick, sister. I'm surprised you never saw it — guess you're too young. In my opinion, this should be required viewing for all high school students as a condition of graduation. That way, if you ever do get married, come home and bust in on a psycho boiling your bunny, you'll know what to do."

Around nine o'clock, Rochelle tipped back the last of her wine. She got up from the sofa on unsteady legs to load the dish-washer.

"You want dessert?" she called out from the kitchen.

"What do you have?"

"I'm having Prozac but there are fudge bars in the freezer if you'd rather have that."

Aspen stifled a chuckle. This could be her in thirty years.

After cleaning up the kitchen, Rochelle strolled out looking refreshed. "Want any-thing else before we hit the sack?"

"I need an alarm clock."

"I'll set the one on my radio. I'll get you up around three and we'll be down at the station by four. Be sure and keep your door closed or Attila will try to smother you. He's a real euthanasia artist. I got him from a nursing home, did I tell you that? He was the mascot but they had to get rid of him. Too many suspicious deaths. The Medical Examiner's Office kept finding cat hairs up the noses of the elderly."

Across the room, curled on a pillow like a sultan's gift, Attila squeezed his eyes. He purred so loudly it sounded like Rochelle had a lawnmower idling in her living room.

They said good-night and headed off to their respective bedrooms. But once Aspen reached hers, she padded back to the kitchen for a water glass. As she flicked off light switches on her way back to the guest room, a silver frame placed facedown on the bookcase caught her eye. She knew, on instinct, that it was the one Rochelle had taken from her room. Aspen gave the den a furtive glance.

She angled over to the bookcase on tiptoes and lifted the frame.

The image of Stinger Baldwin stared back at her.

Aspen gasped.

Why didn't Rochelle want her to see this? Their association could be easily explained. After all, she and Stinger had worked together. He could've given her the picture out of friendship. But if that were true, why would she go to the trouble of hiding it?

Unless there was more to their relationship.

Older woman, younger man?

Aspen didn't want to think about Rochelle being an urban cougar. Behind the closed door of the guest room, her head hit the pillow and she teetered on the edge of sleep with Max's words spinning back to haunt her.

Word of advice . . . watch out for Rochelle.

And then, *Men tell women secrets . . . women guard theirs with a vengeance.*

CHAPTER
TWENTY-FIVE

Monday morning, Rochelle wheeled the Nissan Z into WBFD's parking lot. Gordon's car was in its reserved space but Tig hadn't arrived. She pulled up even with the door and barked out instructions.

"Get inside and check with the assignments desk before Tig-the-pig gets here."

"It's okay, I'll walk with you."

"No. He could careen through here any minute. We both know you're noodle-spined when it comes to standing up to him. So get to the tip box and start scavenging. I'll meet you later. And don't forget your sack lunch."

She handed over a brown bag with lasagna and a side salad. Aspen raced in ahead of her and made a beeline for the assignments desk.

An interesting consumer tip jumped out at her. Her eyes drifted over the page. The man's complaint had to do with a website

— a public forum where dumped girlfriends could go to warn other unsuspecting women not to date specific philanderers and other jerks who feared commitment or those who were just downright liars and con men. While it sounded more like a piece for "Ask Lindsey," it might be worth checking out just for the fun of it.

She'd snagged six complaints from the bin by the time Rochelle came inside dressed in a suit so bright she needed sunscreen just to wear it. The secretary went directly into Gordon's office and closed the door behind her. Gordon got up from behind the desk, walked over to his glass walls and pulled the vertical blinds, effectively shutting them off from view.

Aspen intercepted Reggie as he schlepped to the coffee machine. She asked if he could make himself available to shoot footage for her later in the day.

"Whatcha got going on?" Steam rose from the cardboard cup. He took careful sips, snorting vapors of generic coffee as he drank.

"I'm working a lead." She didn't want to tip her hand in case he and Max were friends. Max, she'd decided, might blab to Tig, who'd try to scoop her on her own story. Honestly, it was like working around

Russian spies. "We might have to be gone all day."

"Fine by me." Reggie took a cinnamon twist from a donut box. He held it up to the fluorescent light for a quick inspection before stuffing it down his throat like a log in a wood chipper. "Holler when you're ready to leave."

"It might mean we'll be late coming back."

"Wouldn't be the first time." He took a sip and did a quick face scrunch.

"We might not get back until tomorrow." Aspen inwardly winced.

"Cool." He walked away, nonplussed, burned tongue and all.

Aspen sat in her office with her back to the door, looking out the windows at a Fort Worth skyline blanketed in twinkling lights. For no good reason, she experienced a neck-prickling sensation. When she spun away from the glass, Mike Henson was easing into a chair.

"How'd you get back here?"

"Nobody's manning the front desk. I decided to snoop around until I found you."

It was a creepy thing to do and she told him so. She felt sorry for Henson and even sadder for the murdered Gabrielle. But his unorthodox way of handling grief was starting to affect her in a bad way.

"What do you need?"

"There's a memorial service tomorrow for Gabby. I thought you'd want to come."

"I'm sorry but I'll be out of town."

"WBFD covered the Drummond case," he said with a touch of petulance.

"I didn't have anything to do with that, but I can do a follow-up interview with you if you'd like."

Henson left disgruntled.

Around six o'clock, Tig glided in like a big fin cutting through water. He was sporting a black eye, and Rochelle lost no time stopping by Aspen's office with her take on the matter.

"Probably hit his head falling out the second-story window of a house he wasn't supposed to be at in the first place. But we'll never know. This could be Inga's handiwork." She struck a pose, meshing her fingers together and batting her eyelashes. "Then again, men brag. He may tell Gordon. If he does, I should know by the end of the day. God, men are stupid. If I ever remarry, I'm finding me an accountant or a mechanic. Preferably a CPA who can tinker with my car. Whenever he's not keeping me out of Leavenworth by doing my taxes, he can gap my spark plugs, if you know what I mean. Anything else I need,

I'll hire it done."

Around seven o'clock, Spike Granger called. The sound of his voice lifted Aspen's mood.

"I'm waiting on you," he said.

She could feel him smiling at the other end of the line. "Where are we going?"

"Austin, San Antonio and Houston. We're transporting four people in a van. I'd like you to ride shotgun with me but I understand if you want to stay with Max."

"Reggie's my photographer today. I'll ask if he minds following us."

"Be here within the hour."

"Who's in Austin? Who's in San Antonio and Houston, for that matter?"

"I'll tell you when you get here."

Before she could get him to raise her comfort level, she found herself listening to dead air.

Aspen grabbed her handbag. She hooked her finger around the jacket she'd hung over the chair back and slung it over her shoulder. Out in the foyer, she found Reggie hanging around Rochelle's desk.

"Grab your gear, get the keys to the SNG truck and let's go," she said. "I'll tell you what I know on the way."

The difference between Max and Reggie was that Max would've given her static until she ran down the particulars. Reggie was game for anything as long as it got him out of the studio and on an adventure.

Snippets of Misty's weather report sounded over the monitor. ". . . chance of showers . . . with some broken clouds overhead."

Rochelle reached into the drawer, pulled out her personal fan and activated the switch.

"Cool," Reggie said.

"Not cool enough," Rochelle snarled.

"Can we bring you anything back?"

"How about a wind turbine?"

While Reggie ventured off to get his camcorder, Aspen pressed Rochelle for information. "Do you know much about Spike Granger?"

"What — you mean that nasty rumor about him taking that Mexican national up in his airplane and shoving him out over the Rio Grande after the guy's murder trial ended in a hung jury? No, I don't know anything."

"Are you serious?" The smile that had formed on Aspen's face when she mentioned the sheriff melted.

"It's probably just talk. Still, you should ask him if he owns a plane." Rochelle, with her head bathed in the glow of the computer screen, paused to consider her empty coffee cup.

A peal of laughter came out of nowhere, followed by a sound byte from Steve Lennox. He poked his head out of the studio and called out to no one in particular.

"Where's Misty?"

"Looking for her sense of humor," snapped Rochelle with her multiple personality disorder. She gave him a frozen stare. The telephone rang and she picked it up. "WBFD," she said sweetly, "how may I help you? Tig Welder? Why, yes, he still works here. I'll switch you to his voicemail." Instead, she disconnected the caller and answered another line.

Aspen mouthed good-bye. With a promise to call in their location, she headed outdoors. Max intercepted her in the parking lot.

"Where are you off to?"

"No time to talk. Gotta run." She cast her mind back to the story of the SMU intern's nose hairs and gave him her biggest smile.

Reggie came out weighted down with camera equipment. Max stopped him in mid-stride.

From the passenger seat, Aspen watched Max making wild hand gestures, casting furtive glances her way. When Reggie finally stowed his gear and took his seat behind the wheel, Aspen asked for a recap.

"You don't want to know."

"I do."

"Ever since Max got that award a few years ago, he's turned into a divo. And he has a certain misguided sense of territory that comes with all testosterone-churning men. Don't worry about it. It'll pass."

"Are you saying he likes me?"

"Not anymore. I told him you were gay."

She stewed all the way to Johnson County, where they found Sheriff Spike Granger at the sally port loading the transportation van with prisoners. One particular inmate, a large African American with a surly attitude, wearing a belly chain and leg irons, refused to climb into his compartment.

"Get your goat-smellin' ass in the van."

"Well, boss," said the slow-talking, slow-walking convict, "I kinda likes it here. Think I'll just stay put."

Granger gave him a brittle smile. "You can climb in under your own steam or I'll Taze you and we'll drag you in like a slab of meat."

"You wouldn't do that, boss." He spoke in a low, forlorn bass.

"You have no idea what I'm capable of. I haven't had my first cup of coffee yet. I'm likely to shoot you in the foot."

"I'd like a cup of coffee. Can you bring me back a cup when you get your own?"

"You got twenty-five years in the pen. They can wait on your goat-smellin' ass down at the Ferguson Unit. Matter of fact, from now on, you won't have to worry about anything but stamps, envelopes and commissary."

Sufficiently sobered, the prisoner climbed aboard. Granger locked up and strode over with an outstretched hand extended in Reggie's direction.

"Spike Granger."

The photographer bobbed his head. "I'm Reggie. Where're we going?"

"Austin."

"I'm not driving to Austin until I know what for."

Granger pushed the brim of his Stetson back and locked Reggie in his stare. "Fair enough. We're dropping in on the Speaker of the House. Then we're stopping by the Lieutenant Governor's. From there we're going to San Antonio where we'll be paying a visit to other luminaries. Is that the answer you wanted?"

"Dude, I just figured out who you are. You're that guy who sneaks into Mexico and steals back airplanes that were stolen in the

States and used for drug trafficking." Reggie's mouth split into a grin. "What're we waiting for?"

Granger thumbed at Aspen. "Just waiting to see if you'll let her ride with me. So she can take notes for the piece." He turned her way, touched the brim of his hat in acknowledgment and slipped her a discreet wink.

Aspen felt a thrill of terror. Remembering Rochelle's words about not irritating the camera crew, not to mention the rumor about the illegal alien's chuteless sky dive, she said, "It's up to you, Reggie. If you'd rather not ride by yourself, I'll stay with you."

Besides, she was safe with Reggie. Granger scared the hell out of her.

The photographer looked back at the sheriff. "Yeah, man. No problem. Y'all enjoy the ride."

CHAPTER
TWENTY-SIX

By Monday noon, a domino effect of outrageous proportions took place.

In a fashionable Austin neighborhood, Emory Fulton, Speaker of the House, awakened from his afternoon nap to the Morse code tappings of an uninvited caller relentlessly stabbing his doorbell.

As Sheriff Granger waited down the street in the transport van, Reggie lit up the camcorder.

Aspen heard Steve Lennox through her ear fob. Before she launched the intro to her exclusive, breaking news, she posed a question to the disembodied voice.

"What's my name, Steve?"

"Aspen."

"Very good," she sing-songed. "Don't forget."

Reggie gave her the heads-up. "Someone's coming down the stairs — three, two, one. You're on the air."

"This is Aspen Wicklow, WBFD, coming to you live from the Capitol City, where we're outside the home of Emory Fulton, Speaker of the House. As you can see —" she made a spectacular hand flourish toward Fulton's front door and the camera panned away from her "— a week has gone by since Sheriff Spike Granger handcuffed the first prisoner to the chain link fence at the penitentiary in Huntsville, and the Johnson County sheriff still isn't taking any guff off the Texas Department of Criminal Justice. In what Granger refers to as his *Adopt-A-Con* program, he intends to rid his jail of convicted felons by adopting them out."

The door yanked open, pulling the prisoner inside. "Rappin' Rodney", the inmate Granger had handcuffed to the handle, sprawled on the floor of the Speaker's marble foyer.

"What the hell?" The Speaker brandished a .38 caliber revolver. Hair the color of a weathered picket fence stuck out on the sides of his head like a couple of currycombs.

Rodney *gangsta*-rapped an annoying explanation, complete with hand gestures.

"I come down to do some time.

" 'Cause my homie dropped a dime.

"Smoked a little crack; smoked a little grass.

"Sheriff Granger hauled off my goat-smellin' ass."

Fulton looked beyond the convict, to the rolling camera. "What the hell's going on here?"

With mike in hand, Aspen trotted up the sidewalk. "Speaker Fulton, can you tell us what you think of Sheriff Spike Granger's Adopt-A-Con program?"

"The what?" He raised a hand to his forehead to shield his face from the afternoon sun.

"Adopt-A-Con. The sheriff of Johnson County is farming out convicted felons to influential people like you who can do something about the prison overcrowding issue."

"Why, that mangy sonofabitch." Incredulity resonated in his voice. "He'll be lucky not to end up dead in a ditch somewhere."

"Do you intend to do anything about prison congestion, Mister Speaker, or must these small town sheriffs continue to deplete their budgets, without compensation, in order to house inmates like Rappin' Rodney, a convicted drug pusher?"

Rodney had finally gotten enough traction to stand. He continued to rap, making subtle background noises that sounded like a helicopter bearing down, bouncing at the knees and jutting his head to and fro like a turkey.

"None of your business." Fulton raked his fingers through tousled hair. "Is that camera on?"

With the weight of the camera on his shoulders and his eyes locked firmly on the viewfinder, Reggie gave him a palsied salute.

"Turn off that damned camera. Don't you air one single frame of this spectacle. You're compromising my safety by showing my address."

Aspen inwardly chuckled. If she knew Reggie, he'd already zoomed in for a close-up on the numbers.

"Who'd threaten your safety, Mister Speaker . . . convicted felons like Rappin' Rodney?"

"Who? That asshole?" Fulton squinted into the sun. "Turn off that camera, boy."

"You have a lovely, spacious estate, Mr. Speaker. I can see why Sheriff Granger would approve your home for placement. Would you be willing to adopt any more convicts under the sheriff's program? Just until the prison overcrowding situation is resolved."

"Listen, bitch. Get off my property. Is that

camera still on? I told you to get off my property, you sonofabitch." His wagging finger shifted to Rappin' Rodney. "And take this motherfucker with you."

Aspen bowed up. "Mister Speaker, shame on you. You're a better man than that. What would your mother say, hearing you talk that way to a lady?"

"My mother's dead. Don't drag her into this."

"I bet she didn't teach you to talk like that. But you and Rappin' Rodney seem to speak the same language. What do you think, Rodney?"

"Fuckin'-A," Rodney rapped. "Mista Speaker got no class. Sheriff gonna haul off yo' goat-smellin' ass."

Down the block, Granger tooted the horn. Aspen glanced his way. He twirled his finger in a *Wrap-it-up* hand spin.

She stared directly into the camera lens. "And there you have it, folks. Speaker of the House Emory Fulton doesn't think much of Spike Granger's Adopt-A-Con program. But the Johnson County sheriff says if the Texas penal system won't take responsibility for its convicted felons, the fat cats at the Capitol complex can by-God do it for him. From WBFD-TV, I'm Aspen Wicklow."

If politicians in the Metroplex had tuned in to WBFD's breaking news, none of them bothered to warn Lieutenant Governor Lance Radcliff of the trouble brewing.

In an even ritzier, old-money part of Austin, Radcliff's next-door-neighbor teetered down her sidewalk with a martini in hand, still clad in a silk robe with a feather boa and satin boudoir slippers. She confronted the WBFD news crew at the curb while Granger was hooking convicted home invader "Dysentery Gary's" handcuffs to Radcliff's front door.

Aspen twirled her finger forward in the *Roll 'em* position. Reggie flipped on the beacon and spotlighted the blowzy blonde.

With a stunned expression on her face, the woman addressed Aspen with a trace of New Orleans upbringing lingering on her tongue. "What do you mean by Adopt-A-Con? Are you serious? My dear, what in the world's wrong with you? One simply cannot abandon a criminal in Austin's nicest neighborhood."

"He's not being abandoned. He's being adopted out." Aspen's eyes slewed to the lady's house. "That's a grand-looking Tudor you've got there. Looks like . . . what? . . . Six, seven bedrooms? Would you be willing to host a convict to relieve the overcrowded prison conditions?" She tilted the mike toward the tipsy woman's face.

"Oh, hell no. I'm callin' the Gov'nor." She swilled back the rest of her drink and placed the empty glass at her feet. Reaching into her pocket, she retrieved a cell phone and tapped out a number. Abruptly, she jammed a finger into her ear to cut the noise.

"Gov'nor, this is your neighbor, Celeste. Now, Gov'nor, there's no delicate way to put this. A man wearing stripes just took a dump on your front lawn." She listened a moment, then snapped her clamshell phone shut and gave the camera an aristocratic sniff. "Lieutenant Gov'nor Radcliff's on the way out. If you know what's good for you, you'll leave. The Gov'nor's a bigwig in the NRA."

Aspen pantomimed the finger-to-throat slit. Reggie kept rolling. She switched off her mike and leaned in close to him.

"We should get out of here. What if he opens fire on us?" Then she remembered what Max said about the gutless nature of the SMU interns. "I'm not scared of him, of course. I'm just worried about you."

"I'm staying. That's why Gordon pays me the big bucks. Turn the mike back on and get ready for your countdown."

On went the mike.

She heard Lennox through her earpiece. "Way to go, Aspen. Ready whenever you are."

She turned toward the camera.

Reggie said, "Here comes the Lieutenant Governor. Three, two, one."

Radcliff's front door swung wide open. The State's second-in-command stepped onto the porch of his Georgian-style home brandishing a shotgun. He vowed revenge on the sheriff of Johnson County and called for a press conference.

Then he came unglued. "Get off my property and take this miscreant with you." Neck veins the size of copper pipe bulged beneath tawny skin. The shotgun swung left to right.

Suddenly lightheaded, Aspen kept her voice even and metered. "We're here at the home of Lieutenant Governor Lance Radcliff, where Sheriff Spike Granger has adopted out another convicted felon under what's becoming a notorious solution to the Texas prison system's overcrowded conditions. Granger calls it the Adopt-A-Con program and says —"

"Where's that crazy motherfucker?" Radcliff screeched like a Chinese monkey. "Granger, I'll get you if it's the last thing I ever do."

Aspen walked briskly up Radcliff's sidewalk. Reggie closed in behind her.

Radcliff leveled the shotgun at them. "Stay where you are."

"Sir, does Governor Woolsey have any plans to call a special session of the Legislature to deal with the prison overcrowding issue?" She backed up a few steps. Reggie did the same.

"Did you hear me tell you to clear out of here before I call in the Texas Rangers?"

"You can't throw us off public property, Governor. This is a city easement. We have every right to be here. What do you think about Spike Granger's Adopt-A-Con program? Would you be willing to adopt more convicted felons from the Johnson County Jail to relieve Sheriff Granger's overcrowding issues caused by the backup in the Texas penal system?"

"Get out." He ratcheted the shotgun. "Granger, you psycho, show yourself."

Aspen's knees turned to jelly. She pressed them together to keep from pitching over, face-first, in a dead faint.

"Way to go, girl," Reggie mouthed without sound.

His praise was enough for her to catch her second wind. With newfound confidence, she flicked her hair behind her shoulders and resumed command.

"As you can see, Steve, Lieutenant Governor Radcliff isn't happy about the Johnson County sheriff's solution to this prison congestion problem. But will the Governor call a special session of the Legislature to cure this situation?" She furrowed her brow for effect. "Or will the sheriffs of the other two hundred fifty-three counties have to start their own Adopt-A-Con program to make their point?"

She'd planned to stop talking, but the devil on her shoulder goaded her. Granger's passion to correct a flaw in the system had rubbed off on her.

"And if they run out of dignitaries, what's next? Will Granger implement a *School-A-Scoundrel* program? Should the Chancellors of our state universities be worried?"

She loved the notion. Ideas germinated in her head. Inspiration seemed to come out of the ether, channeled by the ghosts of past lawmen who'd grown tired of getting the shaft from big-shot politicians.

"How about a *Train-A-Thug* program? Will the CEOs of major corporations be the next to feel the pinch of prison congestion?"

Steve Lennox broke the trance. "All very provocative questions, Aspen. Thank you."

"My pleasure, Steve. Coming to you live,

I'm Aspen Wicklow, WBFD-TV."

An hour and a half later, Granger rolled into San Antonio and turned south on Broadway. He veered off into the posh, incorporated city of Alamo Heights with Reggie hugging his bumper.

The photographer set up the SNG truck in front of the Italian villa belonging to State Representative Lucy Villalpando, Vice-Chairman of the House Criminal Justice Committee. Granger had already triple-belly-chained "Arson Bill" to a concrete support column on her front porch by the time Villalpando wheeled her Lexus SUV into the Alamo Heights driveway.

Aspen checked her watch — five o'clock. Plenty of time left for the evening news.

Villalpando headed up the sidewalk toting a bag full of groceries. She stumbled across Arson Bill and let out a blood-clotting scream.

Wide-eyed and slack-jawed, the Representative stopped dead in her tracks.

"What the hell? Who the hell are you and what're you doing on my porch?"

Arson Bill's eyes thinned into slits. "Got a light?"

She clutched the sack closer and shielded her face from the camera.

Aspen took her cue from Reggie. "We're

here with Representative Villalpando, who has the power to call a meeting of the Criminal Justice Committee to discuss prison overpopulation." She tipped the mike near the stunned woman's chin. "Representative Villalpando, what do you think of Spike Granger's Adopt-A-Con program, and would you be willing to take in more prisoners to relieve the overcrowding situation at the Johnson County Jail?"

Villalpando ripped off a couple of nasty-sounding Spanish phrases that seemed to question Granger's parentage as Reggie filmed what promised to either be award-winning footage or documentation of a mentally unstable woman.

"The sheriff still has a couple of child sexual predators he wants to clean out of his jail and San Antonio's nice this time of year. The sheriff would like to know if he can put you down for one or two?" She tilted the mike toward Villalpando.

"You crazy bitch, I have children. I don't want those sons-of-bitches in my house. They should be in the pen —" She abruptly clammed up.

As soon as she realized her mistake, she unleashed a guts-out, upwardly spiraling, South-o'-the-Border scream, *Aaaaeeeeiiiiiii.* Then she peppered the conversation with profanity — in two languages.

"Can we quote you on that, Madame Vice-Chairman?"

"You can get this scumbag off my porch and take your lily-white ass outta here, too."

"Why, Madame Representative," Aspen said with an expression of mock shock, "that sounds racist. You're not a racist, are you? Because isn't this an election year? And don't you have an opponent in the upcoming race? And when I say 'race' I'm talking about the election, not like 'racist', which it sounds like you don't care for Irish people."

"Get out or I'm calling the police."

Aspen wanted to warn her that if the AHPD was anything like the FWPD, they were either asleep or temporarily distracted by the cell phones growing out of their ears. Instead, she shoved the mike in the inmate's face.

"Arson Bill, is it true you torched an orphanage?"

Villalpando swooned.

Instead of answering her, he directed his comment to the Vice-Chair of the Committee on Criminal Justice. "What's in the bag? Because I don't eat just anything. I have food allergies so I need a special diet. Do you know how to cook steak and potatoes? That's what I'd like for dinner and if you make me sick I'll file a lawsuit with the Department of Justice."

"Have a nice day, Madame Representative."

The lawmaker panicked. "Wait. Don't go. You can't leave this man here. I have little kids. Oh, dear God, we're all going to die."

Buoyed with confidence, Aspen grinned at the camera. "Well, loyal viewers, you heard it for yourself — *Arson Bill should be in prison.* Coming to you live from the River City, it's getting late and I'm Aspen Wicklow, reporting for WBFD . . . where we want to be the station you take to bed with you . . . just as much as we want to be the one you wake up with." She winked at the lens as if she'd claimed it as her new beau. "Back to you, Steve."

While Reggie was unloading his gear into the truck, Aspen trotted up the street. Granger backed up the transport van and met her halfway.

"School-A-Scoundrel? Train-A-Thug?" His eyes twinkled. "That was brilliant. Did you think that up on your own?"

Breathless, she said, "I did. I hope you're not mad."

"Mad, hell. That was priceless. I'll bet the university heads and the leaders of the rest of the corporate world are puckering."

"Did you hear Villalpando say Arson Bill should be in prison?" She clutched her chest. "My heart's about to beat clear through."

"Mine, too." He reached out a finger and lifted a lock of hair from her face. "I think I love you."

"What?" She must've misheard him. Either that or the Partridge Family was making a comeback.

She didn't dare meet his gaze. Granger'd gotten caught up in the victory of the moment and this was his way of showing gratitude. He didn't *really* love her. Probably didn't even have one of those warm, soft spots like the one she was starting to have for him. If she avoided direct eye contact, they could pretend it never happened.

That would be the smart thing to do.

She looked up at Granger past spidery mascaraed lashes. "Do you by chance own an airplane?"

"Why do you ask?"

She gave him a one-shoulder shrug. "No reason."

Reggie rolled up beside them in the satellite news-gathering vehicle. He lowered the canned energy drink he'd been holding and powered down the window. "Ready?"

Aspen turned to the sheriff. "I'll ride the rest of the way with Reggie if that's okay with you. I think I took enough notes."

Around eleven o'clock that evening in Houston, Granger adopted out the last convict at the River Oaks estate of Senator Ditcomb, Chairman of the Senate Criminal Justice Committee.

Reggie unspooled cable and readied the camcorder as Aspen positioned herself beyond the lunge area of Mohammed Jerome Willy. Willy, a huge six-foot-five African American with a shaved head and a toothpick clamped between his jaws, wore a ball-and-chain on each ankle. He sat belly-chained to the wrought-iron architecture holding up Senator Ditcomb's second-floor balcony.

Reggie turned on the overhead light. One by one, fingers curled into his fist for the countdown.

Aspen played to the camera.

"We're here in Houston, at the River Oaks mansion of Senator Ditcomb, Chairman of the Senate Criminal Justice Committee, joining Sheriff Spike Granger as he adopts out another convicted criminal from his Johnson County jail. Mohammed Jerome Willy, known as the 'Greasy Rapist' or the

'Vegetable Oil Rapist,' brought terror to women in Granger's small North Texas county and was recently sentenced to eighty years in the penitentiary. But due to prison overcrowding, Sheriff Spike Granger was notified the TDCJ wouldn't take Willy. Granger's main concern is that the Johnson County jail isn't equipped to deal with maximum security inmates on a long-term basis, and his request that they make an exception and incarcerate Willy in a maximum security prison has fallen on deaf ears."

Heart thudding, she turned in the direction of the prisoner and found him studying her with the intensity of a cobra. She stared into impenetrable eyes that were predatory and flat.

Willy slathered his tongue over his lips. Nostrils flared. "Say, Miss . . . I'd like to bend yo' ass over that flowerpot and stick my big ol' greasy —" The rest of his idea disintegrated. Two electrodes jutted out from his shoulder, infusing a high-voltage jolt of electricity into his system. Mohammed Jerome Willy flopped around like two hundred seventy-five pounds of beached whale blubber as Granger stood beyond camera range and Tazed him into oblivion.

Shaken by the sight of the huge, twitching

man, Aspen struggled to regain her composure.

She tilted the mike to her lips and spoke in a conspiratorial whisper. "I've pressed the intercom and am waiting to see if Senator Ditcomb will come to the door —"

"That rich som-bitch is a coward," mumbled Willy. Gossamer shoestrings of mucous dripped from his nose. He hoisted himself up on one elbow and blinked at his surroundings. Dark eyes scanned the area until he found Granger. "What'd you have to go and do that for, boss?"

"Don't be saying lewd shit like that to her."

"Lemme get one last piece of pus—"

Zap!

Willy curled into a fetal position and groaned out the rest of his sentence. "— before I go to the big house. She looks like she could —"

Granger triggered the Taser. Willy's eyes rolled back in their sockets. Drool oozed from his mouth. He twisted his body and wrapped his massive arm across his chest and over one shoulder, enough to get his huge fingers on the contact leads. His face contorted into a grimace as he ripped them out. For the next few moments he shuddered against the floor like he was in mid-seizure. The faint odor of hot metal and human waste permeated the air.

"Who's there?" The loud male voice vibrated through the intercom.

She darted a quick look at Willy, who played possum by squeezing his eyes closed. "Aspen Wicklow, WBFD-TV, Fort Worth, Dallas. Senator Ditcomb, could you please come outside and talk to us? We have a situation here."

"I'm trying to sleep," he yelled. "Go away before I call the police."

"Well, that's just it, Senator, we have police out here with us." It wasn't a lie; Granger stood on the manicured lawn, holding the Taser, waiting for Willy to get out of line again.

"Dammit to hell, what now?" The intercom shut off but Aspen had a sneaky feeling the seventy-eight year old Senator would head downstairs as fast as he could.

Lights flickered on, casting a butterscotch glow through the sheer curtains. Reggie zoomed the camera lens past Aspen's shoulder as the Senator opened the front door of his mansion. Instead of finding a pleasant surprise at his slippered feet, an ominous baritone boomed out a low-down, bluesy greeting.

"Evenin' Senator." Mohammed Jerome

Willy slid his belly-chained, ham-hock hands up the wrought-iron accents enough to remove the toothpick he'd been chewing on. He fixed almond-shaped eyes the color and dullness of charcoal on the old, white-haired gentleman.

"Been out here all evening, Senator," Willy said. The voice was melodic and taunting. "Hope you've got some grub 'cause I'm hungry and the State's 'posed to put me up but they's all full."

Ditcomb came fully awake.

"What the hell are you doing shackled to my house?"

"It was all a mistake, Senator. I told the judge I wasn't the greasy rapist but he didn't believe me. So I owned up to it, which ought to count toward good behavior, shouldn't it? I told him I wearned my Wesson. Man still didn't believe me."

Senator Ditcomb screwed up his face in disgust.

"Say, Senator — you a gamblin' man? You got a deck of cards in yo' house? We could play a little Texas Hold 'Em."

Ditcomb scoffed at the notion. "You don't have any money. What would a convict be playing cards for?"

"Yo' ass."

Aspen winced. "All in all, I'd say Sheriff

Spike Granger's Adopt-A-Con program is a big hit with the bigwigs. This is Aspen Wicklow, reporting for WBFD-TV, coming to you live from Houston. Back to you, Steve."

She probably could've come up with more clever stuff to say, but with or without Taser wires sticking out of his skin, Mohammed Jerome Willy scared the hell out of her.

Even with Spike Granger close enough to pistol-whip him into a chocolate stain.

CHAPTER
TWENTY-SEVEN

By the time Aspen and Reggie returned to WBFD, four o'clock Tuesday morning had rolled around. Instead of going home to crash, she thanked Reggie for his fine work and planned a retreat to her office.

"There's a sofa in one of the conference rooms," he said. "Max and I usually bunk there if we have to work all night, but you can have it if you want."

"Thanks. You go ahead. You did a great job out there today, Reggie, and neither of us got killed. You take it."

They argued on the walk across the parking lot with him offering her the sofa and her refusing to take it. He'd almost talked her into it when she recalled Rochelle's advice about watching her photographer's back. After Reggie lost the argument, he met her at her office door with a couple of musty-smelling blankets and some chair cushions.

"If you shove these together and wrap them with a blanket, it'll make a nice bed. I ought to know. I've only done it a hundred times." He stacked the trappings of slumber on the floor and hit the light switch, leaving Aspen silhouetted in the window overlooking downtown Fort Worth.

No one bothered her until nine o'clock, when the Asian cleaning woman keyed her way inside and flipped on the light. After a weird face scrunch and shy apology, the lady backed out of the room and closed the door. Aspen drifted back into a deep, dreamless sleep.

Ten minutes later, Gordon, thrilled with the Breaking News pieces, barged into her office and sent her home.

She went looking for Rochelle to bum a ride and found her outside smoking like an Eastern European power station. After burning her skinny cigarette down to a nub, she left Aspen waiting by the Z while she went back for her purse.

Before arriving at Aspen's bungalow, they motored up to the drive-thru, where Rochelle ordered a couple of breakfast croissants. The smell of hot ham wafted out of each grease-stained sack as Rochelle coasted into the driveway.

Aspen, seat-belted into the passenger

compartment of the Nissan, fidgeted in her seat.

Rochelle cut the engine, withdrew the keys and dropped them into her purse, then darted her a look. "You're afraid to go inside, aren't you?"

"A little."

"I'll come with you. I need ice cubes." She patted her handbag. "I have my gun. If I have to kill somebody inside your house, my lawyer says being in the throes of a hot flash is a mitigating circumstance."

Aspen checked the integrity of the perimeter three times before satisfying herself that the window locks were engaged and the house hadn't been breached. After fixing Gordon's menopausal assistant up with a plastic bag of ice cubes wrapped in a cup towel, Aspen asked her to stay.

"Gordon expects me to come back. Want me to leave my pistol with you?"

Big headshake. "I wouldn't know what to do with it."

"Just point it like it's an extension of your finger and fire."

But Rochelle's offer didn't alleviate Aspen's jitters. After the croissants were eaten and the wrappers discarded, she followed the secretary out to the Nissan.

Rochelle hit the remote button and the Z

chirped open.

Plagued by panic, Aspen grabbed her wrist. "Can you come back after work? I'll cook for you." She suddenly remembered she had no food in the refrigerator and precious little money left over from Friday's paycheck. Most of all, she had no transportation. "If you'll take me to the grocery store, I'll buy food and whip up dinner for you."

Rochelle discreetly eyed her up. Irritation got the best of her. "Look, kid, I didn't take you to raise."

Aspen blinked back tears. "I'm sorry. I thought —" her bottom lip quivered "— I thought we were becoming friends."

Rochelle sighed. "I'm sorry, too." Her shoulders sagged. The tension that had her spoiling for a fight seemed to seep right out of her. "I hate my job. Some days I don't even know who I am anymore."

"Maybe you should get a hobby. Like at the nursing home . . ." Aspen said by way of explanation. "They offer free classes for people who want to learn to play bridge or chess or mah-jongg. It keeps their minds sharp while it keeps them out of trouble."

"A hobby," Rochelle said, testing the word. "Why, yes, a hobby might be just the thing to calm my nerves. I secretly yearn to take up knocking cyclists off their bikes with my car. Won't that be fun?"

Aspen gave her a distancing smile.

She placed her purse on the hood. With keys in hand, she grasped Aspen by the shoulders. "Want to calm me down? Then come up with a good slogan for WBFD, win that trip and take me along. We'll spend time on the beach swilling down umbrella drinks, drawing obscene pictures in the sand with our big toes and doing character assassinations on Gordon and the rest of the employees."

Rochelle came up with another idea. She suggested, good-naturedly, that she'd probably die of ptomaine poisoning if she let Aspen cook supper for her, but what the hell? Then she took the reporter by the hand and dropped the car keys into her palm.

"Drive me back to the station. Go to the store and pick up what you need for dinner and come get me in a couple of hours." She dug into her purse and pulled out a ten. "Get popcorn and rent us a movie. Either select something violent or get porn. Don't even think about renting one of those feel-good movies. I need to keep my edge — and you need to develop one."

When Aspen returned to WBFD, Rochelle was waiting at the station's entrance. The women traded places, with Rochelle behind the wheel and Aspen in the passenger seat.

"What's for dinner?"

"Tuna casserole and a Cobb salad."

"You should take a cooking class and learn how to cook." Rochelle winked to show she didn't mean it. "What kind of porn did you rent?"

"No porn. But I did get a couple of 'Dirty Harry' movies."

"Great." Rochelle hit the steering wheel with the heel of her hand. "Those are kick-ass flicks. Let's watch them in order. Did you get wine?"

"Certainly."

"What goes with tuna casserole?"

"Does it really matter?" Aspen said what they were both thinking. "By the way, are you staying over tonight?"

Rochelle slid her a sideways glance. "No. But I don't mind if you pull something out of your closet and come back to my house after we eat."

"Thanks." Her hands had become damp and she wiped them against the fabric bunched loosely around her thighs. "I'm sure this scary feeling will pass by tomorrow."

As soon as they arrived back at Aspen's house, Rochelle loaded the DVD into the player. She fast-forwarded it, stopping at what she called "the good part."

"I love this. Stop what you're doing and check this out. Here's the best part — when he sticks the gun up the guy's nostril and says, 'Go ahead. Make my day.' He's so hot. I'd sleep with him." She clicked the play button and Aspen got to hear it all over again.

"You'd sleep with Clint Eastwood?"

"No, with Dirty Harry. Clint Eastwood's an actor. I want Dirty Harry."

"Dirty Harry isn't real."

"Sure he is," she said with an air of smugness. "He's trapped in the body of that Spike Granger guy you're friends with."

Heat burned her cheeks. "We're not friends . . . not exactly."

"I'd do him." Rochelle punctuated the idea with a nod.

Aspen inwardly bristled. "C'mon, Granger's not even your type."

"What's my type?"

"I picture you with a tall, good-looking younger guy," she said, teetering with the notion of describing Stinger Baldwin. "Maybe a blond. With a great tan and good teeth."

Rochelle gave an aristocratic sniff. "Don't I wish. But these are the rusty years. For the time being, I'll have to make do with what's available. So have you had any more sex dreams about the sheriff?"

"You've got it all wrong." Her protest was about as convincing as the gourmet-to-go meal she was about to pass off as her own creation.

They were halfway through the first movie in the Dirty Harry series, forking salad and sipping Chablis, when Rochelle checked her watch and demanded the remote. The five o'clock news was about to come on.

Rochelle flipped on Channel 18. As the musical lead-in faded out, Bill Wallace greeted viewers with the top story. When he announced the hot topic of prison over-crowding, Aspen sat erect. With chills zipping up her arms, she expected to see cuts from the Adopt-A-Con footage.

Instead, Tig Welder came onscreen.

Rochelle molded her index finger and thumb into a gun and aimed it at the screen. "Go ahead. Make my day," she said in a convincing tone. The gun went off and her hand recoiled, but Tig's eyes still pierced them from the television as she blew invisible smoke from the tip of her finger.

Wine spewed from Aspen's nose. She blinked . . . and blinked again . . . then realized her mouth was opening and closing like a bigmouth bass. Tig was broadcasting from Austin, framed in the backdrop of a pink granite Capitol building.

The Criminal Justice Committee had convened an emergency meeting that afternoon, which resulted in the Governor calling an emergency session of the Legislature to remedy prison-overcrowding issues.

Scorched to the gills, Aspen didn't hear the words being drowned out by the warning bells pealing inside her head; nor was she able to focus over the distraction caused by vibrating retinas.

They were like pirates, this bunch of cutthroats she worked with.

And Granger? Granger was there, too, bigger than life, giving Tig Welder and rival TV stations an interview.

The gut-wrenching betrayal took her breath away.

She panted for breath. Wagging a finger at the television, she could only babble. "He . . . he . . . he stole . . . he stole my story." She got an overwhelming urge to knee the arrogant reporter in the marbles with her eunuch-maker. Mercifully, the ugly visual kept the tears blistering behind her eyeballs from brimming over and spilling onto her cheeks. She looked at Rochelle through pleading eyes. "How could he do that? It was my story. Granger promised to call me if anything —"

The words slid back down her throat, replaced by a newer, more treacherous thought. She measured Gordon's assistant with a look. "Did you know about this?"

Rochelle washed down a mouthful of casserole with Chablis. She dabbed at the corners of her mouth with a paper napkin.

Ha. Stall tactic.

Before she could answer, Aspen's voice dissolved into a whisper. "You knew. You knew and you didn't tell me."

She wanted to cry. Wanted to flop onto her bed and throw herself into the stack of down-filled pillows plumping up the top of the spread and sob until the ache went away.

"You were asleep," Rochelle said weakly. "Gordon said not to wake you. He said you did a fine job but that Tig could handle it."

Aspen drew on all her reserves. She stiffened, gave a debutante sniffle and walked her plate to the kitchen.

The secretary sprang to her feet, following close behind with a half-eaten dinner still on her plate. "Aspen, it wasn't anything personal."

"I understand." But she didn't. In the short time it took to reach the counter top, she'd dreamed up at least five ways to commit murder. Now all she needed was to figure out how to escape prosecution. If she rounded up all of Tig's women and paraded them into the courtroom, she might get off on justifiable homicide. Her cheeks heated up. Rochelle had worn out her welcome.

"I know you're upset. If I'd known you'd be this upset —"

"I'm not upset," she said dully.

"— I would've come into your office and shaken you 'til your teeth rattled. But Gordon said he didn't want you to get burned out your first week."

"Wasn't that nice of him?" She threw her napkin into the garbage, raked the uneaten contents of her plate into a bowl meant for Midnight and reclaimed her dignity with a delicate sniff. "I've changed my mind about tonight, Rochelle. I won't be going home with you."

"I'm so sorry. Look, kid, I'll stay here with you."

"You should leave. Now."

"Aspen . . ."

"Really, Rochelle. I can fend for myself."

"Want me to leave my gun?"

If she did, she'd better drop it and run. Aspen fixed her with a knowing gaze. "Right now, that's probably not such a hot idea."

They exchanged awkward looks. Rochelle

left the house by mutual agreement, free to pursue her new hobby of clipping cyclists with her bumper, and then figuring out ways to hold them responsible.

CHAPTER
TWENTY-EIGHT

After Rochelle left, Aspen quickly packed an overnight bag. She had no choice. The pull of Tranquility Villas tugged at her fear. Hardship be damned, she should've hired a locksmith to change the locks and install new deadbolts and security chains. Until she made personal safety a priority, she refused to stay home alone.

The telephone rang and she answered it.

Margo Sommervel's strident voice vibrated through the phone. "I need to talk to you about my sister's car. Are you still working on that mechanic story for the *Public Defender* spot?"

"Yes, but it won't air this week. Maybe in two weeks. This week's story focuses on the police. Sorry."

"Let's go somewhere and have a drink."

"I can't, Margo. I have to find another place to stay for a few days and I'm packing."

"Use my sister's condo. The police are through with it. Meet me at Chica Tica's and you can follow me over when we're done."

"That's just it," she confessed, "I don't have transportation."

"Tell me where you live and I'll pick you up."

Using Candy Drummond's place seemed like a good idea at the time. Aspen hadn't made many close friends since graduation, so it wasn't as if there were people out there clamoring to invite her as a houseguest. Staying at her mother's house was out of the question. In order to generate income to pay Jillian's nursing home bill, Aspen had the furniture moved into storage so the place could be rented.

Aspen gave Margo her address and waited by the front door. Her mobile phone rang three times . . . Rochelle made two attempts to talk to her, and Granger one. Aspen ignored them, letting each call cycle into voicemail.

She didn't care for this vulnerable feeling, silhouetted beneath the flickering sconce on the front porch. But it seemed better than waiting inside where an intruder lying in wait could descend from the attic or pop out of a closet as soon as the lights went out.

Near the corner, the fuzzy glow of head-lights shimmied down the residential street slow enough for the driver to check house numbers. Aspen reached down expectantly and lifted a small travel bag.

A black BMW bounced onto the driveway. The locks snapped open with an audible clunk. Aspen hurried down the front steps. She tossed her bag into the back seat, climbed into the front bucket and buckled up.

Margo gave her the once-over. "What's with the hair?"

Aspen narrowed her eyes in a *double-dog-dare.* "It's the humidity."

"Well, don't worry. I'm sure there's a curling iron you can use to tame it."

Aspen didn't reply. It was probably an innocent observation on Margo's part, not calculated to inflict pain. But this was the sort of thing the Drummond girls were famous for. They made people who didn't fit their lifestyle feel small and inferior. She reminded herself that Margo was only paying attention to her because she had a job in the media and served a purpose. While police investigated Caramel Jean Drummond's murder, Aspen was the only one willing to deal with the missing car.

Margo backed out of the driveway and threaded the Beemer into traffic. She eased a pair of Versace eyeglasses down over her forehead and seated them on the bridge of her perfectly sculpted nose.

"How come you need a place to stay?"

Her question had the hollow ring of a *Let's do lunch* comment. "Let's do lunch," meant you didn't give a damn about seeing the person again but your brain went dead; or you didn't have the guts to jump-start your dead head with a more appropriate comment such as, "For the love of God, run."

"Aspen." Margo redirected her attention with a finger snap. "How come you need a place to stay?"

"Long story. You don't want to hear it." She leaned against the headrest and closed her eyes. Blue comets arced behind her lids. Her eyes snapped opened and she sat upright. She rifled through her purse and popped two breath chips onto her tongue. "Did you talk to a lawyer about suing Pop's Salvage?"

Margo did a vigorous head bob. "He said my sister received notice the shop would place a mechanic's lien on the car if she didn't pick it up because it was stated in the contract Candy signed. And that they called to let her know it was ready. She didn't pick it up, so case closed."

"Have you spoken to the ME's office about their findings?"

Margo's voice warbled. "They said they'd call when they finished the autopsy report, but they haven't."

"How're you holding up?"

"You're a reporter. I'm not telling you anything that can get me in trouble."

"We're off the record."

Margo's eyes slewed her way. "Really? You can do that?"

"I'll do it for you."

Margo took a deep breath. She did a hand-over-hand move, pulling the steering wheel hard left. They whipped onto the on-ramp and sailed down the freeway.

"Whoever did this to my sister, I want him dead," she said fiercely.

"Let the police handle it."

"They haven't handled it. They don't tell us anything. They don't call. When we call them, they tell us they can't comment on an ongoing investigation." She punctuated her statement with a nod. "For the last week, I've stayed up nights plotting ways to kill the guy myself."

"You realize how unrealistic that is, don't you? Fantasizing murder in a way that won't get you caught?"

"I don't know why you think it's unrealistic. If I knew who I was supposed to be looking for, I'd know exactly what to do."

"And that would be . . . what?"

"Torture him to death."

Aspen barely restrained a sigh. For all of the Drummond sisters' college snobbery, Margo Sommervel didn't have the wherewithal to do someone in, not even a murderer.

As if anticipating her thoughts, Margo glanced over. The contours of her face hardened into a cement eagle expression. "You don't think I can do it."

"I think you should let the police handle it. And even though this conversation is off the record for media purposes, it's not off the record if I get called in to testify before the grand jury for your murder indictment."

Margo's voice went brittle. "Thanks for the warning."

The rest of the ride over to the Mexican restaurant took place in relative silence. At Chica Tica's, Margo demanded a corner table away from the other patrons. She ordered two Swirls, semi-lethal concoctions of green margarita with Sangria dribbled in. The drink had the look of a severed artery.

Margo guzzled her drink too fast, wincing from a brain freeze headache. She shook off the pain and un-scrunched her face. "I keep seeing you on the news. You look good."

"Really?"

"I never realized how pretty you are. I don't know what the makeup people do to make you photograph so well, but the camera loves you."

"Thanks."

They made innocuous chitchat until the Swirl lubricated Margo's tongue. "You frustrate me."

Aspen nodded. "I seem to affect a lot of people that way."

"I never liked you. You always shied away from the popular girls."

"Did you ever bother to learn anything about me, or did you just discount me because I didn't meet your fashion standards? For that matter, what do you really know about me?"

Margo did a slow blink. It was as if she'd been invited to appear on a game show and her allotted number of *Jeopardy!* seconds were about to expire. "You're a Fort Worth girl?"

"That's a given. What else?"

"You went to public school?"

"Good guess." Aspen poked the slushy drink with her straw. "Let me make this easy for you." Feeling the buzz of her drink, she pushed the glass mug aside, rested her hands in her lap and filled Margo in on life at the Wicklow house. "It was hard living at home and commuting to school. After one semester of dorm life, I worked summers just to be able to move into my own house my senior year. Even then, I didn't get much opportunity to mingle with my friends because I was too busy trying to keep my parents from killing each other during the divorce. My father had a wandering eye. Eventually, he wandered off and couldn't find his way back home. Now we understand that he had early Alzheimer's." She laughed in spite of herself, then lifted her Swirl in a toast. "A toast to bread; without bread there'd be no toast. *Sláinte.*" When Margo stared in crosseyed confusion, she translated, "It's Gaelic." Margo blinked. "Irish. It means: to your health." Margo cocked her head. "Oh for heaven's sake — Cheers."

They clinked glasses.

The tension lining Margo's face dissolved. "I'm a terrible person." She slurped down the last of her second drink. Guilt softened her exterior. "I tried to get you blackballed from the sorority during Rush."

"I know." The girl who'd ended up being her "Big Sister" filled her in after she pledged.

A tear slid over one cheek and splashed on the table. Margo took the cloth napkin, folded it into quarters and wiped it away before shaking it out and returning it to her lap.

"You must hate me."

"I should." Aspen swished the straw across the two-colored drink, blending the contents into an unappetizing shade of gray. "But I don't."

"I'm sorry I said all those nasty things back in college. I don't think you dress like a street urchin."

Years of hurt bubbled to the surface. Aspen's eyes misted. "I wasn't exactly a fashion plate back then. But I had no money. I tried not to be jealous of you and your sister — the way you were so close, your nice clothes, the matching Jags. There was no way the daughter of a newspaper printer could compete with you. But it taught me a good lesson."

"What kind of lesson?"

"That there'll always be people who are prettier, smarter, have better clothes . . . but I can still be the best person I can be . . . and I didn't have to compete with others and win in order to validate my own self-esteem."

Margo's quizzical expression wilted. She buried her face in her hands. Her shoulders wracked with sobs.

"I know I don't deserve your help," she announced on an upwardly spiraling wail. "But if you could just forgive me. We were so stupid, Aspen. I'm sorry if I said things to hurt you."

Not if. When. When you said things to hurt me.

"Over and done with."

Big fat lie. Their taunts had shattered her self-esteem.

Margo sniffled back her dignity. Dabbed her eyes with the napkin without any clue that her nose had turned red and mascara had left tracks down her face. "So you'll keep looking into this deal with the car?"

"My pleasure." But behind the thumbs-up, Aspen was thinking ugly thoughts.

Because the way Margo Sommervel made it sound, the car took precedence over her sister.

Margo suddenly brightened. "So how come you need a place to stay?"

CHAPTER
TWENTY-NINE

Aspen took Margo up on her offer to use Candy's condominium. For one thing, the answering machine was still hooked up and she wanted to listen to the message from Pop's Auto Salvage and Repair. For another, the police had finished combing the place looking for clues. If they'd found a breach in Candy's security system, Margo would've mentioned it.

But the main reason Aspen wanted to occupy the condo was to snoop through Candy's things. You could find out a lot about a person by rummaging through their personal files.

Margo gave her the guided tour.

Candy had lived in a two-story condominium in the established, expensive Monticello neighborhood on the west side of Fort Worth. Her father had purchased it for her six months before in an effort to keep her from heading for New York City with a degree in fashion and design — a gift that had not gone unchallenged by Margo.

"He said I'd already married Biff so he knew I wasn't going to leave Texas. But Candy was hot for the Garment District, so Daddy bought the condo. He thought New York City was too violent. I told her she ought to be interning in Paris, not commercializing her talents in New York. Turns out she would've probably been better off on another continent, after all."

Margo flipped on the lights.

The upstairs bedroom had a queen-sized bed with a deep, plush-top mattress and box springs dressed with white damask Waterford linens. Positioned across from a set of French doors that led out onto a small, wrought-iron balcony, the bed looked like a huge marshmallow floating in a cup of hot chocolate against the mushroom-colored carpet. The walls had been painted white with the faintest tinge of buttercup yellow, enough to soften the glare and still reflect the ambient light. A chocolate velveteen settee covered with pale yellow silk throw pillows had been positioned against one wall. An ice green tank top and matching leggings were draped across one arm of the sofa, as if Candy had only stepped out for a moment before returning to dress for exercise class.

Next, Margo ushered Aspen off to the guest bedroom — a childhood re-creation decorated in Barbie pink with trophies, ribbons, a cheerleading megaphone and pictures of Candy as Homecoming Queen her senior year in high school. The bed looked more like a multi-layered birthday cake with its pink silk bedspread and Battenburg lace trim. No doubt, the Drummond sisters had everything a girl could wish for.

Downstairs, the chic living room made a bold statement with its red leather couch and matching club chairs, black Berber carpet and white walls. All of the accent furniture had been lacquered in jet black, including a state of the art entertainment center. Chinese fish bowls popped up throughout the house like toadstools after a steady rain. Ranging in size, they held silk orchids, Ficus trees and even a few palm trees that looked real upon cursory inspection.

The kitchen turned out to be the plainest room in the house. Aspen didn't think Candy spent much time there since the stainless steel appliances appeared unused. The refrigerator contained soda pop, flavored water and an unopened package of processed luncheon meat, three days past expiration. On the countertop, a sealed loaf of wheat bread had already started to mold. The cupboards held food staples of packaged noodles, rice, teabags, salt and pepper and onion powder, along with crystal wine stems and an antique set of Haviland Limoges china.

Margo handed over a key fob. "I'll pick this up from you later. Let's plan to meet in a couple of days and catch up on what you've found out. And don't forget to lock up when you leave."

"Where's the answering machine? I'd like to listen to that message."

Margo ushered her back into the living room, where a small answering machine sat next to a phone. She pressed the button.

"Hi, this is your sister," Margo's recorded voice blared. "Biff has to work tonight and I'm stuck with the kids. If I can get a sitter, do you want to go to the Stockyards?"

Margo's eyes welled. "It's not too far down. I don't know how to work the machine and I don't want to take a chance on erasing anything. The cops have a tape of these, but her voice is still on the recording and I can't bring myself to erase it."

The machine shrilled, then cycled to the next message.

"Candy —"

Aspen recognized the voice of one of the brunette sorority sisters.

"— I simply have to borrow your black Escada. I promise I'll have it dry cleaned before I bring it back. If you'll help me out this one time, I'll loan you my Ungaro. Call me."

The machine shrilled. Another message came on.

"Um, yeah. I'm calling from Pop's Salvage. Your car's ready. You have to settle your bill and pick it up by the day after tomorrow or we'll sell it. Check your contract, it's all in there. We can't store it 'cause we don't have the room, okay? So you have to come get it. We prefer cash but we'll take a check if you can't get by the bank. See ya."

Aspen said, "Replay it."

After listening to it three times, she rifled through her purse and transcribed the message. On the fourth replay, Margo said, "I'll stay here as long as you want to listen to this. But once I leave, don't mess with it. Okay?"

"No problem."

"You need a ride to work tomorrow?"

"I do, but I doubt if you'll want to get up at three in the morning to take me."

Margo scrunched her face. "I don't. I'll

set the alarm and Biff can come get you."

"Not necessary. I'll hitch a ride with someone from work. Or I'll take a cab."

Margo didn't put up a fuss. She wished Aspen a good night's sleep and waved good-bye at the door.

Aspen watched her leave from the balcony. As soon as the BMW's taillights receded to the size of red hots, she snooped. After starting in the master bedroom, she migrated to the Barbie shrine. But for the fact that Caramel Janine Drummond had been murdered, she'd enjoyed a perfect life.

She ended up in the kitchen, unscrewing the lid on a bottle of flavored water. As she leaned against the countertop, her eyes strayed to the refrigerator door. Three magnetic picture frames adhered to the freezer. Only two had photos.

One held a picture of Candy and Margo, their cheeks touching and eyes aglow. The other was of Candy with her arms slung around the shoulders of two sorority sisters.

Outside, the wind picked up. Trees cast spooky shadows across the window coverings. Aspen tensed.

What was that sound?

She hit the light switch and stood, frozen, in the gloom. Seconds later, she eased over to the window and pushed aside the curtain.

She didn't wait to see if her mind was playing tricks. Moving toward Candy's phone, she recited Margo's telephone number in her head.

Margo answered on the third ring. Background laughter pealed down the line.

Aspen's voice trembled. "I heard a noise outside."

"Was it a person? Because Candy used to feed a stray cat."

"I don't know."

"Aspen, if you think it's the guy that broke in, you should call the police."

How'd she know about my break-in? I didn't tell her.

"What do you know about the break-in?"

"The cops didn't find any prints. I got the idea they didn't really think anyone had actually entered the condo."

Aspen shuddered through the hurling confusion. Then she recalled their conversation as she left the wake and realized Margo was referencing Candy's burglary. The one that occurred around the time she disappeared.

Aspen mentally switched gears. "What was taken?"

"That's just it," Margo said with a trace of uneasiness in her voice, "that's why the cops thought we were overreacting. There wasn't anything taken that we know of . . . maybe rearranged. Except for the missing picture on the refrigerator. We've never been able to find it."

Aspen's heart tried to beat right out of her chest. "What was the picture of?"

"Candy. In the nude."

"Nude?"

Margo's voice went testy. "Don't act like you didn't know. My sister had an eating disorder. The picture was to remind her how pretty she was with a little meat on her bones."

"I'm sorry. I didn't know."

"And now you do. You're not going to say anything to anyone, are you?"

"Of course not."

"Because it's not nice to talk about the dead. Candy can't defend herself."

No more than I could when you gossiped about me.

"You should've told me everything you knew about her condo being burglarized."

"What difference does it make now? It's over."

"The reason I needed a place to stay is because someone broke into my house."

Dead air followed.

Margo spoke uneasily. "How come you don't have a ride?"

"The brakes went out on my car."

The silence stretched between them.

Margo's voice came out low and dreadful. "Aspen, where's your car now?"

"At a repair shop down the street from my house."

Candy's sister let out a long exhale. "So you didn't take it to Pop's to be worked on? That was smart."

A shudder went up Aspen's spine. In her heart, she knew where this was all headed.

"I just had a horrible thought," Margo said. "Did that other girl — that girl named Gabrielle — did she have a break-in?"

"Her boyfriend said someone came into her house. The police didn't believe him because nothing was taken."

"Did it occur to you that somebody from Pop's might have a hand in these deaths?"

"It has now." A loud knock sheared her attention. "I have to hang up. Someone's at the door."

"Don't answer it."

She darted a look at the balcony. "Don't worry."

She had no intention of answering it. But she wasn't about to spend the night in Candy Drummond's condo, either.

CHAPTER
THIRTY

On the second floor of the deceased's condo, Aspen tied one of Candy's twelve-hundred thread count Italian sheets to a wrought-iron rung and went over the balcony like Jane auditioning for a Tarzan movie.

She was standing at the corner beneath the glow of a sodium vapor street lamp, waiting for a taxi, when a hulking form stumbled out of the bushes. By the time she let out a guts-out shriek, the man had already pounced.

He clapped a hand around her mouth. "Don't scream."

The voice belonged to Mike Henson.

"I'm not here to hurt you. Please don't scream. You won't scream, will you? Because I have to talk to you."

Aspen tried to shake her head against the strength of the headlock.

"I'm going to let go now." Slowly, he

unhanded her.

She whipped around and took a couple of backward steps, reflexively clutching her neck. "What're you doing here?"

"I followed you. I came by your house —"

"You know where I live?" A chill snaked up her torso and settled at the base of her neck.

"Well, yes."

Her brain did a quick recap. He knew where Gabrielle lived. Gabby's apartment had been burglarized. He'd followed her to Candy Drummond's condo, but had he been there before? Was he the one who broke in? Two break-ins. Two dead girls.

Her mind processed the obvious. He knew where she lived. Her home had been burglarized. If she connected the dots and Mike Henson was the link between the homicide victims, then she'd soon be dead.

"I don't want you following me." Her words vibrated with fear.

"I have to know if you've found anything out. You haven't returned my calls."

"Stay away from me." The taxi she'd called for pulled up to the curb. Emboldened by having a witness, she spoke in a firm, lethal voice. "If I decide to talk to you, I'll ring you up. Otherwise, you're stalking me."

She climbed into the back seat and ordered the driver to take off. She ended up back at the station, bunking on a sofa in a cozy parlor that had been constructed for televised guest interviews inside the studio.

Eventually, she drifted off to sleep wondering if Mike Henson had killed Candy Drummond to throw the cops off the scent before murdering his girlfriend — his intended target.

If so, this guy was the epitome of pure evil.

CHAPTER
THIRTY-ONE

Early Monday morning, three days before Aspen's "Asleep at the Wheel" piece was scheduled to air, the Fort Worth police went on the warpath. Like a nest of spiders, they cast their web by setting up their black-and-whites down the street from WBFD. As employees turned into the parking lot, cops signaled them to pull over.

Aspen was still asleep in the studio when one of the runners shook her awake. She realized she must've been in a deep slumber, because she could've sworn she was wearing a long, emerald green Vera Wang and matching Jimmy Choos while Roger looked on admiringly as she received the Peabody Award.

She hoisted herself up on one elbow and blinked her surroundings into focus. "What's going on?" She fisted her eyes until her hands came away blackened with mascara.

He produced a traffic citation and gamely informed her of the situation. "The cops are going ape-shit crazy over your 'Asleep at the Wheel' piece. They're handing out tickets right and left. Even Gordon's getting one."

Uh-oh.

"Is he mad at me?"

"Amazingly, no. But he sent me to tell you to get your ass outside and see if you can interview them. I'll send Reggie out to meet you. Gordon thinks they'll try to sabotage the morning show by detaining everyone." He touched his lips at the corners. When she didn't get the message, he added, "You have drool crusting around your mouth."

She sprang from the sofa and dashed to the bathroom. After toweling away the black crescents beneath her eyes, she fluffed her wild hair, rinsed out her mouth, applied fresh lipstick and crunched a couple of breath mints. She snagged her jacket on the way out the door, expecting to link up with Reggie in the parking lot.

The cops had a couple of WBFD's fact checkers pulled over and were writing them tickets when she sauntered up with mike in hand.

"Get back in your car," one snarled.

"I'm Aspen Wicklow, WBFD investigative

reporter. I'm not in a car. I'm on foot."

"Then get back in the building."

Across the parking lot, Gordon's face blazed bright red. He yelled, "Don't you dare go back into that building. I want a story."

Aspen stepped back up onto the curb. "Mind if I have your name? I'd like to ask a few questions."

The cop puffed out his chest and shifted his back to her, effectively shielding his nametag from view. He spoke in an over-the-shoulder growl. "You need to leave. You're interfering with an arrest."

Aspen gasped, incredulous. "You're writing a ticket, for God's sake."

"They're still technically under arrest."

"Will you handcuff them?" Her words fell on deaf ears. She took a brazen stance. "I know who you are. I recognize you from the other night. You're just pissed off because you're one of the officers who got caught sleeping on the job."

"You're mistaken. We weren't sleeping."

"Oh, good." She snorted in disgust. "Because for a minute I thought you might be about to invent a lame excuse like . . ." She got caught up in the whirlwind of her own imagination. ". . . like 'they told us at the blood bank this might happen.' Or 'there

342

was a gunman loose in the area so we were playing dead to avoid getting shot.' " This was turning out to be terrific fun. "Next you're going to tell me you were trying to pick up your contact lens off the floorboard." She snapped her fingers. "Carbon monoxide poisoning — you were all overcome with it at the same time."

His jaw flexed. His hand-held radio squawked; he keyed the mike and answered the dispatcher. A "wanted" return from the Texas Crime Information Center revealed that a person with the same name had an outstanding warrant for Interference with Child Custody.

Turning to the driver, his mood unexpectedly lifted. "Now you're officially under arrest."

"But I don't have kids. I'm not even married. Melanie Smith is a common name — I'm telling you, that's not me."

"Tell it to the judge."

Reggie trotted out of the building. His shoulder slumped under the weight of the camcorder. He scanned the parking lot for Aspen and joined her at the curb.

She said, "Light me up."

"I've been trying to, but you never seem to notice me."

She giggled, then sobered when he spotlighted her. "Don't make me laugh. It's hard enough keeping a straight face without you egging me on."

Reggie held up three fingers. He folded them down one by one.

"This is Aspen Wicklow, investigative reporter for WBFD, coming to you live from television headquarters, where at least ten patrol cars have saturated the street in front of the entrance to our station —"

As handcuffs were ratcheted onto the wrists of another WBFD employee, Aspen tilted the mike in the officer's direction.

"— Officer, are Fort Worth police mounting a full-court press in anticipation of WBFD's 'Asleep at the Wheel' piece that's scheduled to air this Thursday?"

"No comment." He steered the employee toward his patrol car. Aspen trotted up behind them with Reggie in tow.

"Are you stopping WBFD employees in retaliation, because you were caught snoozing in your patrol car behind one of the downtown buildings with a bunch of your colleagues? Didn't the chief assign extra units to patrol downtown in response to the unusual number of burglaries in the area?"

Without a word, the officer opened the back seat of his black-and-white and stuffed the poor girl inside. The door slammed shut and he whipped around. "You're in the street."

Slow on the uptake, Aspen blinked.

"If you don't get out of the street I'll arrest you."

Aspen and Reggie stepped up onto the curb.

Near the reserved parking, Gordon stomped around, snot-slinging mad. "I want all those motherfuckers on camera."

Max drove past with a police car on his tail. He pulled over to the curb with a defective taillight winking as he applied the brake.

Aspen motioned Reggie to follow. They headed toward Gordon. While the cop wrote out the citation for an expired inspection sticker and ran a warrant check on the station manager, Gordon bellowed, "Are you getting all this?"

The camcorder continued to roll.

Gordon turned to the cop. "Hey . . . I recognize you. You're the guy in the picture on my mistress's night stand." He twirled his finger in the universal *wrap-it-up* motion. "Could you speed it up? You're wife's expecting me at the motel and I don't want to disappoint her. You know how she gets."

The policeman torqued his jaw. His face flamed and he fisted the ticket. With an angry wish for Gordon to, "Have a nice day," he presented it to him like an invitation to a gala.

Across the parking lot, the police officer scribbling out Max's ticket abruptly halted. Aspen was close enough to hear his handytalkie squawk. By way of answering the dispatcher, the cop ducked his chin and keyed the microphone clipped to his collar.

A computer check showed Max had warrants for unpaid parking tickets.

The cop stuffed the ticket book into the waistband of his Sam Browne with one hand and pulled out his handcuffs with the other. With the agility of a chimp, he spun the stocky cameraman around and ratcheted on the cuffs.

Gordon barked, "Get that on video. Get all these sons-of-bitches on video."

Max probably wouldn't have banged his head against the patrol car as the officer helped him into the back seat if he'd refrained from mouthing taunts.

"Hey, didn't I watch you getting your ass kicked on *COPS* the other night?"

The arresting officer traded insults. "You're so hairy Bigfoot snaps pictures of you."

With a lopsided grin angling up his face, Reggie switched off the camera and waited for the next bad driver to show up for work.

Fort Worth's finest bagged Steve Lennox for failing to stop behind the painted white line at the traffic signal — what Reggie called a real chicken-shit infraction. When Lennox tried to speed up the officer by saying, "Just give me the damned thing; I've got a show to do," the cop gave a brittle laugh and said, "Not if I have anything to say about it."

Overhearing this ominous comment, Gordon rushed inside with a contingency plan for anchoring the morning show.

Misty Knight failed to use her turn signal. Not that it made much difference to all the pedestrians out there jumping for safety. Careening into the parking lot with one hand on the wheel, she focused on her reflection in the rearview mirror while whisking on mascara. Beautiful Misty, with her water wing-sized chest and pea-sized brain, might've skated from getting a ticket on good looks alone. But she cemented her fate when she handed over her driver's license and lipped off.

"Bad cop! No donut!"

The officer returned a sinister smile. "Aren't you the weather girl?"

"I'm a meteorologist."

"I'm not sure you ought to be calling yourself that," he said wryly, "when the closest you'll ever come to a brainstorm is a light drizzle."

It took a few beats before Misty figured out she'd been insulted. With an audience of colleagues, she showed the policeman what she thought of his authority by committing an act of defiance. She crumpled the ticket and tossed it on the ground.

The cop promptly wrote her another one for littering.

"Don't mess with Texas," he said, tearing it off the pad and handing it over.

Bill Wallace got written up for failing to come to a complete stop at the intersection. He remained a perfect gentleman throughout the ordeal.

The officer handed him the citation and said, "How come you're so cheerful about all this?"

"Son, you're still young but I'm sixty years old. If there's one thing I've learned, it's don't sweat the small stuff."

Marginally relenting, the uniform explained how Bill could put a check in the envelope and mail in the fine.

"Thank you, officer."

"Just doing my job. Mailing the fine is for your convenience."

"I understand completely. You've been extremely professional in the way you've comported yourself this morning. But if it's all the same to you, I think I'll set it for a jury trial. Have a nice day."

The cop must've thought Bill intended to ridicule him. He snarled, "See you in court," and strode toward his patrol car.

Bill piped up. "I'm afraid I won't be seeing you again and that's a crying shame. By the time my case comes up, I'll be dead. You see, son, I have terminal cancer." The cop turned around. Bill gave him a wan smile. "Be careful out there, young man. Life is short. Treasure each day as if it's your last — the way I plan to treasure this ticket."

The patrolman frowned, confused. "You're glad you got a ticket?"

Bill glanced heavenward. "I thank the Lord for it because it means that I woke up on this side of the dirt today."

The officer stood slack-jawed. He returned to the anchorman with precision in his step.

"Let me see that." He snatched the ticket from Bill's hand and tore it into quarters. "But next time, you need to come to a complete stop. This isn't California."

Reggie edged too close to the curb and his foot slipped off. He was immediately detained for jaywalking.

Aspen rushed to his defense. "He wasn't jaywalking. He lost his balance."

The cop continued writing. He ripped the citation off his ticket book and pushed it at the photographer. "Try to see this from my perspective. The roadway is for cars. If you step into the roadway, you could get hit."

Seemingly engrossed, Reggie looked over the ticket. "I'm trying to see things from your perspective but I can't seem to get my head as far up my butt as you can yours."

Gordon burst through the glass doors and hurried her way. Caught up in the moment, Aspen grew rebar for a spine.

She spoke loud enough for the station manager to overhear. "You know, officer, I'd be the last person to tell you how to do your job. But you should remember that the badge you have on only covers a small part of your shirt — not your ass."

Gordon fidgeted like a dancing Rottweiler. "You tell them, Wicklow. You set those sons-of-bitches straight. That badge won't cover your ass."

The only major player who came away unscathed during the blitz was Rochelle. Tig Welder drew unwanted attention when he cut her off trying to beat her into the parking lot.

"Oh, no." Rochelle strutted up to the nearest cop with her eyebrows lifted like wings. A look of desperation rode on her face. "You're *not* going to look inside his Hummer, are you?"

They tore into the vehicle like gorillas on banana bread. When they came up empty, they cited him for reckless driving.

"He should treat me with more respect, you know?" Rochelle muttered to no one in particular. "Especially since we all know my taxes will be paying for his prison cell one of these days. You ask me, Tig has a real future making license plates. I have a good mind to call WBFD's legal counsel to find out if the 'because he needed killing' defense is valid in this state."

Aspen heard Steve Lennox's voice through her ear bud. The morning team had taken their respective seats and Aspen was about to be on-air.

She spoke directly to her new best friend and confidante, the camera lens.

"The police aren't asleep at the wheel this morning. But does the Mayor know about what might be considered an abuse of power? For that matter, is this an act that's been sanctioned by the police chief, or is it the work of a few renegade cops, retaliating for getting caught sleeping on the job? Since the chief has asked for additional funds to hire sixty new officers, is this the way taxpayers want to see their money spent?

Coming to you live, I'm Aspen Wicklow, WBFD-TV. Back to you, Steve."

CHAPTER
THIRTY-TWO

At few minutes before seven that morning, Aspen took a phone call from Spike Granger.

"Good morning, gorgeous-and-talented. I just watched the news. You looked wonderful. I'm particularly fond of that just-laid look. What's that hair-do called? The bed head?"

Still miffed, she pretended not to know him. "Who's calling?"

"Spike." When she didn't react, he added, "Granger."

"Oh . . . because you sound a lot like Benedict Arnold."

It took a moment for her little dig to soak in. "Wait a minute . . . are you lathered up about me going down to Austin without you?"

"No. I'm angry because you didn't give me the exclusive. You said you'd let me know when you were going to pull another one of your dumb stunts."

"Dumb stunts?" Clearly, she'd wounded him. "I'd hoped you thought I was clever. Man, did I ever miss the boat."

"How come you got Tig Welder to cover that piece? You know he's my arch-rival and yet you did it anyway." Words poured out pouty and furious. Suddenly, she disliked herself immensely for getting worked up over this hayseed sheriff with the Coke bottle lenses, leathery face and balding head. "Never mind. I apologize. Look, I'm really busy. I have to go now."

"You like me."

"What?" Her pulse thudded in her throat.

"You like me. *You love me.*" He drawled out the words, then let out an Arizona chuckle that sent chills up her ribcage. "That's the way it always happens. The ugly ones get the pretty girls."

"I don't know what you're talking about," she said in a made-up huff, wishing for another layer of clothes to put on. Granger had a knack for seeing right through her.

"It's because the ugly ones try harder. Like Avis. We know we can't compete with the Welders and Lennoxes of the world, so we excel at other things." He gave a roguish laugh. "Guess you'll have to take my word on that — for now."

"I don't care if you stand on your head and push B-Bs up the wall with your nose. I think you're a horrible person and I hope I never see you again."

"The reason I called . . . I'm heading back down to Austin. I need to be there by eight or nine tonight."

The disclosure piqued her curiosity. "What does that have to do with me?" she said in her best *Big deal* voice, but her heart was pounding out *Take me* in Morse code.

"I want you to come along. I promise it'll be worth your while."

Mildly intrigued, Aspen still stung from yesterday's snub. "How come you didn't invite me the last time you went?"

It turned out he did. But when he asked to speak to her, Rochelle told him she was out for the rest of the day and couldn't be reached. Then she routed his call to Tig.

"So . . . can you and your cameraman come down here around three this afternoon? We'll leave at four, arrive by seven or eight and I can do what I need to do."

"Might as well get the hell outta here," she said. "Gordon's madder than a blow-dried wolverine. If his neck veins get any bigger, he'll pop all the buttons off his shirt and turn into The Hulk."

"Sounds like a real guy's guy."

"Gordon's a psycho. They all are. Only Misty Knight seems like a normal person and the rest of them all think she's as weird as me."

"I like you," he said reassuringly.

"No, you don't. If you did, you would've tried me on my cell phone when you didn't get me at the office the day you went to Austin."

"I did call you. You never called me back."

Ha.

She grabbed for her cell phone and scrolled through the missed calls. Sure enough, Spike Granger's number popped up on the digital display. Sufficiently humbled, Aspen apologized.

"I'll let you make it up to me when we get back from Austin," he said with a wicked inflection.

"Before Reggie and I come down there, I have to know why we're going."

"Remember our conversation about Tent City?"

She got an ugly visual of a tent encampment ringed in barbed wire and her body tingled with chills. Surely he wasn't stark-raving mad enough to pitch tents on the Capitol grounds. "You're crazy."

"Crazy about you. The same way you're crazy about me."

"Am not."

"Are too."

"I'll get over it," she said before hanging up to track down her photographer.

Aspen and Reggie arrived at the Johnson County SO a few minutes before three o'clock that afternoon. The secretary directed them to the jail yard where Granger had twenty prisoners lined up in front of him. Knapsacks rested at the feet of each inmate.

Granger lifted a whistle hanging from a cord around his neck and blew three sharp trills into it. He thumbed the start button on a stopwatch and studied the men like a coach at practice the night before the big game. Inmates collectively grabbed their gear. They worked as a team, ripping into their knapsacks like jackals on a prime rib. With the last pup tent pitched, Granger consulted his stopwatch.

"Billy Ray, if you don't improve your timing when we get down to Austin, I'll shoot you where you stand."

"Yes, boss."

"Leander, if you move any slower I'll handcuff you to the front doors of a nursing home."

"Yes, boss."

"Jimbo, Skeet, Ruben . . . nice job."

"Yes, boss," they chorused.

"The rest of you ladies —" that evoked a series of groans "— need to try harder. Think of this exercise as a scene from *Stripes* where that rogue platoon out-performed all the other platoons."

The one called Leander launched into a couple of dance moves, hollering, "Boom-shaka-laka-laka, boom-shaka-laka-laka," and the others merrily joined in to show Granger they remembered the movie.

"Any of you run, I'll put a bullet in your back. Deliver a great performance and I'll credit each of you sixty days off your sentence for each day you stay camped out there. Anybody doesn't know what to do?"

The one Granger called Billy Ray lifted a hand and pointed. "Is she going with us?"

"Yep. And if you know what's good for you, you'll get these damned tents put up in under a minute, crawl inside them and let her cameraman film you. If she decides to interview you with your head sticking out of the flap, there are three rules: no cursing, no spitting and no playing with yourselves. Just because you're on display doesn't mean you can act like gorillas jerking off in the primate cage. Now pack up your gear; then get on the bus."

Granger blew three staccato bursts into

the whistle. Inmates sprang into action.

Billy Ray said, "Boss, do we have to wear these pink skivvies under our stripes?"

"Quit whining."

"But everybody'll think we're gay."

Granger looked at him squinty-eyed. "You shot your old lady in the back and you're worried people will think you're gay? Quit carping and load up."

With Reggie still filming, the sheriff took a brass spittoon and a handmade sign on a stake that had Hug-A-Thug printed on it and headed for the Bluebird.

"So what's the spittoon for?" Reggie wanted to know.

"Donations."

"For what?"

"To feed these sons-of-bitches. I'm not doing this as a publicity stunt, despite the fact that at least ten sheriffs a day call me to accuse me of that. I'm doing this because my budget's bone dry and I don't have money to feed these people. I'm not running a concentration camp. These people have the right to eat. I'm sick of hearing these Oliver Twist types telling my jailers they want more every time they finish their bowls of watery gruel. If the State won't house these convicted felons, the least they can do is reimburse me for feeding them.

Fair's fair."

"Why would people want to donate money to feed a bunch of crooks?"

"Because I'm turning it into a game: Hug-A-Thug. And you're going to help me promote it. 'Want to hug one of the biggest, baddest thugs in Johnson County? Come hug-a-thug. Oh, you say you'd rather not? Then drop a dollar in the pot.' "

Reggie got on board with the idea. "It's like being at the carnival and buying three balls to throw at the guy in the dunking cage."

"Right. If you want to gawk at the miscreants, then you have to pay admission, like when you go to the zoo. I even brought along a Polaroid camera and ten boxes of film in case civilians want their pictures taken with a convicted felon — murderer, arsonist, rapist, burglar or kidnapper. That'll cost 'em five dollars a snapshot. Only I'm calling them mug shots." He turned to Aspen. "What do you think?"

"Great marketing technique." She turned serious. "What happens if one of these guys tries to take a hostage or hurts a civilian?"

"I'll cap him between the eyes. And you'll have your next breaking news story."

CHAPTER
THIRTY-THREE

Granger'd heard enough complaining to last him the rest of the year. With Aspen riding shotgun in the bus while Reggie followed in the SNG truck, they could hardly carry on a conversation without the convicts' constant interruption.

Leander wanted the radio turned up. Skeet wanted it volumed down. Billy Ray wanted the channel changed and Jimbo wanted it off. The ride down to the Capitol had been like hauling around a bunch of whiney, snot-nosed brats — except that a couple of these cons had killed people. They took turns bitching about the chill on the bus and when Granger flipped on the heater, they bitched about the heat.

"Boss, we been in the tank with nothin' but green baloney and we need real food," Leander said in a plaintive wail.

"Boss, I bet you didn't know I'm diabetic, did you?" Jimbo.

Granger pulled down the visor and glanced in the mirror. "If you slip into shock, we'll call you an ambulance. Otherwise, I don't need to hear it." He made a sharp right turn and a dozing inmate slid off the slick metal seat and thudded to the floor.

Aspen found Granger easy to talk to. Eventually, the conversation turned to Mike Henson. Aspen thought he was creepy, but to be fair, she included information that would suggest that the grief-stricken Henson just wanted justice for his dead girlfriend. Granger called him a stalker.

"Can you do a background check on him?"

"Are you asking me to run a criminal history?"

"Yes."

The sheriff nodded. "A CCH will show if he has any arrests or convictions — or both. Where's he from?"

"I don't know. I've spent so much time giving him the bum's rush that I haven't asked many personal questions."

"Let's start with Texas. Then I'll run him through NCIC — the National Crime Information Center — to see if anything comes up out of state."

"You can do that?"

"Little darlin', I can do anything."

"Do me one more favor?" She did a quick lean in. Her smile slipped away. "Run a check on Rochelle LeDuc, too."

Streetlamps blinked on as the Bluebird rolled past the Austin city limit around dusk Monday evening. Before heading for the Capitol, the Sheriff pulled into the first McDonald's he saw, wheeled into the drive-through and ordered twenty Happy Meals with burgers, fries and diet cola — cut the toys. He didn't want his prisoners on a sugar high any more than he wanted them fashioning their prizes into weapons. Instead of clogging the pass-through artery, Granger parked the bus on the far side of the fast food restaurant and waited for one of the employees to bring out the order.

For himself, Aspen and Reggie, Granger brought along a cooler filled with home-made corned beef and baby Swiss sandwiches on rye. They ate outside at a picnic table near the Bluebird, far enough away from the taunts and jeers of the inmates; close enough to keep an eye out in case the prisoners went mad cow on them.

"Excited?" Granger asked of neither in particular.

Reggie head bobbed. "It's cool." He polished off the last of his sandwich, then washed it down with an Evian from the truck.

The sheriff looked over at Aspen. "What're you going to say on camera?"

"Don't know. Depends on what happens when your Boy Scouts jump out and pitch their tents."

She didn't want to tell him that the main thing she'd learned so far in the short time she'd done the investigative reporting thing at WBFD was that even if she started out covering his Hug-A-Thug stunt, she'd probably end up reporting a shooting if the convicts made a break for it. She wanted Granger's plan to work and she wanted to be the one breaking the exclusive when it did. What she didn't want was to end up testifying before the grand jury for three hours, explaining, play-by-play, the footage Reggie shot of Granger picking off inmates like a greenhorn at the carnival shooting gallery.

At nine o'clock, after they'd finished their sandwiches, she said good-bye to the sheriff and joined her photographer in the truck.

They followed behind the Bluebird as Granger motored down the freeway toward the Capitol. He took the designated exit and coasted to the curb. Reggie pulled up next to the driver's window and Aspen powered down the glass.

Granger said, "When I was here the other day, I found a nice spot to set up camp. Problem is, with the Special Session in progress, Capitol Police may be crawling all over the place. What I need," he hesitated, "is for someone to make a drive-through."

He wanted them to scout for cops. Gordon's warning rang in her ears.

Never become part of the story.

Reggie volunteered to swing through. No one would think twice about the WBFD truck if other stations were covering the Special Session.

Meantime, Granger ordered the convicts to slump down in their seats so they couldn't be seen from the roadway. Or from a passing patrol car.

When they'd gone the equivalent of a block, Aspen twisted in her seat. "Are you nervous?"

"Heck, no. This is great. He's so cool. Man, I used to hate cops but this guy's rad. He doesn't just sit there going *Wah-wah-wah* when something ruins his day — like all those lazy bums, sleeping on duty, turning around and retaliating by writing chickenshit tickets — he takes action." He expelled a passionate breath. "I love it when the little guy wins."

"Ever hear about him pushing a Mexican national out of an airplane?"

Reggie corkscrewed his face. "Where'd you hear that?"

"Rochelle."

He debunked the notion with a heavy eye roll. "Rochelle's in charge of Black Ops."

He'd used the unconventional warfare term for Black Operations, comparing Rochelle's methods of disseminating misinformation to covert missions that are highly secret due to questionable ethics and legalities. Reggie's description fit Gordon's assistant to a "T."

"So he didn't shove the guy out of a plane?"

By way of answering, Reggie gave her a slow headshake. "When you're dealing with Rochelle, you've got to take things with a grain of salt. It'd be different if she mentioned that ugly business about Gordon killing his first wife —"

"Gordon killed his first wife?" Aspen's voice nearly went ultrasonic.

Reggie let out a belly laugh. "That's what I'm talking about. Stop being so gullible."

"So Gordon didn't kill his first wife?"

Reggie shook his head. "Gordon's first wife is his only wife and she's very much alive — heaven help him — and I only say that because she's high-maintenance."

"So that stuff about the sheriff was just —"

"Rochelle messing with you."

The tension in her neck instantly unwound. Relieved, she sank against the seat back and reflected on scencry so beautiful that it almost took her breath away. "Then Granger's cool?"

"Ubercool," Reggie said.

Aspen smiled inwardly. Granger was like a . . . super hero.

Up ahead, a Capitol police car turned into a parking lot. With the reconnaissance mission completed, Reggie doubled around and returned to the bus.

"There's one prowling this area," he told Granger. "We left him cruising one of the parking lots."

Granger fired up the Bluebird. The bus lurched forward and rumbled up the curve in the road. He picked his spot and killed the engine. Reggie parked the SNG a few car lengths ahead in case things went south and Granger needed to make a quick getaway.

Trees cast shadows across the Capitol grounds like gray doilies pulsing on the lawn.

"All right, you guys . . . move like your

hair's on fire and your goat-smellin' ass is catchin'." The sheriff blew three short whistle bursts and stepped off to one side as the prisoners scrambled out of the bus. They set up their tents and disappeared inside them.

Granger's next act of defiance was to sledgehammer the Hug-A-Thug sign deep into the ground. He loaded the Polaroid with film and waited for civilians strolling through — or Legislators packing it in for the night.

Aspen listened for the voice of one of the anchors to come over her ear fob. When she heard Misty Knight say they were standing by, she gave Reggie the OK sign.

The overhead spotlight lit up the night.

"Ready anytime you are, Aspen," said Steve.

Reggie did the countdown.

"Good evening, I'm Aspen Wicklow, reporting live in Austin where Spike Granger, Sheriff of Johnson County, has implemented his Hug-A-Thug program at the State Capitol. Granger, who infuriated members of the Criminal Justice Committee several days ago when he launched his Adopt-A-Con program, refuses to take the Texas Department of Criminal Justice's housing freeze on inmates lying down. Tonight, the sheriff's inviting law-abiding citizens to venture down to the State Capitol and select an inmate from Granger's tent city and . . . well, as he says . . . 'hug a thug.' "

She didn't mean to slide him an adoring glance, but when they made eye contact and he winked, her eyes crinkled at the corners and her lips turned up.

"The inmates, who are all convicted felons, are being housed in the Johnson County Jail until the prison overcrowding issue is resolved, and Granger says he doesn't have money in the budget to feed them. Anyone wanting to have their mug shot taken with murderers, thieves, kidnappers, rapists, robbers and burglars can donate five dollars to Granger's Feed-A-Felon fund and take away a Polaroid memento to commemorate the event and impress friends."

Reggie zoomed the lens on a family of five who strayed into camera range.

As Granger hawked photo ops, they shooed the children back into their protective embrace. A young couple seemed to be game. After a brief chat, Granger hollered for Leander to come out of his tent and have his picture taken with the man.

He took the five dollars and dropped it into the brass spittoon.

"Who's next?" he shouted to no one in particular. Several more takers strolled up and paid. Within a few minutes, bystanders were on cell phones making calls.

Aspen continued her presentation. "Well, Steve, it looks as if Sheriff Spike Granger's Hug-A-Thug business is booming. The Committee on Criminal Justice met in an emergency session over the weekend and Governor Woolsey has called an emergency session of the Legislature, which is meeting now."

An elderly couple who'd been hanging around like cloves on a ham found themselves in her path. Aspen made a quick decision to conduct a man-on-the-street interview.

"You, sir . . . and you, ma'am . . . would you mind if your taxes went up a few dollars if it meant keeping prisoners behind bars?"

The lady gripped the old gent's arm. She spoke in a quavering voice, dripping with sugar. "Well, honey, I believe I'd be all for it. But even if they let 'em run around loose, that'd be fine, too. Eldon and I — Eldon's my husband; we've been married more than fifty years — we carry his-and-hers Sig Sauers, equipped with laser sights, so it doesn't matter if they're locked up or running around. We'd just as soon cap 'em as not, wouldn't we, Eldon?" She glanced up at her spouse. Old eyes brimmed with love.

Aspen blinked, slack-jawed. Mental note for new investigative story: Interview DPS on their mental health criteria for issuing permits to carry firearms.

Granger's Hug-A-Thug program turned out to be a rollicking success.

Then Billy Ray decided to escape.

Granger whipped out his Taser and fired. Contact leads hit the convict in the middle of the back and Billy Ray went down like a tranquilized buffalo.

Jimbo and Skeet started to bolt, but Granger grabbed a shotgun. The bone-chilling sound of a ratcheted round in the chamber filled the night.

Aspen went rigid.

Both men froze.

"One more move and you sons-of-bitches will lose more than just your good time."

CHAPTER
THIRTY-FOUR

After Granger ran out of Polaroid film, he retrieved all the money from the brass spittoon, counted it out and pocketed it.

"Not a bad haul." He winked at Aspen.

"C'mon Reggie, let's call it a day." She moved toward the SNG truck but Granger called them back. The inmates, belly-chained and wearing leg irons, had a special performance for the Criminal Justice Committee.

"We're paying them a visit," said Granger.

"Holy cow." Aspen's eyes bulged. "You'll never get inside the Capitol with these prisoners. I can't believe you made it this far without getting run off by Capitol Police. What happens if the cops don't let you inside?"

"I'll worry about that when the time comes."

She looked over at Reggie, who'd apparently grown testicles the size of medicine balls. He said, "I'm game."

"Come on, ladies, you know what to do," Granger yelled.

The inmates lined up, military style.

Granger took out a bag of handcuffs. He hooked each inmate's belly-chain to the belly-chain on the prisoner in front of him until they resembled a trotline of bottom feeders. If anyone tried to make a break for it, they'd be moving at the speed of a centipede wearing cinderblock sneakers.

Reggie posed a question to the sheriff. "Do you really think you'll be able to sneak these men inside?"

Granger tilted the brim of his Stetson up. "This is an open meeting. Anybody can observe."

"But what if the cops say these guys are dangerous?"

"Then the story is that we're here for them to give testimony on the overcrowded prison conditions."

"What happens when they're through testifying?"

Aspen did a heavy eye roll. Reggie could be gullible at times.

Billy Ray, the leader of the chain gang, still had the contact leads to the Taser stuck in him. Granger warned him not to pull any crap. Then he gave Billy Ray the go-sign.

The inmates launched into military marching cadence that bore all the elements of a nursery rhyme delivered while on PCP. They tuned up and sounded off a variation of the Duckworth chant.

"I don't know but I've been told,

"Penitentiary's mighty cold.

"Jury said I did the crime,

"Now I got to do the time.

"Sound off, one, two,

"Sound off, three, four.

"Sound off, one, two . . . three, four."

They were halfway up the Capitol steps when Capitol Police intercepted Granger on the landing. The prisoners marched on as if Granger had already scoped out the location of the Criminal Justice Committee and told them which way to turn. Strong male voices echoed through the Rotunda.

"Warden, he says keep us out.

"Sheriff had to use his clout.

"Now we're at the CJC,

"Give us food and a place to pee.

"Sound off, one, two,

"Sound off . . ." Their voices faded.

Reggie and Aspen trotted up the steps, past Granger and the police, and trailed the prisoners to the Criminal Justice Committee meeting room. Billy Ray banged the door open. The rest of the chain gang followed him inside. Everyone sat in stricken silence as the convicts trickled into the gallery.

"We joined the chain to have our say,
"And tell the Ledge we ain't goin' away.
"If we don't get a place to stay,
"We be in your 'hood, havin' our way.
"Sound off, one, two . . ."

Aides and pages scurried to the telephones.

"Sound off, three, four . . ."

Senate Chairman Ditcomb grabbed a gavel and bellowed, "Who brought these miscreants in? What're these thugs doing here? Where are these damned convicts supposed to be?"

The chain gang chorused, "In the pen, men."

Without warning, they shuffled toward the nearest pillar, chanting, "Boom-shaka-laka-laka, boom-shaka-laka-laka." Once they'd completely encircled it, Billy Ray came up behind the last man and clicked a handcuff onto the back of his belly-chain.

Granger's men were there to stay.

House Chairman Villalpando roared out a string of profanity in Spanish. Whatever she said needed no translation.

Leander shouted, "Whatsa matter, Senator? Everybody go runnin' out? Better stick around. You wouldn't want to miss all the excitement."

"Where in the hell is that psycho Granger?"

The chain gang let out a collective yell. "On the bus, Gus."

Billy Ray locked eyes with Representative Villalpando. "I'm partial to Mexican women. Why don't you come on over here and rub some of that Spanish fly on my hot tamale."

Villalpando filled the room with one of her South-o'-the-Border shrieks.

Reggie caught it all on video.

State troopers fanned out through the corridors with guns drawn.

Aspen tilted the mike to her lips. "It appears Sheriff Spike Granger, like Elvis, has left the building. And now it's up to the Criminal Justice Committee to figure out what to do with the chain gang. Reporting live from Austin, I'm Aspen Wicklow, WBFD-TV, where we want to be the station you take to bed, as much as we want to be the station you wake up with. Back to you, Steve."

The Bluebird was nowhere in sight.

Aspen turned at the sound of Granger's voice and saw him waiting behind the

WBFD truck. While Reggie unloaded his gear, the sheriff pulled her off to one side.

"Want to ride back with me?" His soft, hypnotic voice almost convinced her she should.

She cut her eyes toward Reggie. Dog-tired, she was sick of keeping vampire hours. At least with Reggie, she could curl up in the seat and sleep. Granger, on the other hand, would expect her to keep him company.

"I can't ask him to make the trip back alone."

"Scared?"

She took stock of the tips of her shoes. "Maybe. I don't know. Should I be?"

"I'm crazy about you." He stuck out a meaty hand and gently grazed her cheek. "You're an amazing woman, Aspen. I can't stop thinking about you."

"Really?" She stared into the gray depths of his eyes, wanting to believe it. But she had a sneaky suspicion he was proposition-ing her with lines collected from a TV soap opera, or worse — from the Lifetime Movie Network. Without warning, old self-esteem issues tugged at her. If it wasn't for the new job, would he still find her amazing?

She stared up into a pewter gaze that sparkled with vitality.

"It's not healthy," he said. "I've found myself out on calls, distracted. You have the potential to turn my birth certificate into a worthless document."

"What's that supposed to mean?"

"You could get me killed."

"Then stop thinking about me."

"I know what would help." His voice trailed. "If you'd just go ahead and kiss me, I'd stop thinking about what it'd be like. How about it? Care to save a man's life?"

The thought sent a thrill up her neck. She looked around for spectators. They were too close to Reggie, still rummaging through the SNG, securing camera equipment and re-spooling cable. Still, if she worked fast, she could probably sneak in a peck on the cheek . . .

Granger slid his hand around her neck and pulled her close. Slowly, softly, their lips met. Her name was a rasping cry against her mouth. His tongue forged its way in.

The sheriff's kiss was delicious.

The man downright took her breath away.

He pushed her far enough away to make eye contact. "I think of you all the time."

She closed her lids, lulled by the hypnotic resonance of his voice. Gripping his arms to keep her balance, she melted into his body.

He issued an invitation. "Come home with me."

Aspen barely repressed a giggle. Reggie was so sweet, looking anxious and vaguely resentful, sitting behind the wheel of the truck, pretending not to see them in the rearview mirror.

"What's your next move, Sheriff?"

"I thought I'd take you to this little place I know —"

"I'm speaking in terms of your next political stunt. I want an exclusive."

He did a non-committal shoulder lift. "Inmate Idol. A talent competition. Like *American Idol,* only with crooks. Want to be a judge?"

"You can't be serious." But already, she was thinking of herself as the new Paula Abdul of music entertainment.

"Why not? We could sell tickets. That would cover the cost of watery gruel and green bologna. Meantime, I'm working on another idea: *Pretty in Pink.*"

"What's that?"

"I'm having new jail uniforms made. I figure now that I've emptied out the last of the convicted felons, I'll implement one of those prevention programs," he deadpanned in that deep baritone. "Get booked into the Johnson County Jail and you wear a pink jail uniform. If they don't want to look like flaming fairies, then they can go somewhere else to commit their crimes."

Rednecks in pink?

Granger might be onto something. And he had another bright idea in the works.

"A magic show. Remember me telling you about Buster Root, the jailhouse Houdini?"

Only a vague recollection sprang to mind.

"Buster and I go way back." His hand dropped from her waist. "We were good friends once upon a time, but now he's locked up in my facility. Only Buster doesn't much care for the accommodations and now he's become a flight risk. So I found a way to turn that to my advantage."

Aspen cocked her head.

"See," he explained, "I need to put on a campaign fundraiser in case I get an opponent in the next election. And since my intelligence-gathering sources keep telling me Buster's plotting a jailbreak, I figured I might as well invite him to perform a few magic tricks at my fundraiser for old time's sake and maybe it'll get this escape nonsense out of his system."

"Isn't that a bit cavalier? What if he really flees?"

He rested a hand on the butt of his Colt. "Unless he can run faster than a thousand feet per second, I'm not too worried. Now kiss me again."

She did. This time it was even more dizzying than before.

In a lightheaded rush, she backed away with reluctance, wondering when she'd see him again.

Instead of returning home, Aspen spent the rest of the night crashing at WBFD, in the parlor used for guest interviews on the morning commute show.

Early Tuesday, around ten after four in the morning, Rochelle entered the staging area carrying two cups with the Starbucks logo on them.

"I understand why you think I'm a jerk, but I never intended to do anything underhanded. I don't want you to think badly of me, so here."

While Aspen fisted away sleep, Rochelle handed over a steaming chocolate mocha. "Surely you know I couldn't possibly think any less of you," Aspen said.

It took a moment before Rochelle realized she'd been insulted. "Touché."

Aspen peeled off the lid and let the vapors snake up her nose.

"I want to clear the air. You've been working hard. Gordon's insensitive. Tig's a world-class jerk, bless his heart. My body's a chemical and hormonal battleground. And if you win the slogan contest and still don't have a boyfriend, I want you to take me on the four-day trip to the Bahamas."

"A cup of coffee in exchange for a cruise?" She oozed sarcasm. "Sounds fair to me."

Tig walked by and they immediately clammed up.

Without invitation, he insinuated himself into their conversation.

"How's it going, Barbie?" He raised a finger to Rochelle. "I want you to call Red Hot Tunes again and tell those mouth-breathers to quit sending that heavy metal shit. I got something in the mail yesterday by some group named Addicted Devil Whore. With a hit song called *Sucking Ice Cubes in Hell.* I don't want rap, I don't want heavy metal, I don't want rock-and-roll, I don't want their damned CDs, period. Got it?"

Rochelle uttered a mournful, "Bless your heart." She twisted her head to meet his gaze. "You're like a booger I can't flick off."

Tig's startle reflex engaged.

"Swear to God —" Fake sweetness and light drained from her face, replaced by daggers and slander. "Tig, if you ask me to do one more thing for you today, I'll slap you so hard they'll have to excavate through the body impression in the sheetrock to dig you out. Bless your heart."

WBFD's uberstar beat a hasty retreat.

Apparently, venom was acceptable as long as Tig's heart was blessed with each new indictment.

Rochelle unexpectedly brightened. "So, what'd you do over the weekend?"

They traded details of their escapades, with Rochelle mentioning she had a nice visit with her son who'd dropped by to dump his two dogs on her while he left town for a week to look for a job. Aspen shared the story of discovering Wexford Wicklow in bed with her mother.

Once she finished painting that raw picture, Rochelle said, "Think about it — here they hated each other for decades and now they've found love again during the twilight years of their lives. Don't you think that's kind of romantic?"

About as romantic as two naked fat guys slathered in bacon grease.

"I see the makings of a feature story. If you run up on a week where the only tips coming in are from pissed-off Texans complaining about all these Spanish billboards popping up like weeds at the Yard of the Month club, you could do a slice of life piece on your parents."

"I'm glad you find my pain entertaining," Aspen said sarcastically. "It's a wonder the man can get his shoes on the right feet. He's got a mind made of mush and the sexual stamina of a mechanical bull."

Rochelle handed over a bunch of faxes, rolled into a cylinder and rubber-banded. "Here. Don't say I never gave you anything."

"What's this?"

"I scrounged through the tips. You have some good ones in there."

"Thanks. I need a favor."

"Anything. Need a kidney?"

"I'd like to borrow your Z. I need to check in with Tranquility Villas to make sure those dements haven't tied the knot."

She met Rochelle at her desk to pick up the car keys and found her examining a hand-written placard someone left on her blotter that read *Does Not Play Well With Others.* Rochelle was holding a magnifying glass up to a document signed by Tig, while performing a handwriting comparison on the placard.

"I've asked Gordon to fire Tig five times. Each time I asked, he said he couldn't. This time, I told him if he doesn't fire him, I'll throw him through the plate glass window."

"Don't worry about Tig," Aspen said reassuringly. "You can't go through this world annoying people and still lead a charmed life. He'll get his."

"Soon, hopefully. But just to speed things along, I stopped by the porn store last night on my way home and pulled out all those subscription cards from the grossest gay magazines I could find. Before I leave work today, I'm going to fill them all out and drop them in the mail. He should start receiving his subscriptions in a few weeks."

CHAPTER
THIRTY-FIVE

In the director's office at Tranquility Villas, Harriet Ramsey had her chair positioned so she could see out her corner windows. When Aspen sauntered in late Tuesday morning on a couple hours' sleep, the director was on the phone with an angry caller, attempting to pacify the person at the other end of the line about what happened to "poor Mr. Gentry." Seeing Aspen enter the doorway, Mrs. Ramsey held up her hand like a traffic cop, halting Aspen in her tracks.

She spoke into the mouthpiece. "A problem just cropped up. I'll call you back." After replacing the receiver in its cradle, the woman rose and lumbered around the desk.

"He's incorrigible." Her lips thinned into a crimson thread.

"Now what?"

"He masterminded a wheelchair race and took bets on it like a common bookie."

"You're talking about a man who picks up

the salt shaker to sugar his coffee."

Mrs. Ramsey gave a derisive grunt.

"Where were the staff members?" Aspen shot a furtive glance at the nurses' station. "Why didn't they stop it?"

Mrs. Ramsey wagged her finger. "He's cagey, that Wexford Wicklow. He made up some cock-and-bull story to get the attendants out of the courtyard and they fell for it. Once they left the group unattended, that's when the crazy bast — your father — started the wheelchair races. Poor Mr. Gentry got rammed from behind and now he has whiplash. He's at the ER getting an MRI."

"Where's my father?"

"I have no idea. If there's a God, he's wandered off and doesn't remember how to get back."

Aspen grew a backbone. Wexford Wicklow might be a pain in the ass, but he didn't deserve to be wandering around out in the elements, scared and alone and vulnerable to criminals; or lingering near death by isolated, backwoods railroad tracks.

"You damned sure better hope that doesn't happen." She imagined herself dolled-up, out in front of the portico, doing an exposé on nursing homes.

The director said, "They should both be

thrown out of here."

"Not both of them. Look at it this way, Mrs. Ramsey, at least my mother's a calming influence."

"You call dancing topless on top of a cafeteria table a calming influence?"

"Hey, if God didn't mean for women to dance on table tops, He wouldn't have created busboys to clear off the dishes." She clapped a hand to her mouth. Where'd that come from? For God's sake, she was starting to spout Grangerisms.

Mrs. Ramsey had a talent for bringing out the absolute worst in her.

"Half of these men are demanding Cialis. Your father helped them circulate a petition. He's a menace, I tell you. Since that crazy Irishman came to Tranquility Villas, the nurses are calling the place Chaotic Courts."

"I have to leave. I have to get back to work. Just don't let them get married. I don't care what you have to tell them; I don't care what you have to do. Just don't let that chaplain go near them. Understand? I'll figure out how to get them under control, but *do not let them get married.*"

Aspen's heels clicked loudly against the sidewalk as she headed for Rochelle's Z. Without warning, Mike Henson popped up in her path. Aspen sucked air.

"I'm sorry. I didn't mean to scare you."

"Stop following me."

"I'm not following you."

"What do you call this?"

"I have to talk to you about Gabby."

"If you have anything else to discuss with me, make an appointment." She hit the remote and the locks on Rochelle's Z popped open. Aspen got inside, closed the door, fired up the engine and watched Mike Henson recede in the rearview mirror.

Back at the station, a man from the car repair place called to say the Accord was ready to be picked up. Aspen found Reggie and asked for a lift, but he was about to leave the station with Tig "to shoot Golden-Throat's eight-liner story."

Overhearing the conversation, Steve Lennox chimed in. "I can take you."

"Really? You don't mind? It's about five miles from here."

Steve assured her distance wasn't a problem. He told her to get her stuff and meet him in the parking lot. When she came outside, she didn't see him. But she did hear music filling the air. When she walked toward the sound of Roy Orbison, she caught Steve lip-syncing behind the wheel of a canary yellow Corvette.

On the way to the auto shop, they talked about the trip to the Bahamas.

"I liked your slogan." Steve shot her a sidelong glance. "If you win Gordon's contest, you should definitely take me."

"Rochelle already hit me up. Frankly, I don't think I stand a chance. It wasn't something I gave a lot of thought to. I was miffed and feeling a little snippy. Suffice it to say, my thoughts were hotwired to my tongue. I figured Gordon probably wouldn't be watching, so what harm could it do?"

"Gordon's always watching. He's omnipotent. You know that show *Cheaters*?"

Big head bob.

"Well," Steve continued, "some of us have a pool going that Gordon has them on retainer to follow us around."

"You're kidding."

Of course he was. He gave her a big grin to show he was just having fun with her.

Aspen made a subtle observation. "I can't believe your wife lets you drive around in a babe magnet like this." She caressed the buttery leather seat.

"I'm not married."

"You're not?" Unbelievable.

"We should go out," he said.

"That'd be wonderful." Her voice came

out so breathy she wished she'd exercised more restraint.

"That way you'd get a chance to talk to everybody away from work. Misty's an airhead but she's fun. We had a thing going a few months ago but it didn't work out. Thank God for EPTs. When the pregnancy test came back without a line through the round window, I bailed. And Bill —"

He's suggesting we go out in a group.

Should've known he wasn't asking me for a date.

You're just not that interesting.

"— Bill Wallace is the greatest guy you'll ever meet. I don't know anyone who knows more about the business. He taught me everything I know."

Lennox glanced at her. "Gordon's cool if you don't mind working for a confirmed perfectionist. Changing his mind once he makes a decision is like trying to herd cats. Tig's way cool. Have you had a chance to talk to him? He can really help you spiff up your presentation."

"I'll remember that." Stated politely. Aspen pointed. "Up ahead. See the sign?"

The anchorman pulled off the road, into the unpaved parking lot of Eugene's Auto Repair.

"Want me to wait?"

"Not necessary. Thanks for the ride." She couldn't bail out of that Vette fast enough.

Inside the bay area, she watched Steve Lennox churning up dust.

At the counter, the cashier presented the invoice.

Aspen did a double take. She put a hand to her mouth to stifle a gasp. Eugene's had gouged her with their prices.

"You didn't tell me I'd have to take out a second mortgage just to get my brakes repaired. And what's this extra charge for photos?" Her heart fluttered with the panic of someone who'd have to write a hot check and hope it didn't clear until Friday payday.

A fleeting thought flashed into mind. Now she understood Mike Henson's frustration when trying to settle Gabrielle's bill.

"Demitrius wants to talk to you. He did the work. He said to make you wait if he wasn't here."

"And?"

"He ain't here. He's taking a smoke break."

Aspen waited fifteen minutes before a tall, black man with angular features and skin the shade of hot chocolate sauntered in with a cigarette filter stuck to his lip. He pulled it out and stubbed it in a metal ashtray. When he shifted his stance, she saw the name *Demitrius* emblazoned on a patch stitched onto the front of his uniform shirt.

He looked at her slitty-eyed. "That's your Honda?" When she owned up to it, he said, "I had to fix the brake lines."

She rattled the invoice. "This is higher than a Georgia pine. I don't understand. I thought pads and shoes —"

"Somebody cut your brake lines."

"What?" Aspen blinked through the hurling confusion. "I don't understand."

"You owe anybody money? Pissed anybody off? 'Cause somebody sure don't like you. Matter of fact, they want to kill you. Either that or it's a case of mistaken identity. So here's what I did . . ."

She heard his voice resonating in the airspace between them; she watched his lips move and saw his tongue forming words. But she didn't hear a thing he said over the tinny, distant ring in her ears.

". . . and that's why I took pictures," Demitrius said, "because you need to take them to the police and have them look into this."

"You're saying somebody tried to kill me?" she repeated dully.

"Looks that way." He pointed to a signature blank on the invoice. "You need to sign here and pay out before I can release your car."

She pulled out her checkbook and spoke in a zombie voice. "I need to post-date this. I'd appreciate it if you wouldn't cash it until Friday; otherwise, I'll be overdrawn."

"You're saying if I throw it against the wall it'll bounce?"

"If you'll wait to deposit it on Thursday, it should go through." She abruptly stiffened. "Who'd want to kill me?"

Her mind spun with suspects.

Tig, wanting to eliminate the competition?
One of those cops?
Stinger Baldwin, for taking his job?
Somebody who had a beef with Granger?

She shook off the rest of her wild ideas.

"Sometimes it's a drug deal," Demitrius offered helpfully.

Aspen flung daggers with her eyes. She signed the check and took her keys from him. "Will you give the police a statement?"

"Reckon so. Matter of fact, I even saved the parts in case they want them for evidence." He darted out of the room long enough to retrieve an opaque plastic bag. "Sorry about the bill."

But Aspen sensed she'd dodged a bullet. "Cheap at twice the price."

Now she wanted to get Granger's take on the matter.

CHAPTER
THIRTY-SIX

By the time seven o'clock rolled around that evening, Aspen left Fort Worth Police headquarters totally disenchanted. For starters, the initial interest the detective took in her plight waned as soon as she furnished her name for his report. It was that damned "Asleep at the Wheel" piece that was about to air, and now she couldn't even get enough attention from the cops to get herself locked up. Go figure.

Then she missed the evening broadcast and had no idea what Tig reported.

She dialed the telephone number for a locksmith and waited on her front porch with Midnight until he arrived. No way would she go inside that house until deadbolts had been drilled and the locks had been changed.

As she killed time stroking the cat, she put in a call to Spike Granger. He sounded genuinely glad to hear from her. But once she gave him details of the Honda's severed brake lines, she detected an urgency in his tone when he invited her out.

"How'd you like me to buy your dinner tomorrow night?"

"I can't tomorrow," she said, remembering she'd decided to give the five-minute-date event one last shot. "But I'm free tonight."

"Give me your address and I'll be there in fifteen minutes."

Aspen laughed in spite of herself. "You can't get to Fort Worth in fifteen minutes."

"I can if I go Code-Three," he said, referring to the patrol car's overhead lights and siren.

It took only twenty-two minutes for him to arrive. The locksmith was packing up when he showed up dressed in his trademark leather vest, starched pinpoint oxford shirt and khakis, lizard boots and Stetson. A crooked grin angled up his face when he saw her. Behind the Coke-bottle lenses, nickel-colored eyes thinned until the corners of his lids crinkled.

He gave her the once-over. "You look nice."

Aspen thought so, too. For the first time in several days, she'd spent long enough in front of her closet, picking out just the right thing to wear, without listening for the haunting sounds of creaky floors or watching for phantom shadows in her peripheral vision. Tonight, she'd selected a sea green silk jacket and matching slacks over a festive Hawaiian print shell with bright pink peonies, splashes of yellow and the same sea green accents.

The cat slinked up and did a figure eight through Granger's legs. "Who's this?"

Remembering Rochelle's admonition on pedigrees, she introduced him to the stray. "This is Dammit Midnight Wicklow."

He got it immediately. "You're funny. And you're fun. So where do you want to go?"

She wanted Mexican food and he wanted Italian. They settled on burgers at Wild Dick's, where Granger insisted on eating in the corner booth. By the time the occupants left the table the sheriff set his sights on, the waitress had already seated three couples who came in after them.

The waitress jotted their order on a guest ticket; one Dickburger for Aspen and a Double-Dick with cheese for the sheriff; two colas, one diet, one regular; an order of fries and O-rings to split between them. Aspen had barely settled in and was trying to come up with something clever to say about the Austin trip when Granger stuck his hand inside his vest. He removed a couple of papers, quartered, and unfolded them.

"Mike Henson," he announced, removing his glasses and wiping them off with a napkin. He slid them back on and consulted his notes. "Seems he got in a little jam down in Houston not so long ago. Over a girl — that goes without saying. She filed a Protective Order against him and then never showed up for court. Case dropped." He stopped reading and locked her in his gray gaze. "I told you he was a stalker."

"I'll tell Gordon in case he starts lurking around the station."

"Call the cops."

"The cops aren't real thrilled with me at the moment. The piece we're airing Thursday night is called 'Asleep at the Wheel' and it's about FWPD snoozing instead of patrolling." She recounted how everyone but herself, Rochelle and a couple of maintenance people had received tickets in retaliation.

"Speaking of Rochelle —" he removed the paper on Mike Henson and slid it behind a second sheet "— I ran her license and got a copy of her driving record."

The sheriff handed it over.

Aspen scanned it with a sharp eye. Rochelle had aliases. And while she was known at the station as Rochelle LeDuc, she'd clearly been married several times because at one time her name had been Baldwin.

Chills crawled up Aspen's arms.

Stinger Baldwin.

"I love Stinger," Rochelle had said in an airy confession that came after one-too-many stems of white Zin.

The waitress slapped two frosted mugs down on cardboard coasters and sashayed off to another table.

"What's wrong?" Granger reached for her hand.

Aspen sat stricken. "I just figured it out. Rochelle LeDuc is Stinger Baldwin's mother." Her voice dissolved to a whisper.

"The investigative reporter guy?"

"*Former* investigative reporter. I took his place."

The waitress backed through the pass-way door with a tray of burgers and trappings balanced on one shoulder as Aspen returned the papers. For the next few minutes, the sheriff did most of the talking. Tuning in and out of the conversation, Aspen reflectively considered what to do to prolong her survival at WBFD. Apparently no one knew Rochelle and Stinger were a mother-son team. Maybe WBFD had a nepotism rule. Rochelle probably hired on first; Stinger came along later. Having different last names made it unlikely for any potential relationship issue to pop up. It was only in hindsight that Aspen noticed the resemblance.

A slim woman with her back to them, with long, dark hair, got up from a nearby table. She left the handsome cowboy sitting, thunderstruck, with a look of bewilderment on his face. The lady paused at the cash register before exiting. The next time Aspen shifted her attention to the table, it was empty.

Halfway through his burger, Granger stopped in mid-bite.

"What's wrong?" She wondered if he'd bitten down on glass. If the meat had a bone chip in it. If the lettuce had sand on it. Her mind raced ahead with any number of problems that might cause a person to make such a face. Heart attack? Stroke? Choking? "Are you all right?"

He shushed her with a hand, inclining his head toward the window.

Suddenly, he bolted from his seat. "Wait here."

"The heck you say." Aspen threw down her napkin and sprinted after him.

Everything happened so fast that, later, before she went to bed, she scribbled down details in a spiral notebook while the event was still fresh in her mind.

Following hot on Granger's heels, she'd arrived in the parking lot in time to see a tragic event unfold in slow motion. The cowboy from the next table wielded a pipe overhead. She sucked air as he brought it down hard against the brunette's head. A sickening thud filled the night. The woman crumpled in a heap to the asphalt.

Granger yelled, "Freeze, police." With his badge held aloft, he went for his gun.

The cowboy whirled in their direction. An orange blast lit up his hand, as if he'd hurled a bolt of fire at them. Granger grabbed Aspen and flung her into the hedge.

"Call nine-one-one," he growled.

Aspen groped for her mobile. She felt a chunk of ice where her heart should've been.

He pushed her further behind the brick wall and took cover. Balancing on one knee, he aimed his gun.

Aspen heard the squeaky hinge of a vehicle door opening. She maneuvered herself where she could see past Granger's shoulder. Her warm breath against his neck must've given away her position. Granger's hand shot up, grabbed her by the shirt and yanked her back down.

Another gun blast exploded in the distance.

Granger said, "What the — ?"

Aspen scrambled to her feet, expecting to see a dead woman's brains on the parking lot.

Instead, the cowboy lay face-up on the pavement.

Distant sirens screamed in the night. They ran to the truck: Granger, with his gun drawn and his finger whitening against the trigger; Aspen with the dispatcher still on the line, speaking in a calm, collected manner.

The cowboy's eyes were open, wide and unfocused. The woman lay on her side with her skirt on cockeyed and the hem hitched up, as if she'd dressed in the dark.

"Tell dispatch to send an ambulance." Granger picked up the cowboy's pistol and shoved it into his waistband.

Aspen rushed to help the injured woman.

Even with a bloodied head, the lady still had a death grip on her gun. The smell of cordite hung heavy in the air. Aspen lifted the victim's head and cradled it in her lap, hoping fervently that Tig Welder wouldn't show up, or any of the other stations either, for that matter.

Then she brushed the hair out of the

woman's face.

"Ohmygod. It's Rochelle."

Granger said good-bye to Aspen in the ER and accompanied a detective down to the FWPD to give his statement. Aspen stayed with Rochelle while an intern stitched her head. On the other side of the curtain, a police officer waited to get her account of the aborted abduction.

Aspen glanced around furtively. "Was it him? The guy . . . your friend's daughter?"

"Shhh. Unless you want to testify before the grand jury, let's not talk about it."

"I brought your car down here but I'll take it home with me if they keep you overnight."

"I'm not staying."

"You can't drive yourself. And you should have someone stay with you tonight in case you have a concussion."

"Fine. You can drive me home and stay over."

"I can't. Not tonight. But I called someone who can."

"Please don't say you called Misty. In a battle of wits, she's unarmed. If you stand close to her, you can hear the ocean. Don't do this to me."

"I didn't call Misty."

"You didn't call Gina from accounting,

did you? The girl's all bubbles and no cham-
pagne."

"How would I know to call Gina? I don't
even know Gina."

"You called Melanie. She's proof positive
that evolution can go in reverse. Please tell
me you didn't call her."

"I called Stinger Baldwin. *Your son.*"

CHAPTER
THIRTY-SEVEN

If Rochelle had any doubts about her value at WBFD, she only needed to shore up her self-esteem by missing work. Wednesday morning, Gordon staggered in looking like he'd been dragged through a knothole backwards. Bleary-eyed and grizzled, he started the nine o'clock meeting by reporting that he'd been to see Rochelle, and that she planned to return to work in a day or so.

"Do we have meat?" he asked the room at large.

Lennox piped up. "We have meat, boss."

Gordon went around the table. He wanted to know what each person was working on and when it would be ready. The station had moved into sweeps month and Gordon didn't want to end up in last place again. Eventually, his attention landed on Aspen.

"Will the 'Asleep at the Wheel' piece be ready to air tomorrow night?"

"It's ready now. Reggie and I put the finishing touches on it this morning."

"Fine." The lines in Gordon's face relaxed. "We'll take a look at it after the meeting. What else are you working on?"

"The Spike Granger story has tons of footage to edit but we'll be ready," Aspen said.

Gordon cut his eyes to Reggie. "You'd have to shoot ten miles of video just to make that guy look sane."

Reggie mumbled, "Coolest dude I ever met."

Aspen considered Granger a friend. Hearing Gordon poke fun at him smarted.

"He's colorful," she piped up, trying not to sound defensive. "And he probably saved Rochelle's life. I think he's a hero."

"Apparently CNN thinks he's colorful, too. They bought the footage from the Austin–San Antonio–Houston debacle."

"They what?" Aspen sat erect.

"And they bought the stunt that maniac pulled at the Capitol, too."

The news siphoned the air from Aspen's lungs. CNN? Airing her footage? The thought was exhilarating.

Across the table, Tig stewed in his own juices.

Gordon poised his pen to write. "What

else are you working on?"

"I want to do a piece on the Katrina evacuees — the ones who live downtown."

"What's so special about them? What's your angle?"

"That's just it. There's nothing special about them. They masquerade as homeless people even though FEMA gave them money. I'd like to expose the ones who're cheating the government. The night I discovered the cops sleeping on the job, I sat around the campfire with a handful of FEMA scammers. They said when the money ran out, they'd pulled little capers that would funnel them into the county's mental ward."

Tig scoffed. He picked up his Mont Blanc and doodled on his notebook.

"They were trying to get into the nuthouse?" A frown of confusion deepened between Gordon's eyes.

"Right. Once the money ran out, they'd wear tin foil on their heads or talk smack about aliens and God and CIA conspiracies. That got them locked up in the mental ward for seventy-two hours, long enough for psychiatric evaluations to be completed. The best of the con artists ended up at the North Texas State Hospital in Wichita Falls for ninety days at a cost of three hundred taxpayer dollars per day. They get free housing, free medical and free meals. I think there's a compelling story and I'd like to develop it."

"Three hundred dollars a day? I think you may be right," Gordon said. "Go for it."

Tig did a heavy eye roll. She looked at his drawing and recognized Barbie with a little microphone in her hand. Next to Barbie stood a gorilla with a camera.

Investigative Reporter Barbie.

Aspen set her jaw. Her eyes stung. Her nose burned.

"What else?" Gordon's lids thinned into slits.

"There's this mechanic . . ." Her voice warbled with the effort of speech.

Tig guffawed. "Lame. Mechanic stories are a dime a dozen."

Aspen held Gordon's gaze. "What makes this one different is that I've discovered a tie-in between Caramel Janine Drummond's murder and the murder of Gabrielle Foster. They both used the same mechanic and both of their cars were sold for scrap when they didn't pick them up on time. I pirated an invoice where it says they can do that — sell the car if the person doesn't come pick it up — it's in small print, but it's there."

Gordon listened, spellbound.

"And here's another tie-in — both girls had their homes broken into shortly after dropping off their cars for repairs."

"Interesting. What do you make of that?"

"I don't think it's a coincidence." Aspen consulted her notes. "There was no sign of a break-in, so it appears each girl either left the door unlocked or someone let themselves in with a key."

"You think the mechanic took their keys?"

"I think he may've made copies. But that's still conjecture at this point."

"Wait a minute. You're thinking he killed them?"

"There's nothing to suggest that. As a matter of fact, there's this creepy guy who's been hanging around —"

"Gordon, I hate to cut this short, but I have to leave. I'm working on the Big Kahuna and I have to meet some dignitaries," Tig said, straightening his papers into a neat stack. "Before I go, I want to discuss that matter we talked about in your office."

Gordon gave him the go-ahead.

Tig addressed his colleagues. "Yesterday, I forwarded my phone to my house. After I left, someone reprogrammed it to one of those gay sex lines. I had to do a quick soft-shoe to undo the damage with the people who called. Whoever's pulling this crap, knock it off."

Aspen's thoughts turned to Rochelle, *in absentia,* kicked back on her sofa with a fruity umbrella drink in one hand and a cordless in the other. She'd probably forwarded Tig's phone to her own home and was dishing out the dirt on him while he perfected his second career as a comic strip artist.

Gordon shuffled his papers into a neat stack. "One more thing," he said as the rest of the employees suddenly remembered they had things to do. "I've considered each of your suggestions — those who turned in slogans for the new WBFD trailer — and I decided to go with Aspen's. From now on, memorize it: *'Have dinner with us. Come to bed with us. Wake up with us. We have the news that'll make you more interesting.'* "

The announcement scorched Tig. He scurried out of the meeting like a fat rat with cheese.

Applause sounded all around. Aspen did a little chin duck in the scant hope she'd appear gracious; but inside her head she danced the tango.

Bahamas, here I come.

"So here's my idea," Gordon went on. "I want Aspen, Misty, Gina from accounting and the SMU interns to go to Victoria's

Secret and pick out some skimpy lingerie. We'll move a bed into the studio for the shoot and you'll all pile on and say, 'We're the girls at WBFD. Have dinner with us. Come to bed with us. Wake up with us. We have the news that'll make you more interesting.' " His gaze flickered to Reggie and Max. "Shoot the footage and we'll look it over. Now get on it. Procrastination's like masturbation. It seems like a good thing at the time but in the end, you're just fucking yourself."

The SMU interns wore mortified expressions.

"I'm not jumping into bed with a bunch of girls in my underwear," Misty snapped.

"I'll jump into bed with you," Steve said helpfully.

Misty scowled. "I know what . . . why don't you jump up my ass?" She turned to Gordon. "It's too suggestive. Viewers will think we're lesbians."

"It shows we're cosmopolitan. That's our target market. Just buy the damned lingerie and put it on."

"Fine," Misty said, picking up her pace as she headed for the exit, "I'll be the one wearing footy pajamas."

Aspen rose. For the first time in over a week, she felt like she belonged here. She'd made Gordon proud. He liked her ideas. Best of all, she'd left Tig Welder as bent out of shape as a pretzel.

She strode to the door with the grace of a runway model.

Gordon called her back. "I'm not accustomed to answering the telephones, but some asshole kept calling until I finally picked up Rochelle's line. It was for you. He said his name was Roger."

CHAPTER THIRTY-EIGHT

The right part of Aspen's brain wanted to return Roger's call.

The left part wanted to return Roger's call, too — once a little contact switch to trigger an explosion had been imbedded in his phone.

Her heart drummed in her chest as she fingered the pink message slip. What could he possibly want? Maybe he'd seen her on TV at the Drummond crime scene. Maybe he wanted to praise her for a good job.

Maybe he wanted to tell her his mother disapproved of the new girlfriend and insisted he escort someone more presentable to the Steeplechase Ball.

Aspen shuddered.

Just when she thought she was over him . . .

Her right brain tortured her with a series of "What ifs."

What if he's sorry he cheated? What if he

wants me back?

Her left brain mounted a counter-attack.

He doesn't want you back. Stop thinking about him. He doesn't deserve to share your space.

But what if he's finally come to his senses?

Or maybe he wants your address so he can invite you to his wedding.

Emotionally whipped, she crumpled the telephone slip and tossed it at the wastebasket. It circled the rim and disappeared. This must be how alcoholics felt when confronted with the opportunity to drink.

All she needed now was a sponsor and a twelve-step program.

Before heading home Wednesday afternoon, she stopped by Tranquility Villas. Mrs. Ramsey must've seen her through the corner windows, because she rushed out of her office and intercepted Aspen before she reached the nurses' station.

The drawn, gaunt look on the director's face telegraphed trouble.

Aspen said, "Oh, no. What happened?"

"You should be sitting down for this."

As Mrs. Ramsey herded her to the arranged seating area, she couldn't help wondering if her father had walked away from the facility. Her heart picked up its pace. "He's dead, isn't he?"

"I wish he was."

"What?"

"You said not to let the chaplain anywhere near him, but he pulled a con job on the night nurses and convinced them he was dying. He said he wanted Last Rites administered and asked for the chaplain. When the poor man got here, Wexford talked him into marrying them."

Aspen buried her face in her hands. With her elbows on her knees, she slumped forward and wept.

"If it's all the same to you, they seem very happy."

"My poor mother." She swatted off Mrs. Ramsey's attempt to pat her shoulder and groaned out her rage. "It took years for her to recover from his philandering. And now you're telling me they're married? Which way is the kitchen? I need a large butcher knife."

"For what?"

"I thought I'd go into the lobby and impale myself on it as a warning to others."

"You're overreacting."

"Am I?" Her voice spiraled upward. *"Am I?"*

She rocketed from her seat and stalked down the hall toward her father's room. When she tried the door, it was barricaded

416

from the inside by a piece of furniture. She braced her arms and threw her shoulder against the door until she forced it open a sliver.

Wexford Wicklow was deep in the throes of old-man sex.

Startled by her presence, he took her in, in a glance.

So did the woman he was screwing.

And the woman wasn't Jillian Wicklow.

"What the hell do you think you're doing?" Aspen yelled.

"What does it look like? I'm having sex with my wife."

"Your wife?"

"Damned straight. I'm on my honeymoon. Will this go on my permanent record?"

She turned to Mrs. Ramsey. "What the hell kind of place are you running here?"

The hatchet-nosed matron cleared her throat. "That's what I've been trying to tell you. This is Nellie Wicklow. Your new step-mother."

Aspen found her mother in one of the parlors, watching four women playing bridge at a card table. She set her handbag on the settee and pulled Jillian aside.

Her mother cupped a hand to her mouth and whispered, "They won't let me join them. I'm a liability because I can't remember what's been played. But they still let me watch. Isn't that nice?"

"Do you know about Daddy?"

"What about him?"

"He's married."

"Poor woman." Her brow knitted in confusion. "Wait — is that supposed to mean something?"

"Don't be upset. You were going to marry him."

"I was?"

"You know what, Mom? Never mind." She'd gotten ten steps from the front door before remembering she'd left her purse on the sofa. When she returned, her mother had already re-seated herself and was bent in concentration on the game. Aspen leaned over and kissed her cheek.

Jillian looked up surprised. "Aspen, how nice to see you." She got up from her chair and cupped a hand to her mouth. "They don't actually let me play bridge with them. I can't remember what cards have been played so nobody wants to be my partner. But they let me watch. That's nice, isn't it?"

Aspen's eyes welled. She blinked back tears. This was how all of their conversations went since the wreck — déjà vu all over again. She swallowed hard. The words she wanted to say slid back down her throat.

It killed Aspen's spirit that there seemed to be no improvement in her mother's short-term memory loss. It also simultaneously thrilled her. Jillian had no recollection of Wexford Wicklow's promise to remarry her.

That, in and of itself, turned out to be a blessing.

Aspen spent Wednesday evening back at the sports bar on the speed-dating circuit. The women were each seated at a table for two; the men lined up to join them. When the chime sounded, potential suitors rushed the tables like cowboys at a calf scramble.

Aspen ruled out her first date. It wasn't the lisp, or the toupee, or even the fact that she towered over him by a good five inches. At the sound of the tone, after she declined to give him her phone number and suggested they chalk it up to a lack of chemistry, "manly" Marvin moved on to the next table.

"Coarse" Craig took his place. Did he really pick his teeth with a toothpick during the five-minute speed date? Ugh.

She finished drawing a line through Craig's name when a shadow fell over the table. As she looked up from her tally, Mike Henson had seated himself across from her.

Aspen's jaw went slack. At this rate, the only thing left was to have a duel at dawn.

Henson held out his hand for a shake. Aspen recoiled. Her date settled in to make small talk.

"Tell me about yourself."

"I have a better idea. Why don't you tell me about you? Let's talk about why that girl in Houston filed a Protective Order against you."

The disclosure jarred him.

"Yeah. Uh-huh," she said through a nervous laugh. "You think you're the only one who can dog people? So what happened? How come she didn't show up for court? Did you do something to her? Did she go to Rhode Island to visit her aunt, too?"

Henson's jaw flexed.

"Well, come on. You wanted to talk? Let's talk."

In an amazing turn of events, Mike Henson couldn't end their speed date fast enough.

CHAPTER
THIRTY-NINE

Thursday morning, Aspen watched dawn break through her office window. She might not be important enough to demand the same square footage as Tig, but having the corner office gave her two sets of windows. As streetlights shut down in a domino effect, she swiveled her chair around, grabbed a pen off the desk and prepared to make notes on the new tip sheets she'd snagged out of the box. A plastic surgeon had botched a tummy tuck and breast augmentation on a patient's body. The woman claimed she knew others who had pending lawsuits and felt that viewers should be warned. When Aspen saw the pictures, she agreed.

Another consumer report came from an anonymous tipster who'd leaked information about pharmaceuticals being found in the municipal water supply. According to the tip, several cities in the Metroplex tested their drinking water, only to discover significant traces of anti-depressants, anti-psychotics and anti-convulsants seeping into the supply. One drug remained in the water even after treatment. Aspen caught herself nodding as she read along.

Wow.

Good news.

She should encourage her co-workers to forego bottled water and drink straight from the tap.

For no good reason, she felt the uneasy presence of an interloper in her workspace. Hairs prickled her neck.

When she glanced up, Mr. Duplicity stood framed in her doorway.

Very *Nice Day for a White Wedding.*

For a few seconds, she thought her lungs had collapsed.

Smartly dressed, with a deep, rich suntan that brightened his blond hair and made his crystal blue eyes practically jump out of his head, the guy hadn't changed a bit.

White lies, bedroom eyes, just like the song.

The cabin pressure instantly plummeted. She needed a snort of pure O_2, but the oxygen mask she fantasized would drop from the ceiling never descended.

"What're you doing here?" She barely

found the emotional strength to speak.

She busied herself by scraping her notes together and tapping them into a neat stack. It gave her something to do instead of fixating on whether the lavender pantsuit and purple knit shell set off her hair enough for Roger to realize she'd never looked better.

"I was in the neighborhood and decided to stop by."

It made no sense. They hadn't spoken since — had it really been five months? She mashed her knees together to keep them from shaking.

Her heart did a little tap dance. "How'd you know I worked here?"

"You've got to be kidding. I saw you on TV when they found that girl dumped in a ditch."

"But you don't watch WBFD. You've never watched WBFD. You said they have the lowest ratings in the Metroplex and that only boneheads watch this station." She had to remind herself that this was the man who said he wanted to marry her just as soon as he got a raise. The only raise she knew of was the one between his legs when she walked in on him and the stripper.

"That was before Satin and I saw you on TV at the sports bar."

"Satin?" she asked with a smile so forced she thought her jaw would go numb. She wanted to thunk her forehead with the heel of her palm. Of course. Satin. The ecdysiast. "Right. Your girlfriend." She could actually feel her retinas pounding.

"It was a flirtation."

An insult to her intelligence. It was enough to make her grind her molars. Someone should tell him that a flirtation meant coy looks, sly winks and sheepish chin ducks. Not being caught in their bed getting his carrot waxed.

"I'm sorry to hear that." Aspen's heart thudded. Her pulse fluttered in her throat. The right side of her brain wanted her to scream, *Take me back.* The left side thought she should stab him through the heart with her pen. The middle part wanted to analyze the odds of successfully pulling off an office murder in broad daylight, and to determine whether extra-strength Tide with bleach would degrade blood evidence without taking the color out of her clothes. She decided to take her options under advisement and get back to him.

"Well, look . . . I hate to cut this short but I have to take a call from CNN. They bought my video. I've even heard talk they want me to fly up for an interview."

He stared in disbelief. "They offered you a job?"

Without invitation, he slid into the nearest guest chair, looking hot in navy Dockers and a blue oxford shirt.

"It's only an interview. They want me to talk about the Johnson County sheriff." She realized she'd been rattling the papers and stopped fidgeting. Letting go, she rested her hands in her lap. At least that way he couldn't see her picking at her cuticles.

"Listen, I came to ask if you wanted to go to Steeplechase with me this year. My parents reserved a table and my mother said I should invite you to be my date."

Her heart beat so fast it echoed in her ears. "She didn't like your friend Satin?"

"Satin's history. Anyway, that's not her real name. It's Tammy. She just goes by Satin when she's working."

"How nice, having a street name. Very handy."

"I didn't come here to talk about her." Roger flashed one of his gorgeous, *Don't be mad* smiles. "So, will you go with me?"

"Can't." She gave him one of her *golly-gee* shoulder shrugs. "Already made plans."

"You don't even know when it is."

"Doesn't matter. I have plans."

"Please, Aspen, can't you find it in your

heart to give me another chance?"

"No."

"Why not? I said I was sorry."

As if words would undo the pain.

"Do you remember what you said to me? The reason you gave for dumping me?"

"I . . . don't."

"You said I just wasn't that interesting."

"I must've taken leave of my senses. You're one of the most interesting people I know."

Aspen barely contained a smile. She checked her watch for effect. In under five minutes, she'd gotten everything she thought she wanted.

"I really have to go." She stood, snatched her jacket from the back of her chair and whirled it around her shoulders. "I have an appointment."

"Why won't you let me make it up to you?"

"I don't want to hurt you."

"What?" he demanded, palms up and clearly frustrated. "Is playing hard-to-get your idea of payback?"

"No." She started for the door. "Look, if you want to talk you'll have to walk with me. I'm not kidding about the appointment. I can't be late."

Roger followed her out. In the corridor, he caught her by the sleeve and hauled her close enough for her to sniff the remnants of corn nuts on his breath. "I want another chance."

She braced her palms against his chest to keep him at bay.

He needed an explanation as much as she did back when he'd unceremoniously dumped her. If she deserved to know why, did he deserve any less?

"After you left —" she took a deep breath and slowly exhaled "— I met a man. We've grown quite fond of each other."

Roger scoffed. "You'll be back. You'll never find anyone like me."

"You're right. He could never be like you," she said without guile. "He's a whole lot more interesting."

Around noon, Rochelle returned to work with a gauze pad that looked like second base taped to the side of her head. She walked into Aspen's office on unsteady legs, carrying a brown bag with manicotti and a side salad.

"I brought lunch. It'll give you a chance to tell me who that guy was, and to thank you for helping me."

"I'm pretty sure there's an old Irish custom that says you have to support me now. I'll put together a list of regular expenses so you can start right away." Aspen gave her a seal hug — half embrace, half flipper hand pats — and took the sack. She spread the contents out on the blotter, lifted the lid and inhaled the vapors of Italian food.

Rochelle pushed the door closed. "Did you tell anyone?"

She knew exactly what Rochelle was referring to but she decided to play dumb — make her sweat — before answering.

A lengthy silence passed between them.

"What difference would it make if I did?"

Rochelle gave a nervous exhale. "The station has a nepotism rule."

"They hired Misty, didn't they?"

"Not until her father retired. If anyone finds out, Stinger won't be able to return. I need some discretion here."

"Gordon fired him. What makes you think he can come back?"

"I'm lobbying for it."

"You're lobbying for me to be out of a job and you want my help? Pretty ballsy, even for you."

"I want Stinger to have Bill's anchor job."

Aspen agreed to keep the secret.

Then Rochelle asked another favor. Stinger had to leave town for an interview out of state and the doctor thought she needed someone nearby in case of complications. She wanted to stay overnight at Aspen's.

"I've been having blurred vision. Imagine walking in and seeing two Tigs."

This proposition sounded marginally fun. They could watch the *Public Defender* spot on the news and share a bottle of wine. She'd give Rochelle the lowdown on Roger and confess how much she wanted to hear from Spike Granger. It would be kind of like life at the sorority house, only without the dues, the Drummond sisters, their cruel friends and the etiquette lectures.

The phone rang. "Aspen Wicklow."

"This is Nellie." Seconds passed between them. "Your stepmother?"

She preferred to think of her as Wexford's latest victim.

"Oh. Nellie." She gave a heavy eye roll. "Hello."

The woman probably called to invite her for coffee. Or to apologize on behalf of her father for not inviting her to the wedding. How ghetto. Wexford Wicklow didn't need to share his heart one-tenth as much as he needed a bypass for it. "Best wishes on your marriage to my father. I can't tell you how glad that makes me."

"Wexford's missing."

429

CHAPTER
FORTY

After leaving Rochelle with the key to her house, Aspen headed for Tranquility Villas in a whirlwind of apprehension. She strode into the building spoiling for a fight with Mrs. Ramsey. The administration should've called her. Should've let her know her father had wandered off. Should've filed a police report and had officers out beating the bushes for him. Instead, she imagined the director celebrating with cake, toasting Wexford Wicklow's disappearance with the rest of the staff.

With her sleep-deprived patience slipping away, she intercepted the woman at the nurses' station. "Where's my father?"

"I have no idea. We have people out looking for him."

"Why didn't you call me?" she asked, carefully modulating her voice to conceal her anger.

"You're no longer his next-of-kin."

Reality set in. If Mrs. Ramsey had hauled off and boxed her jaws, she couldn't have been more stunned.

"Fine. You don't want to discuss emergencies with me? Then don't contact me when the bill comes due. Get the money from his wife. From Nellie."

She dug out her mobile phone and tapped out nine-one-one.

Then she went in search of her mother. When she didn't find her, she called Spike Granger. He couldn't come to Fort Worth until he finished booking in Choya Fletcher and his crazy cousins. He told her he'd decided to handcuff the three men to the doors of the County Commissioners' Office. Maybe then they'd approve the emergency budget where he'd asked for ten extra deputies and a couple of portable buildings they could turn into makeshift jails. Once he put out that brushfire, he promised he'd meet her at Tranquility Villas.

A brisk wind whipped leaves across the pavement. Disheartened and afraid, she left the facility and set out for seedy places Wexford Wicklow might be inclined to go.

Granger still hadn't arrived by the time Aspen returned to Tranquility Villas. She decided to scout out the courtyard one last time before going inside to look for her mother. Even though Jillian and Wexford were no longer married, the poor woman had the right to know he was missing.

Near an outbuilding close to the pool, she heard rustling in the shrubs. She called out for her father, but no one answered. She circled the shed and ended up back on the paved area next to the Jacuzzi. The place had a creepy feel and she didn't want to investigate alone.

She wandered into the lobby in search of an attendant. One of the nurses summoned a tech. Aspen stared up at the hard-looking man with processed blond hair moussed into spikes and made a request.

"I need a flashlight." When he hesitated, she asked about the outbuilding with the latticework door.

"It's the pool shed. We store the grounds equipment inside it."

"I heard noises. Get the flashlight while I stand guard."

They met outside, where the tech handed it over. As the door creaked open, she flicked the switch and cast the ghostly circle of light over the inside of the building.

She viewed the contents of the shed in stages: pool vacuum, skimming net, push mower, weed-eaters, leaf blowers, man, rakes, riding lawnmower — *man?*

She reversed the stream of light.

The beacon hit a lean, spectral figure with a pasty white countenance and hollow-eyed stare. The ghoulish apparition hunkered over a smaller form. It took a few seconds for Aspen's eyes to make out the details. The naked figure beneath him was bent over at the waist, braced across the back of the riding lawnmower, sucking air and looking vaguely resentful at the interruption.

Aspen sealed her eyes tightly against the vision rising before her, only to have a blurry version of it pop back up in a reverse image behind her lids.

She tried to back out slowly and hoped no one noticed both parents' new high water mark, but she only managed to flatten herself against the tech.

Her eyes telescoped back into their sockets. She took deep breaths until she got a dizzying rush. What a ghetto experience. Not that it surprised her. Wexford Wicklow had probably been seduced by the unseemly location.

She left the pool shed buoyed by a cheery thought.

If Tranquility Villas didn't make it as a nursing home and rehabilitation center, it could always be turned into an insane asylum for old people.

CHAPTER
FORTY-ONE

When Aspen could no longer stand to watch Nellie Wicklow weeping into her hands while Wexford spun his lies, or hear her mother asking for the hundredth time whether she'd finally gotten a job, she left Mrs. Ramsey to sort out the chaos at Tranquility Villas.

Granger hadn't called back, and that wasn't a good sign.

That she found herself worrying about him wasn't a good sign, either.

But Rochelle's red Z was parked in the driveway and that was a very good sign, especially since Rochelle had her house key.

She walked up the sidewalk with Midnight prancing beside her. As she pressed the doorbell, she looked down to see him gazing up expectantly, as if to say, *What's for dinner?*

After waiting more than a minute to be let in, she resorted to using the brass doorknocker. Midnight was performing a figure eight between her ankles, rubbing his silky fur against her skin and making throaty chatter. Without warning, he went rigid. His head inclined to the right. Before she could track his gaze, he streaked across the porch, into the bushes and disappeared into the darkness.

Fifty feet away, a shadowy presence moved among the hedges.

Her pulse thudded in her throat; her heart tried to beat through her ribcage.

On instinct, she thought of Mike Henson.

The sinister-looking form slunk behind a tree.

Aspen beat her hand against the molding. Panic set in. Crying out Rochelle's name, she tried the knob and forced her shoulder into the door.

It unexpectedly gave way, spilling her headfirst onto the carpet.

She scrambled to her feet and bolted the lock behind her.

"Rochelle," she shrieked. "It's him. We've gotta get out of here. That guy, Mike Henson, he's out there. He'll do something."

No answer came from inside the house.

Still calling out for Rochelle, Aspen ran to the kitchen and double-checked the locks.

Convenient scenarios played out inside

her head. Maybe Rochelle couldn't hear over running water. She could be taking a shower. Or washing her hands. She had the television turned low. That would mute the noises in the rest of the house. She probably took a painkiller, went to bed and had fallen into a deep sleep.

Or Mike Henson had killed her.

Her breath quickened.

Aspen rushed down the hall toward the guest bedroom with self-preservation on her mind. She should buy a gun. Make that several guns. A gun for every room. And for the car.

The door to Rochelle's bedroom was closed.

She burst inside, screaming the woman's name as she flipped on the light.

Rochelle lay on top of the bedspread, on her side, with her head facing away and her skirt hiked up around her hips.

Thank God. She's only napping.

But wait . . .

In a glance, Aspen took in the room. This made no sense.

"Rochelle?"

The secretary rolled over. Her mouth and hands had been duct taped. Her eyes grew wide with fright. Her blouse had been ripped open and her bra cut away to reveal scar tissue from a mastectomy.

Terror gripped Aspen's throat.

She rushed to Rochelle's bedside and grabbed her hands, pulling the secretary upright. Picking at the tape was a losing battle. She needed scissors.

Low, throaty moans came from Rochelle.

Aspen never heard him approach. But from the fear telegraphed in her house-guest's bulging eyes, she instinctively knew.

He appeared from behind, fisting her hair savagely and pulling her to him, clamping a hand over her mouth as he pressed the cold, indifferent blade of a knife to her throat. Out of the corner of her eye, the blur of a large, grimy hand flicked out and shoved Rochelle back down on the bed.

He spoke in a raspy voice. "Calm down and you won't get hurt."

She nodded understanding. Her eyes darted over the room in search of something sharp to lunge for. Nothing.

Rochelle had a gun.

It was probably still in her purse. She scoured the corner in a glance and saw only the secretary's hard-shell suitcase, open, with tomorrow's blouse and skirt laid neatly out.

"I'm gonna take my hand away and you're gonna be quiet, or I'll kill your loudmouth friend. Understand? I want to, anyway, so anything you do is just gonna give me an excuse."

Aspen gave him a careful head bob. The knife felt icy and lethal against her skin.

He released his hand. She stumbled away, deliberately falling to the floor near the suitcase. She glimpsed Rochelle's purse on the side of the bed next to the wall. On some level, she knew she'd never reach it before he was upon her, stabbing her until she looked like a ragged piece of cloth with a hundred crimson buttonholes stitched into it.

This wasn't Mike Henson.

Mike Henson couldn't have gotten into the house that fast.

She turned to look, staring up into the flat, expressionless eyes of the mechanic.

He tossed her a roll of duct tape. "Pull off a piece."

"Why are you doing this? Is it money? You need money? We can drive to the ATM —"

"Shut up. You bitches are all the same."

"I'm trying to understand. If you're in need of something, I'll see if I can get it for you."

"What I need . . ."

Flashes of light arced from the knife blade as he sliced the air. She recognized the wicked curve of a rarely used filet knife that had come from her kitchen.

". . . is for you to shut your trap. What I *need* is to fuck you up. And when I'm done, I'll find your replacement."

Aspen thumbed at Rochelle. "Let her go."

"I have plans for her."

A tear slid out of one corner of Rochelle's eye. Her face drained of all color. Aspen sensed Rochelle had heard this part before.

"What plans?"

She wanted to keep him talking. To see if she could fling herself between the bed and the wall before he dragged her out and cut her throat as an example to Rochelle.

"Like I said —" he stared at the secretary through dead eyes "— you, I'll gut like a fish and throw you to the dogs."

A low, eerie wail bubbled up from Rochelle's throat.

"Shut it. And you — motor mouth — get that tape out."

She wrenched a small piece of tape away from the spool.

He could cover her mouth, fine. But she couldn't let him bind her hands. A scream probably wouldn't save her, but with her hands secured, she'd lose the last bastion of defense. With both of them hogtied, he could do anything he wanted.

He could torture them.

He took a step toward her and ran the knife through a section of tape. She knew, instinctively, what he expected of her. Just before she pressed it over her mouth, she discreetly wet her lips.

"Now your hands."

She pulled the tape off her mouth and desperately tried to reason with him. "I won't do anything. I promise."

"They all say that. Next you're gonna tell me you'll do whatever I say."

Aspen swallowed hard. "I will."

He gave a brittle laugh. "What if I say I want to watch you kill your friend? Huh? Your life in exchange for hers?"

"I have money." She wanted a reason to go into Rochelle's handbag. To pull out that pistol and brandish it in his face while Rochelle called nine-one-one.

"They say that, too. Women are so predictable. You think you can buy your way out of trouble. You bitches with your fancy cars . . ." Demonic flashes sparked from his eyes.

"You saw my car. I'm not like that."

She instantly realized, against all hope, that his contempt for women had nothing to do with beefing up his nest egg.

"Slap that tape back on."

She made the decision not to go like a lamb to the slaughter. She'd probably survive a knife plunging into her side as long as it missed her heart. Maybe he'd panic and run off.

More likely, he'd disable her enough to slit her throat and then gut Rochelle for having witnessed it.

Still, she had to try. Cooperation might buy them another half hour, but in the end, they'd still be as dead as Candy Drummond and Gabby Foster.

Aspen stiffened. "You put it on."

His cheeks flamed beet red. Veins plumped out from his temples. He turned snot-slinging mad. This was not the reaction she'd hoped for.

Between gritted teeth, he explained why requiring his assistance was a bad idea.

"If you don't cooperate and I have to put it on you, I'm going to wrap your friend's head with duct tape until she looks like a mummy. Understand?"

Rochelle's lids fluttered. Her eyes rolled up into her head.

Aspen stared long and hard, searching for any sign that Rochelle hadn't actually fainted. She wanted a wink, or to see her eyes crack open enough for Aspen to know she could still be of help.

"Put the damned tape on. I'm not gonna tell you again."

She cupped a hand to her mouth, subtly slathering her tongue over her lips before affixing the tape.

"Now your wrists. Pull off another piece. Enough to wrap around your wrists."

Aspen tugged at the tape, inwardly flinching at the ripping sound as it came away from the roll.

Outside, a cat meowed.

It wasn't Midnight.

It wasn't a cat at all.

It was a person trying to sound like a cat.

Mike Henson stood off to one side of the window, staring in at her. He pressed a cell phone to his ear and his lips were moving.

A half-whimper, half-laugh erupted from Aspen's throat.

"Crying ain't gonna get you out of this. Now hurry up."

She held out the strip of tape and he sliced it, barking orders as she made furtive glances outside. Mike Henson had receded into the darkness. In her frantic state, it occurred to her he might be in on it. Tears brimmed against the rims of her eyes, then slid over her cheeks in rivulets.

They were going to die. All because she'd agreed to help a cruel, heartless woman and her shallow, self-absorbed sister . . . girls who'd never been anything but hateful to her. All because Jillian Wicklow had raised her to do the right thing. Turn the other cheek.

Where was the justice in that?

After the mechanic had bound her wrists, he shoved her onto the bed next to Rochelle. Then he pulled a small bottle from his back pocket, along with a red oil rag similar to others she'd seen tossed around the bay area at Pop's Salvage.

Rochelle slitted her eyes open. The look in them suggested they should make a break for it. He couldn't control them both if they bolted for the door. If they rushed him, one of them had a chance. Aspen saw a flicker of dread and knew Rochelle was offering to run interference.

The mechanic folded the cloth into quarters.

He twisted the cap off the bottle. Covered the opening with the oil rag. Flipped the bottle over until he'd saturated the fabric.

Chloroform.

The pungent smell drifted into their shared space.

Rochelle emitted a low, guttural moan. She closed her eyes halfway, as if to say, *You go.*

When the mechanic came within a few feet of her, Rochelle moved with the speed of a striking snake. Her legs came up off the floor. She delivered a kick to the chest that packed the wallop of a mule. The blow sent him reeling into a small vanity. The bottle fell to the floor.

Aspen broke for the door.

She grabbed the knob and slammed it shut, then bolted down the hall with the thunder of footfalls closing in on her.

She could almost feel his hot breath singeing her neck.

Her decision to dive through the plate glass window was instantaneous. She'd never make it to either door. In the time it'd take to disengage the deadbolts and twist the knobs, he'd be on her like an alligator on an impala.

She closed her eyes and tucked her chin. Ducked her head and threw herself, shoulder first, fully into the pane. Glass exploded into white fragments. The sting of a sharp edge cut through her jacket and lacerated her skin. The next few seconds passed in a smear of muted colors. Shards of glass rained down upon her. She hit the porch with no time to think.

The front door swung open. A slice of light swept across the porch.

The mechanic came out with the rag in hand.

Aspen rolled through chunks of glass, off the porch and into the hedges. She took a hard hit against a couple of paver bricks, forcing a low groan from her throat. She dug for a fistful of dirt to fling in his eyes, even as she worked her tongue against the formidable seal of duct tape.

The mechanic trundled down the steps, thrashing the bushes to get to her.

Distant sirens wailed in the night.

He stood over her, cursing, and grappled at her sticky clothes. As he dragged her from the safety of the landscape, his mouth was an ugly gash against his face. He'd come to kill them but he'd picked women who knew the value of life and friendship and what mattered.

They wouldn't go quietly. Which meant their deaths would make a far worse crime scene than any indignity or pain and suffering foisted on Candy and Gabrielle.

With that grisly realization, everything shifted into slow motion.

Mike Henson's warning about the neighbors hearing weird noises coming from the salvage yard rushed back to her. His words echoed in her head.

"They said it happens at night. They said it

sounds like whining. Whining coming from Pop's place."

The mechanic had a dungeon. Or barracks. Or a torture chamber.

She and Rochelle were supposed to be taken prisoner. They'd be allowed to live until he tired of them. Candy Drummond went missing a week before they found her, dumped, like putrefied garbage.

As he dragged Aspen through the yard, her mind conjured up horrible scenarios, each worse than the one before. She recalled the wounds on Candy Drummond's body — electrical burns and dark rings around her wrists where she'd obviously been shackled. Or handcuffed. Or, God forbid, strung up.

He'd torture them. He'd get off on their screams. And when he had no further use for them, he'd dump their corpses next to some desolate roadway like roadkill.

The yelp of sirens grew louder.

She struggled against him, wriggling to break free. The mechanic jerked his head toward the street. She tracked his gaze in time to see two sets of headlights rounding the corner. Beyond his shoulder, she watched Mike Henson rush toward them. With his arms upraised, he came down hard with — a stick?

The grease monkey whirled on him, sending Henson street-proned with a mean right cross. He grabbed Aspen's wrists and dragged her along, clutching the duct tape as if it were a handle.

They moved toward a pickup.

The wail of sirens filled her head.

He lifted her from the ground and tossed her, hard, into the bed of the truck.

She'd barely raised her head enough to see over the edge when she heard the hard crack of his fist against her ear. Trees swayed overhead. Cloud cover broke to reveal a mirrored moon.

Mirror, mirror on the wall . . . who's the deadest of them all?

No!

She couldn't give up. To give up meant certain death. She'd fight for her life right here.

A faint voice that sounded remarkably like Rochelle's carried on the breeze.

"Go ahead, punk. Make my day."

Aspen imagined the secretary in a stance on the porch, her wrists still duct-taped together with the Smith & Wesson trained on their tormentor.

It made for a nice, cozy feeling, even if it was probably the delusional belief of a woman slipping into unconsciousness.

A lightning crack echoed in her ears.

Warm droplets misted her face.

Misty finally got it right. She'd predicted rain and now fat drops were falling, sliding down her cheeks. She liked rain. Rain was good.

Rain would wash the blood off.

Then Aspen slumped, sleepily, against the hard, cold surface of the truck bed.

CHAPTER
FORTY-TWO

The first voice Aspen heard when she came
to belonged to Spike Granger.

The second belonged to Rochelle.

"It's always been my dream to meet a man
like Dirty Harry," she said, speaking clearly
into the mike of an investigative reporter
from a rival network. "No, I haven't taken
lessons. It's instinctive. Like when a mother
points a finger in her child's face. It's a
natural reaction. I think that's why women
make better shots."

Granger, who was pacing beside a couple
of paramedics working over her, knelt on
one knee and took Aspen's hand.

"You okay?"

"You should stop Rochelle. She's talking
to the enemy."

"Actually, she just put in a plug for your
Public Defender slot for sweeps next week.
That woman's no fool."

The paramedic broke in. "You need

stitches, lady. Lots of them."

"I'm going to look like Frankenstein, aren't I?"

Granger said, "I'll run her down to the ER."

Aspen blinked. "What're you doing here?"

"I stopped by the nursing home. They said you'd already left."

"That guy — Mike Henson — he's not a stalker. He's a hero," she said, watching the emergency medical technicians pack up their gear.

Granger looked up and scanned their surroundings. "What guy?"

"Mike Henson. Gabrielle's boyfriend. He called the police."

Granger shook his head. "If he did, he didn't stick around."

"We've got to find him. I need an exclusive interview before another station gets to him. And I need to tell him I'm sorry." Thoughts turned to the mechanic. "Is he dead?"

"No. But Rochelle parted his hair down the middle. And she blew off an ear. FWPD transported him to Our Lady of Mercy to get stitched up."

"Gordon will be so mad at us. I'll probably lose my job."

"Screw the job. I don't want you doing

that job anymore. You'd be safer hopping trains."

"Spike — ," it was the first time she'd called him that, "— you don't get to pick what I do for a living."

"Maybe I get a say-so, though."

"Why do you get any input at all?" She thought she knew the answer, but she wanted him to say it.

"I want you to stick around for a long time."

"Why?"

"So you can take care of me when I'm old."

"I'll put you in Tranquility Villas with mean old Mrs. Ramsey."

He was about to set her straight when the *whuppa-whuppa-whuppa* of rotor blades drowned out the conversation. Overhead, a powerful spotlight lit up the grounds like the mothership. Aspen shielded her eyes from the glare and saw so much blood spatter on her hand that it resembled measles. The helicopter buzzed the house — Chopper Deke — and for a fleeting second she swore she'd seen Tig riding shotgun with his face buried in an airsick bag. For a moment, the light utility aircraft dangled above them like a huge spider before lifting upward and floating out of sight.

The sheriff leaned in and pulled her to him. "I'm so glad you're still here." With an *Aw-shucks* grin angling up his face, Granger looked down at his boot tips and toed the ground. "I love you."

"You do? You're not just saying that because you're caught up in the moment?"

"I never say anything I don't mean. Just ask the warden. And the governor. And the nitwits on the Criminal Justice Committee." He met her stunned gaze. "Besides, I need you to oversee my convict work crew while they're painting the cell blocks pink."

"Pink?"

"Yeah. The clink needs feminine touches and I want you to show the crooks where to paint the little flowers and butterflies."

"Wait. You're painting the jail pink?"

"Hey," he said with a nonchalant shrug, "if they don't want to wear sissy pink jumpsuits with slides and live with Pepto-Bismol walls, they can, by-God, stay out of my jail. And I've requisitioned those tents."

"You're really planning to house inmates in tents?" She cracked a smile. This was a real "Git-R-Dun" sheriff she'd fallen for.

"Why not? We have troops overseas who're living in the desert in tents — and they're not even crooks."

"Can I have an exclusive?"

"Darlin' —" he fisted a hand to his heart "— no matter what, you've always got an exclusive here."

EPILOGUE

Aspen entered the TV station to the cloying scent of flowers. A crush of roses similar to the tribute to Princess Diana overran Rochelle's desk and accumulated along the walls. Helium balloons tied with festive streamers had floated to the ceiling, blown along by the gentle current from the air-conditioner vent.

At first, she thought this must be Bill Wallace's last day, especially when she saw the morning show host seated outside Gordon's door on the same guest couch that she'd sat on her first day at WBFD. Then she noticed boxes with her name on them, stacked at the end of Rochelle's desk.

Rochelle was flopped in her chair with her eyes closed. She had a box fan positioned to blow up her skirt and an oscillating fan perched on the file cabinet behind her, aimed down her back. Stinger Baldwin stood beside her. As he sifted through the leftover tips from the assignments desk with one hand, he waved the paddle fan with the funeral logo near Rochelle's face. It was like watching a eunuch fan Cleopatra.

"See, Rochelle?" Aspen bit her lip until it stung. The last thing she wanted was to get misty-eyed. "These people do appreciate you."

She walked up to Stinger with her hand outstretched. Obviously, Gordon had given him his old job back. He'd already reclaimed his old office or her stuff wouldn't be sitting out in boxes, waiting to be carted off.

"We've never formally met." She offered him the firm handshake of a professional. "I'm Aspen Wicklow."

"Stinger Baldwin." He pumped her hand. "You're a slow learner. Thought I warned you to run like hell." He did a conspiratorial lean-in and pointed to Rochelle. "Listen, you're not going to mention anything to Gordon, are you?"

He meant the nepotism clause.

She shook her head. "I'm just here because Rochelle called me to pick up my last paycheck." She barely restrained a sigh. "For what it's worth, I'm glad you got your old job back. Half the time, I was scared to death. I don't know how you do it." She lifted her palms in surrender mode. "I'm a researcher. I'll always be a researcher."

She turned to look at Rochelle and put on a brave face. "Do you have my money?"

"What I have is a bunch of calls for you to return." She glanced up at her son. "Go get Aspen's messages."

He returned wheeling a dolly stacked with two large cardboard boxes.

Aspen stared, incredulous. "Those are messages?"

"You should probably call CNN back first. They want an exclusive. I already purchased your airline tickets. Gordon says he'll fire you if you say anything bad about us."

"But I thought — I don't understand — I'm already fired. You said I should come pick up my last paycheck."

The anchors were ricocheting off each other in their rush to the studio. They had less than five minutes to get into position for the morning broadcast. When she gave them a little finger wave, activity faltered.

Abruptly, Bill Wallace turned to face her.

He rose on rickety legs and began to clap.

Then everyone clapped.

Rochelle opened her drawer and thumbed through a stack of envelopes. She pulled one out and handed it over. "This is your last paycheck as an investigative reporter."

She looked over her shoulder and back. "Now go on in. Gordon wants to see you."

"I don't understand. Is he keeping me? Is the research assistant position I applied for still open? Do you think he'll give it to me?"

Rochelle's lips thinned into a crimson thread. She zipped them with an invisible zipper, then locked her mouth with an invisible key that she tossed over her shoulder.

Five minutes later, Aspen walked out of Gordon's office, ashen-faced. She staggered to Rochelle's desk in a drunken sailor walk.

The woman was on the telephone again, listening to one of the demon voices that guided her. "I'm telling you, shady characters keep buying stuff in his backyard. Then you never see them again. He probably has bodies stacked up like firewood. Otherwise, why else would he have rented a back hoe and bought all those bags of lye?" Rochelle looked up and covered the mouthpiece. "Be right with you." She went back to her call, adding, "Sure I'll testify. My name? It's . . . Inga."

When she hung up the phone, Aspen said, "Gordon told me I should see you if I wanted the job."

"Do you?"

"Do I?"

"Don't be naïve. Of course you do. The

pay's different but you'll get used to living on it. Shall we go re-introduce ourselves to the big shots?"

She was talking about Steve, Misty and Tig.

"Let's go see Tig first, shall we?" Rochelle flashed a devilish smile.

They walked down the corridor of offices with only the whisper of skirt hems swishing between them. The secretary pushed Aspen back from the entrance a few inches before giving Tig's door a light knuckle rap. "Got a minute?"

Aspen heard the squeak of his chair swiveling around.

"What's up?" he said.

He had no idea.

Rochelle handed him a message slip. "The IRS called. Someone told them you were laundering money and they want you to come down and talk to them this afternoon."

"What?"

"Yeah . . . bummer. It took a lot of doing, but I finally wormed it out of them. They said it was a woman who called in. You really should learn to become a better judge of character with these females you date," she said airily, "but that's not why I'm here."

"The IRS? Is this some sort of sick joke?"

"Hey, if you don't want to call them, that's up to you. But I knew a guy once who crumpled up his message the same way you just did and he's doing life in Leavenworth. The Feds don't give good time, by the way. You have to serve out your sentence day-for-day."

"You'd better not be yanking my chain."

"Want me to call them for you? I can tell them all sorts of good stuff if you like. Hey — remember that sheriff, Spike Granger, from Johnson County?"

"That lunatic?" Long pause. "What about him?"

"I heard the Feds hired him on as a consultant. He's sending them a packet of suggestions on the effect of painting jail cells pink and telling them how much red dye to use to turn white coveralls pink. Stinger found out an investigative reporter over at one of the independent stations is doing a story on how big, ugly bruisers go into his jail and come out fairies."

"Is that what you came to tell me?"

"No. Actually, I'm doing orientation for new-hires this morning. Well . . . that's not exactly true. In this case, it's more like re-orientation." She reached out, grabbed Aspen's wrist and yanked her through the doorway. "Tig, it's my great pleasure to re-introduce you to Aspen Wicklow."

Tig's fake grin melted. "I thought Gordon gave Stinger his old job back. I saw him slide his name tag into the slot on the door."

"He did."

"But —"

Aspen almost felt sorry for him, the way his sluggish brain took a few moments to piece it together. His sick expression suggested he thought he'd have to share the limelight with two investigative reporters instead of one, thereby decreasing his odds of winning the Peabody or Scripps-Howard or Pulitzer or any number of other awards for excellence in broadcasting.

"But I thought he fired her." Veins plumped in his neck like garden hoses. "Don't tell me we have three investigative reporters?" His voice pitched up in an unflattering whine.

"Don't worry, Tig. You're safe. You still get to be the big dog — for now. Aspen's not taking your job, so you can't go around referring to her as Investigative Reporter Barbie any more."

Relief died on his face.

Suddenly, he got it.

WBFD's superstar wore the expression of a has-been.

"Tig Welder," Rochelle's mouth split into

an evil grin, "it's with great pleasure that I present to you . . . Anchor Barbie."

That night, Granger arrived at Aspen's house an hour early. When the doorbell rang, she was standing in front of the bathroom mirror, half dressed, dusting herself with perfumed powder.

She shrugged into her robe and walked briskly to the front door. Plywood still covered the broken window, so she viewed him through the peephole before opening her home.

She took in Granger's features in a glance. Cowboy hat riding low on his forehead. Pewter irises staring out behind thick glasses. Leather vest with the gold sheriff's badge reflecting the porch light back into her eyes.

She slid off the new security chain and opened the door. "You're early."

Instead of the kiss she'd been expecting, he pushed past and strode on in. "Turn on the TV. Then go pack a bag. You're coming with me."

"I can't. I'm flying out tomorrow for the CNN interview — you know that." It made her feel desirable knowing Granger was hot for her. But their first bedroom experience should be slow and deliberate, not haphazard and rushed.

She flashed a smile. It felt good knowing he wanted her as much as she wanted him.

But Granger had a grim set to his face, not the look of a man wanting a quickie before the flight out. "Spike . . . what's wrong?"

"The mechanic escaped from the hospital."

ABOUT THE AUTHOR

Laurie Moore was born and reared in the Great State of Texas. After receiving her B.A., she spent several years as a police officer and District Attorney investigator, and is currently a practicing attorney in the Cultural District of Fort Worth. A fifth-generation Texan, she lives with a fractious Siamese and a rude Welsh corgi. She is the author of ***Constable's Run*** (2002), ***The Lady Godiva Murder*** (2002), ***Constable's Apprehension*** (2003), ***The Wild Orchid Society*** (2004), ***Constable's Wedding*** (2005) and ***Jury Rigged*** (2008). Her Young Adult novel, ***Simmering Secrets of Weeping Mary*** (2005), written under the pseudonym Merry Hassell Frels. Laurie is a member of the DFW Writers Workshop. Visit her website at www.LaurieMooreMysteries.com.